Blood-Stained Justice

A Novel

Rick Ward

SPRING
MORNING

PUBLISHING

"Congress Shall Make No Law Respecting an Establishment of Religion, or Prohibiting the Free Exercise Thereof; or Abridging the Freedom of Speech, or of the Press; or the Right of the People Peaceably to Assemble, and To Petition the Government for a Redress of Grievances."
—First Amendment

Dedicated to Pam McPhail

"First Amendment freedoms are most in danger when the government seeks to control thought or to justify its laws for that impermissible end. The right to think is the beginning of freedom, and speech must be protected from the government because speech is the beginning of thought."
—Supreme Court Justice Anthony M. Kennedy

Chapter One

Delivery Down

*Men acquire a particular quality by constantly acting
a particular way... You become just by performing just
actions, temperate by performing temperate actions,
brave by performing brave actions.*
—Aristotle

Armed with intelligence and dressed in camouflage, the agents lay flat on their stomachs, peering upward through the tall grass.

They watched as the makeshift lights flickered on and heard the engines overhead slowing down so the aircraft could make a quiet landing. On its final approach, the target of their stakeout—a mostly white, dual-engine plane with full flaps, gear down and landing lights off—was visible only through night-vision binoculars.

The pilot came down low, causing the agents to cover their heads reflexively. The plane set down just past the cab of an old truck parked on the end of the runway. Batteries in the back of the truck were being used to power a string of runway lights through a jumble of jumper cables and extension cords.

Once the aircraft had touched down, its engines again started to roar as it turned around and taxied closer to the truck and its two passengers. One of them turned on the parking lights to guide the pilot back down the grass-strip runway. The other jumped out with a huge rotary-magazine-equipped shotgun and placed it in the back of the open truck.

"Stay down." A crackling voice was heard over the agents' radio earphones. "Wait until they start loading the truck, then listen for my cue. I have a visual on an armed suspect."

The plane stopped and turned around just before reaching the truck; the noise of its turbo prop drowned out any other sounds before it went completely quiet.

The aircraft's right door flew open and the Hispanic copilot appeared on the wing. The agents could make out the outline of an assault rifle positioned across his body and a bandolier of bullets forming an X across his chest.

"Damn it, these guys are armed to the hilt," Captain Veazey whispered to his men through the radio. When he saw the pilot step out, he added, "We have two at the truck and two at the plane, and at least one at each location is heavily armed."

Suddenly the pilot reached back into the plane, slid the front passenger seat forward, released it and threw it out onto the ground.

"Pronto, pronto," the copilot called to the truck attendants. No other voices were heard. It was clear that this was not the first time the group had acted together.

The two men ran to the trailing edge of the wing as the copilot stood guard on the ground. Falling at his feet were tightly wrapped, shoebox-sized packages that the pilot threw from the aircraft. When the truckers finished loading their vehicle, it was time for the agents to move in.

"Sierra One, are you there?" Captain Veazey whispered over the radio.

"Yes, sir. I have a fix on the armed suspect," the sniper replied.

"It's too risky to rush them in the dark with the copilot keeping guard. You need to wait 'til he turns the rifle in our direction before you fire, which I'm sure he will when our lights come on. After that, we move in…but that guy's gotta go first."

"Understood, sir."

"The lights will drown out your night vision, so you'll only get one chance. Are you ready?" Veazey asked.

"Waiting on you, sir," the sniper said with confidence.

"Okay, Team Humvee, when you hear the shot, do your thing," the captain's voice crackled.

Spotlights suddenly flooded the darkness. Within two seconds, a sharp shot rang out and the copilot's head exploded; his back slammed against the wing as his knees buckled and he fell to the ground face-first, though he didn't have much of a face left.

The three other men had no time to react as Humvees with grass netting and huge spotlights on their cabs came screaming toward them through the weeds. The agents followed behind these powerful vehicles, guns raised, as the night-blinded truckers threw their hands in the air. The pilot, however, managed to jump back into the plane and start the engines, almost cutting one agent in two with the propellers.

The aircraft started moving out of the spotlights. As the agents shot blindly in its direction, one of them jumped into a Humvee that had no top and two more jumped in the back with their weapons in hand. They caught up with the plane as it was about to lift off of the ground.

One agent fired a specially configured explosive-round shotgun at the wheel; the blast collapsed the landing gear, dropping the right wing of the plane to the ground as the propeller slung dirt and weeds into the air. The plane, looking like a wounded dove, spun in a quarter circle and stopped at the edge of the field.

"Get out with your hands on the back of your head!" an agent yelled as his colleagues jerked the plane's door open and stuck their guns into the cabin.

"*Si, si, señors... No habla Ingles,*" the pilot rambled on as he nervously climbed out of the plane.

"Get on the ground facedown!" an agent ordered. "You understand English if you fly in US airspace."

"Yes, sir," the pilot said in a heavy Spanish accent as he quickly complied.

Another Humvee arrived and agents boarded the plane with handheld spotlights. The front passenger seat was still on the ground where it had fallen, and there were no seats in the back of the plane. Instead, agents found a large, flattened-out, rubber bladder that resembled a waterbed covering the plane's back floorboard.

One agent removed the filler cap, resulting in a strong smell of aviation fuel, and another held up a small, clear, plastic line connected to a brass valve between the two front seats. Though the hundreds of packages that had not yet been unloaded were now clearly visible to the agents, no papers could be found on the plane, and it had an altered US-registry N number near its tail.

Captain Veazey stepped up and took one look at the plane's insides. "Our suspects are airplane-thieving, dope-dealing Colombians," he announced while opening one of the packages with his knife. White powder poured from the cut.

"Millions of dollars' worth of coke, my boys. You see that valve on the floor between the seats? These guys filled that bladder tank with fuel somewhere around here, then flew to Colombia. By the time they got there, the tank was empty and collapsed flat, leaving room for the cocaine. Then they flew back here on the wing tanks."

As Veazey stood there, shaking his head in wonderment, an agent on the ground called into the cabin. "Captain, the pilot's singing like a bird to our translator. He swears the plane isn't stolen but owned by a big businessman who hired them to make this load."

"What big businessman?" Veazey asked.

"He says he doesn't know, sir, but is willing to cooperate."

"Okay, let's get this crime scene policed up," the captain said. "Get the coroner and an evidence-collection team out here before we load that stiff into the ambulance and head back to the station. Lieutenant, leave a team to secure the aircraft until morning. We'll get the serial numbers from the frame and have the FAA match it to the real N number."

"Yes, sir."

Veazey watched his men scurrying around as they carried out his orders. He stood alone in the cabin, hands on hips, surveying the scene. "That leaves just one more thing to do," he said to himself. "Find out who the fat cat is."

Chapter Two

The Performance

My passions were all gathered together like fingers that made a fist. Drive is considered aggression today; I knew it then as purpose.
—Bette Davis

One Year Earlier

"Dope dealer... Dope dealer... Dope dealer!" the district attorney yelled out with more vigor and volume each time, simultaneously slamming his fist on the antique, hardwood podium in front of the jury.

The strength of his last blow lifted his feet off the floor and severed the top of the podium from the square, wooden post. As it fell to the floor, the jurors' eyes got wider. They moved back in their chairs as if trying to get away from a mentally deranged man—who was now approaching them with disheveled hair and anger in his eyes.

The boards in the old floor creaked with every step the DA took toward the jury box. Echoes of his ranting and raving still bounced off the high ceilings of the mostly empty courtroom and ricocheted off the torn-plaster walls.

District Attorney John Chastain didn't skip a beat. With both hands he grasped the scarred, wooden rail that separated him from the jurors and leaned in, making slow, deliberate eye contact with each of them. His tie was hanging askew and sweat poured from his brow as he said in an uncharacteristically soft tone, "This...this is what's killing our children, ladies and gentlemen. You know what you have to do."

He leaned his head down as if in prayer, but his eyes were wide open as he gazed under his arm at the bailiff, who was picking up the pieces of what was once the podium behind him.

Chastain had delivered a classic theatrical performance, but the jurors saw it as a sincere plea. It wouldn't take them long to find the defendant guilty, not after Chastain had succeeded in painting the small-time drug dealer as a serial child killer.

Wayne Lott sat in the front row of the courtroom, taking in the show. He was riveted by the impassioned, dark-haired DA, who was so well built for a man in his early forties that he looked like a force of nature. As if he weren't tall enough at six foot three, he also had on cowboy boots. And not just run-of-the-mill ones but sharp-looking boots that actually complemented his suit, if that were possible. There were no wing-tip Oxfords for this guy.

This was the man Wayne hoped to emulate. He wanted to be a strong, robust prosecutor, not just another assistant US-attorney flunky in an air-conditioned office in Jackson.

Although Wayne was on the fast track—moving quickly from a private law practice to the legislature, then becoming a government informant honored with an appointment as an assistant US attorney—he felt stuck in the center lane. He had started out naïve and idealistic but the constant temptations that tormented him and influenced his colleagues, as well as his exposure to the criminal element and the true intent of many unscrupulous lawmakers, had changed him. Each new political scandal hardened him more, filling him with a desire to retaliate personally against those who betrayed public trust. For Wayne, that meant one thing: becoming a full-fledged prosecutor.

Because he had moved so quickly into his current, high-level position, Wayne had not had any prosecutorial experience. Most of the cases handled at the federal level were preapproved by the US attorney's office before FBI agents even pursued them. The assistant US attorneys were there generally to guide the cases and ensure that sufficient evidence of the crimes existed before presentation to a federal grand jury was even allowed.

To gain the real-world experience he lacked, Wayne had gotten approval from his boss to tour his choice of the state's twenty-five circuit-court jurisdictions and watch district attorneys in action prosecuting cases. Many more cases were tried in the lower courts, usually due to poor preparation by local cops.

Wayne was most fascinated with Stonewall, a delta county in the twenty-third judicial district located on the river near Greenville, not far from Oxford, Mississippi, where Wayne had lived. The small town of Puknik was the county seat of government and the location of Stonewall's courthouse as well as its most prominent leaders. Jack Burchfield, one of Wayne's best friends from law school, was the assistant DA there and had recommended that Wayne come up from Jackson.

Still, Wayne had not been prepared for what he had seen. Mere minutes after the jurors left for deliberation they returned to give their resolute verdict. Deputies placed handcuffs on the defendant, who by then was looking at his lawyer with equal parts anger, surprise and helplessness. His knees were shaking as the leg irons were snapped shut. The last Wayne saw of the convicted man was the expression on his face as he looked back in disbelief before being whisked outside to a waiting police car.

A few lawyers and a young, female reporter milled about in the courtroom; investigators and an undercover agent shook hands, with smiles on their faces, as they saw justice served; and the defendant's family, too shocked to move from their seats, broke down in tears.

Among all the mayhem, District Attorney John Chastain walked tall, striding toward the courtroom exit like a cowboy heading into the sunset.

Chapter Three

The Meeting

You learn more quickly under the guidance of experienced teachers. You waste a lot of time going down blind alleys if you have no one to lead you.
—W. Somerset Maugham

"Mr. Chastain," Wayne called in the hallway, trying to catch up to him. "I'm Wayne Lott, an AUSA from Jackson. I've been watching your trials and, after reviewing several others, I find your prosecutorial style the most, uh, intriguing. I hope you won't mind my using you as a mentor."

"Not at all," Chastain said, clasping Wayne's hand in a firm shake. "Jack already told me about you. Said he'd like to be here but he's helping out the sheriff's chief investigator on some other drug cases today." The DA looked Wayne over and smiled, sensing he was a bright, earnest young man. "So you're looking for a mentor. Do you also want a job?"

"No, I have a job. I just need to learn how to do it," Wayne said.

"Too bad. I need another assistant DA," Chastain replied. "It doesn't pay as much as you feds make, and we work much harder. I've got more bills than my old coon dog's got fleas. Hell, I have to sell soap and cows to make a living here and I'm the DA. I just hope my assistants aren't selling dope to make ends meet," he said with a sideways grin.

"I wouldn't want to be them and have to face you if I was," Wayne said. "You sure were convincing with that jury. I thought that guy would garner sympathy but you made him look like the leader of a drug cartel."

"Yeah, he made the mistake of selling blotter acid on cartoon-character stamps to an undercover agent. But his Memphis lawyer was an asshole, unwilling to take a pretrial diversion program I offered. I warned that guy not to start nothin' he couldn't finish, but he didn't listen. That scumbag defendant of his had an attitude, too. Laughed about a twelve-year-old who took the same type of acid and thought he could stop a train. Kid's family couldn't even make a positive ID of his body."

"Jesus," Wayne gasped.

"Well, I just taught him and his lawyer a lesson. Tennessee lawyer anyway… Who cares? The doper could've had an expunged record after probation if he'd taken the deal. Now he's a convicted felon for good," Chastain said with some degree of satisfaction.

"Think he'll appeal?" Wayne asked.

"Doesn't matter. Judge Cates never has a case overturned." The DA draped an arm around Wayne's shoulder, clearly happy to have an audience. "C'mon over to my office. I'll have my secretary put on a pot of coffee."

Wayne walked across the square, trying to talk to his new mentor, but was first interrupted by an old man in coveralls and a straw hat selling sorghum molasses and fresh tomatoes from the bed of his old, beat-up, green truck with homemade sideboards. Next, a frail, blue-haired, retired high-school teacher stopped by to reminisce with her favorite former drama student as she kept pushing her glasses up on her nose.

"Did you know John could've been a movie star?" Mrs.

Hedgspeth asked, looking directly at Wayne as if she had known him all her life.

"No, ma'am, I didn't," he said with a smile as he looked over at Chastain, who was blushing and motioning for Wayne to keep moving, in fear of a long lecture.

"Well, it's true. He was the best. I wanted him to go to acting school but he wanted to be in politics. Not just a lawyer, mind you, but in politics. Hmm, of all things, I swear. He was also president of the debate team. Won the impromptu speaking challenge at the state Jaycees convention his first year out of college," she insisted, raising her head upward and pointing her bent index finger in Wayne's face. She reminded him of a fire-and-brimstone country preacher giving his last sermon to his tent-covered revival congregation.

"Who knows what he'll do next?" Mrs. Hedgspeth asked in a shrill voice as she walked away, hunched over with a cane and sporting a long dress, worn-out flats and bobby socks. "Say hello to yo' mama and cousin Elmer for me," she mumbled to the thoroughly embarrassed DA.

She stopped a short distance away to throw sunflower seeds to the squirrels on the courthouse lawn, which was cluttered with towering oaks from the previous century that had become sanctuaries for chirping birds.

"Didn't you see me looking up at the clock in the courthouse tower, Wayne? That was your signal to hightail it or that old woman would talk your head off," Chastain chided.

"You liked the drama club, huh?" Wayne laughed as they walked between cars, crossing the one-way street that went around the square.

"You mean you couldn't tell from my performance in the courtroom?"

"Guess that's true. So, what *are* you going to do next?" Wayne asked curiously.

"Getting ready to run for the US Senate," Chastain said ambitiously. "That's why I need another assistant to pick up the load while I'm out campaigning."

"Well, good luck," Wayne said, admiring the man's confidence.

"Thanks." Chastain winked. "I just hope Mrs. Hedgspeth doesn't find out."

Chapter Four

The Office

Make no little plans; they have no magic
to stir men's blood...Make big plans,
aim high in hope and work.
—Daniel H. Burnham

A s Wayne and Chastain stepped into the DA's office, Betty Sue, a bleach-blond secretary with an eyeful of cleavage, was busy smacking on a piece of gum. She pulled a pencil caked with makeup from behind her ear, scribbled one last note and handed her boss at least ten phone messages. He quickly scanned each one before throwing them all in the trash and sitting down in his private office.

"Have a seat," Chastain said to his guest before calling out, "Betty Sue, can you bring us two cups of fresh coffee?" He leaned across his desk toward Wayne and whispered, "I just want you to see her new miniskirt."

Wayne rolled his eyes and blurted out, "One with cream and sugar...please."

Chastain just grinned.

"Mr. Chastain..." Wayne said, getting back to business.

"Call me John."

"Okay, John, do you have any other interesting cases on your docket that I can watch?"

"Depends on what you'd call interesting," Chastain replied. "I've got a murderer, a couple more drug dealers, an arson case and a lawnmower thief."

"You mean you're trying someone who stole a lawnmower?" Wayne asked, surprised.

"Listen, my friend, you don't tell one of your biggest supporters that his lawn mower being stolen is insignificant, especially when you're seeking a higher office," Chastain said. "Besides, it was one of those new gadgets that turn on a dime and cost thousands, not hundreds, of dollars."

Wayne wondered—but didn't ask—whether the DA would have taken the same stance if the victim had not been a major supporter of his campaign.

As one might suspect from his past encounters with crooked officeholders, Wayne was by then very leery of political motivation. But his friend Jack felt pretty comfortable with Chastain for having known him only a short while, and Wayne was definitely impressed by what he'd seen so far.

"I have two more weeks away from my office. Might as well watch as many trials as I can," Wayne said.

"Suit yourself," Chastain replied. He leaned back in his chair, propped his feet up on the desk, picked up an old cigar that was resting on the window sill and lit it. "But, between us, which of those cases do you personally find most interesting?"

"Murder, I guess."

"Been watching too much TV, Wayne. Murder is almost always a simple, open-and-shut case. It's not like in the movies where there's some mysterious plot or motive. Hell, people kill each other over the damnedest things."

"Like what?" Wayne asked with a great degree of curiosity.

"Like arguments over kids shooting off fireworks, infidelity, loud music, a neighbor's dog shitting in their yard. I even had one old guy kill his young, live-in girlfriend over an egg. One damned egg. Can you believe that?"

"No. Tell me about it," Wayne said.

"The fellow stumbled home drunk in the wee hours of the morning, slept a little before having to leave for work and woke up at six a.m. wanting breakfast. He kicked his girlfriend out of bed to fulfill that need and started getting himself ready for work. He walked past the dining table and saw two fried eggs lying there on the plate next to a few strips of bacon, a biscuit and a pile of grits. He went back in the bedroom, got his gun—a blue-steel, five-shot revolver—then came back and shot her...right between the eyes."

"Holy shit! What did he do that for?" Wayne wondered.

"Said in his statement that he had told her time and again he wanted three eggs for breakfast, not two. Didn't want to have to say it again, so he shot her. Had no problem with it, either...no remorse. Even helped the ambulance drivers load her up. They assumed she'd shot herself—so did the cops who arrived on the scene. One of the young officers asked why she'd wanted to kill herself, and the old man started running off at the mouth, explaining why it had to be done. The cop was stunned—slammed the guy against the ambulance to search him. The old man just calmly told him that he wasn't armed and directed him to the gun still sitting on the kitchen table."

"You've got to be kidding me," Wayne said.

"Nope. That's life here in Stonewall County. Interesting, huh? Shoot, I told his lawyer that if the old man ever got out of prison and remarried, I'd bet his new wife would fix him a dozen eggs and the chicken that laid them. Not likely that'll ever happen, though," Chastain said with a smile.

"So what's the deal with the murder case on your docket?"

"Nothing new. Just a jealous wife killing her husband. She's going to claim he was abusive and she was in fear for her life when she killed him. There's some merit to that claim, but we'll probably end up with a manslaughter plea. Turns out her panties weren't always in the up position, either. Maybe the poor, stiff bastard had a reason for slapping her around," Chastain said.

Wayne bit his tongue. He was too mesmerized by the DA's stories to argue the finer points of domestic abuse. "If you don't mind, then, I'll stick around for all the trials, watch you, take notes and try to learn something."

"Don't mind at all. But today's Friday, and it's about time to feed the cows, so I'm going to get going," Chastain said, standing up. He had already given up on Betty Sue bringing any coffee, fresh or otherwise. "Got my monthly Amway meeting tonight and a meeting this weekend with some Senate campaign supporters from out of town. Hope they bring plenty of money with 'em... We're gonna need it." Chastain smiled. "Court starts at nine o'clock sharp Monday morning. You stayin' in town?"

"No, heading back to Jackson," Wayne said, rising from his seat. "But first I'm stopping in Oxford to have a home-cooked dinner with my friend Wallace Tischner, the FBI special agent in charge there. Used to work with him in Jackson."

Wayne didn't know if Chastain was aware of his role in last year's much-publicized case against legislative and lobbying corruption in Jackson, and he didn't want to seem like he was bragging by mentioning it. Resigning from the legislature in less than two years had not made Wayne a very well-known politician, which his father, Will, a retired officer in charge of the state's Organized Crime Strike Force, was glad about.

"Take a copy of my arson-case file with you to look at over the weekend," Chastain said. "Let me know what you think when you get back. It'll probably be tried later next week—and the defense might just be surprised."

"How so?" Wayne asked.

"Well, defense lawyers are pretty cocky about winning arson cases, and rightfully so. Don't know about the federal system but in state court you just about have to catch the arsonist on video with the match in one hand and the accelerant in the other to get a conviction," Chastain explained. "And this particular defense lawyer is a hotshot from a family of lawyers living on the other side of the state. Thinks he owns the courtroom. That's exactly the kind I like to bury the deepest under their own piles of bullshit."

Chastain handed the file—covered in cigar ashes—to Wayne, who was surprised by how easily the DA found it among the other stacks of paper that completely hid the top of his desk.

Wayne placed the file under his arm, shook Chastain's hand and walked out into the main office. When he jerked on the front door to leave, a cowbell at the top of the doorframe rang.

Betty Sue looked up mid-manicure; her smile was at once seductive and coy—and, perhaps, Wayne thought, a little cunning.

"That old, sticky door and cowbell are my announcement system. Wakes me up when people kick it open."

"Maybe they're just kicking their way in to get their hands on your, uh…"

The buxom secretary sat up straight and raised her eyebrows expectantly.

"Coffeemaker," Wayne finished. "You should probably check to see that it's still there." With that, he bid Betty Sue goodbye.

Chapter Five

Old Friends

You have to recognize when the right place and the right time fuse and take advantage of that opportunity. There are plenty of opportunities out there. You can't sit back and wait.
—Ellen Metcalf

As Wayne drove to Oxford, he reminisced about the town where he'd once lived. He turned onto University Avenue off Highway 6, wondering what it would have been like if he had stayed, then passed his old rental house and noticed that the new tenants had removed the wheelchair ramp his father once had used.

The square hadn't changed much: old buildings with wrought-iron balconies protruding above the sidewalks, students scrambling about in Ole Miss attire, which was unmistakable and would have made them look out of place anywhere else in the state. Square Books was as busy as always and the stately courthouse in the middle of the square looked like no other. A stone-cold Confederate soldier made of granite was still on guard, reminding residents of years past and the willingness of this quaint, little town to take up arms against its enemies.

As Wayne turned into Wallace Tischner's driveway, smoke poured from the side of the house as if it were on fire. Wayne hurried to the white-picket fence and peered over; he saw Tischner's wife scurrying off the back porch with a pitcher of water in her hand. She was screaming at Wallace, who had fallen asleep on a patio lounge chair and burned the steaks he was grilling for dinner.

"Tisch," Wayne called out, "are you okay?"

"Yeah, I'm fine. Must have been that new charcoal," Tischner complained, heading out the gate.

His wife, Ann, stood in the back yard mumbling something about it not being the fault of the new charcoal but of the old man who'd bought it.

"C'mon, Wayne, let's drive to the square. Plenty of good places to eat there. I want to talk to you privately without being nagged, anyway."

"Stay away from fat and salt!" Tischner's wife screamed out to her husband as he was getting in the car.

"See what I mean?" Tischner asked in a low voice.

"She's still on your case about your health only because she loves you," Wayne said, smiling.

"She must love me worse than ever. Let's go to City Grocery. They've got these braised pork shanks and soft-shell crabs…" Tischner licked his lips. "We can top it off with my favorite bread pudding… Just don't tell Ann."

They went to the restaurant and got a seat on the balcony overlooking the street. It was an early May evening with a cool, northwesterly breeze blowing in from a cold front that was trying to keep spring away.

This reunion was more than just a couple of friends getting to shoot the shit; it was two men who shared the same ideals, the same interests and the strong desire to eradicate corruption in the state.

"How's your dad?" Tischner asked, making small talk.

"He's fine. Travels around in his motor home, just him and his new dog," Wayne said.

"What kind does he have?"

"A Gulfstream," Wayne answered.

Tischner look startled for a second. "I meant what kind of dog."

"Oh, a Min-Pin. Mean little bastard, at least to everybody else. Dad adopted him from an animal shelter in Jackson. They told him this dog, Sinbad, was the most unadoptable animal they had of the over three hundred there. Bit everybody. Dad had to beg them to let him have it. They said he couldn't be around kids but my little girl, Dawn, pulls his ears and sticks her fingers in his mouth, and he does nothing. But raise your hand to her and he will take it off for you."

Tischner smiled. "Well, if anyone could tame a dog like that, it'd be your dad."

"He sure did. Even renamed him 'Been-bad' because he may have been bad in the past, but he's not anymore. Dad says the nine months the poor little guy spent in solitary confinement would've turned anyone bad." Wayne laughed.

"I'm glad to hear he has a good road companion," Tischner said.

"Yeah. While he's out there, he's also trying to get a book published that he just finished about the evolution of Mississippi politics. Learned a lot from it myself. In fact, if I had read it beforehand, I might not have run for the legislature."

"Enlighten me," Tischner said, biting into his braised pork shank.

"Well, did you know that the King Edward Hotel used to be the seat of governmental power in the state? Since the nineteen-twenties legislators lived there. But when segregation came along and a black gentleman checked in, they all moved out. It met its demise shortly afterward and, until recently, just stood there slowly decaying—a symbol of an old era and an outdated way of thinking."

"I didn't know that," Tischner said.

"Yep. And those guys haven't changed much, either. Maybe on the surface. But I gotta tell you, when I walk by the Capitol, I feel dirty. Some of those bastards who've been there for years keep dictating the law. We need term limits in this state worse than anything. Don't expect those power-hungry pocket stuffers ever to vote for it, though. We need a referendum on the ballot to let the people decide."

"That why you resigned so quickly to become a fed?" Tischner asked.

"Let's put it this way... I never could have made a difference. Couldn't have passed the first law—neither could have anyone else, in my position. If you don't become a part of the machine and cooperate with the old-timers you don't get any support on your bills, you get no important committee appointments, and you're worthless to your constituents. That's the old-timers' argument *for* term limits: 'If you get rid of us, our district loses power.' Of course, it has nothing to do with district power. It's all about lobbying and special interests."

"What do you mean?" Tischner asked innocently, digging into his dinner.

"I mean that lobbying should absolutely be illegal. I was elected to represent the people of Oxford—not the gaming industry, not the medical industry, but the people! These are folks with median incomes of less than $40,000 per household. Why should any industry with big money and lobbying funds be able to influence me on *its* behalf, not theirs?" Wayne said, clearly getting worked up.

"I agree with you, Wayne," Tischner said calmly. "So what did your dad think when you resigned from the legislature?"

"C'mon, Tisch, you know he was elated. Hell, he's convinced the system is broken and will never be fixed. He thinks the New Madrid Fault should open up and the whole damn Capitol should get sucked into it during full session so we can just start over. In his mind, that's the only way we'll ever be on an equal playing field, nobody with any more power than another."

"Yeah," Tischner said between mouthfuls. "I've heard Will compare the senior members of legislature to a varsity football team playing against junior-high kids."

"He even said that with the renovation of the King Edward—the project of two wealthy African-Americans—the legislators who are descendants of those from the sixties should move back in and have a black man as a landlord. Now, that would be justice in my mind…and, finally, an equal playing field."

Tischner began to laugh as Wayne swatted away mosquitoes with such vigor that he almost fell off the balcony.

"What's so damn funny, Tisch? I damn near broke my neck."

"You've been so busy talking and getting fired up that you haven't eaten a bite of that soft-shell crab, and I'm ready for dessert. If you show that kind of fierceness in a courtroom, you'll be a sight to watch," Tischner said with a broad smile.

"You got me all worked up on purpose, didn't you?" Wayne claimed as he wiped off some of the sweet tea he'd spilled on his lap. "I haven't thought about half those things since we worked together. What have you got up your sleeve?"

"That depends. You happy down there in Jackson?"

"What do you mean by 'happy'?" Wayne asked. "That's a relative term."

"You know damn well what I mean. Do you like being a federal prosecutor?"

"I'm really not a federal prosecutor. Seems like every time I have a case about to come up, the defendant pleads. I do a lot of work to further prosecutorial preparedness, but it never comes to fruition," Wayne said, taking a sip of what was left of his tea. "I'd really like to be in a district that prosecutes big cases, which doesn't happen much in Jackson. Seems like y'all get the big ones—Memphis mobsters trying to infiltrate north Mississippi, corrupt lawyers, judges and other state officials here in the northern district."

"Yep. We sure are lucky." Tischner laughed before suddenly turning serious. "I want you in this office, Wayne. We have some important issues coming up and I'd like your help. You still have the passion in you. What do you say?"

"Nah, I don't think so, Tisch. I'd love to work with you again, but Julie and I have a nice loft apartment overlooking the city. It's just down the street from my office, and I don't want to start dragging her and the baby all over the state."

"Look, my friend, let me know how you feel next week after you've learned all you can about being a tough guy in circuit court. You'll be back up here in weeks! Besides, you don't want to raise a child in Jackson… You need a yard, a dog, a place for a swing set and a wading pool. Oxford's a nice, progressive town. There are a couple of houses for sale on my cul-de-sac. Julie would love them, the prices are right—and we can get together for barbecues."

"That's damn close to blackmail, mister, and you know I don't take kindly to that methodology," Wayne said laughingly. "Besides, I don't know if I can live next to a guy who likes to play with fire."

Chapter Six

The Weekend

*Destiny is no matter of chance. It is a matter
of choice. It is not a thing to be waited for,
it is a thing to be achieved.*
—William Jennings Bryan

"Honey, I'm home," Wayne yelled out as he closed the door behind him and flipped on the light. It was shortly after 10:00 p.m. and he was still wired from his meeting with Tischner.

Dressed in her pajamas, Julie rushed into the living room with her finger in front of her mouth. "Shhhh, you'll wake up the baby. She's been cranky all day from teething and I'm exhausted," she said, rubbing her eyes. Still, she managed a smile as her husband hugged her. "Glad you're home, though. How was your trip?"

"Good," Wayne said as he and his wife sat on the couch. She put her tired head on his shoulder and he held her silently for a few moments. "Jules," he whispered, "I was wondering something…"

Julie lifted her head and looked at him through sleep-deprived eyes.

"Have you ever thought about living back in Oxford?" Wayne asked.

Just like that, Julie was suddenly wide awake. "Wayne, that's not just something you casually wonder. Is there a problem with your job?"

"Not at all—other than the fact that I'm not happy doing what I'm doing."

"Then why are you doing it?" she asked matter-of-factly.

"Stability. I didn't want to move the baby all over the place."

"Stability?" Julie repeated incredulously. "You think we have stability? You aren't happy where you are. We live in an apartment, not a *home*, and we're not building any equity. Your dad's always traveling. I don't work. We're not near family—"

"I didn't know you felt that way," Wayne said, cutting her off.

Julie just kept going. "Well, there's something else you don't know that I've been meaning to tell you," she said. "I was thinking about going back to Ole Miss to get my master's. If I attend night classes, you can look after Dawn…or we'll be near enough that my parents can help out. By the time I graduate, she'll be in pre-K and I can have a career."

"So you actually *want* to move back?" Wayne asked, surprised.

Julie smiled. "I was just giving you a little time in your new job, but that was my plan in a year or so."

Wayne laughed. "Thanks for letting me in on it."

"No problem." She smiled. "So, what brought about this brilliant idea of *yours?*"

"Tischner wants me to help him develop some big case he's embarking on. He said he'd have his US-attorney contact mine and it'd be a done deal. You may not know it from looking at him, but he's a legend in the FBI who carries a lot of clout with US attorneys everywhere he's ever been."

"I can't believe you wouldn't seize that opportunity immediately," Julie said with a shocked expression. "Listen, Wayne, it'll be better for all of us. We can get a house, Dawn can have a big backyard and her grandparents can be close by to spoil her to no end. It's a perfect plan."

"Oh, yeah? I'd like to hear you say that if we end up living next to the Tischners." Wayne laughed.

"I don't care who we live next to as long as we're together and both have chances to do what we really want," Julie said.

Wayne saw just how impassioned she was about starting a new career for herself and a new life for her family. Her fire and determination made her irresistible to him. He looked at his wife, naturally beautiful without a drop of makeup and sexy even in her comfortable, old pajamas, and realized again what he had known about her all along: She was smart as a whip yet had been willing to put her own dreams and desires on the back burner for the sake of her husband and daughter. But she wouldn't sacrifice her talent and education forever—and he wouldn't want her to.

"Let's go to bed, honey. What are we waiting for?" Wayne asked excitedly.

"Not just yet," Julie said with an innocent yet seductive smile. "My poor hubby looks tired and all stressed out. Why don't you take off your shirt and I'll give you a nice, slow backrub? Dawn's asleep. We have all night."

"I won't argue with that," Wayne said as he unbuttoned his shirt and lay across the couch.

"Just relax and close your eyes, sweetie," Julie said. "I'll make you feel so good."

"You always do," Wayne said softly.

As Julie continued to massage his shoulders, she heard a light snore and started grinning. As the snore got louder, she realized her husband was out cold. She got up quietly and gathered a few things to take into the bedroom.

When she was finished with her plan, she walked back out to the living room in a stunning, sheer negligee. Wayne was still asleep. She sat down next to him and began rubbing her fingers gently across his lips until he opened his eyes. The sight of her with her long, auburn hair falling past her shoulders took his breath away.

Julie took her husband's hand and led him silently to the bedroom. Candles were lit on the nightstands on both sides of the bed and a CD was playing softly—Faith Hill singing of love and longing.

As Wayne stepped toward the bed, Julie held his hand to stop him. "Uh-uh, honey. Not so fast. Let's take a shower first," she whispered as she started to disrobe.

"Together?" Wayne asked, unable to believe his luck.

"Mmmm hmmm," she purred, enjoying herself thoroughly. She loved teasing him and seeing the look of anticipation on his face.

Inside the shower, Wayne pulled his wife's warm, wet body close to him and kissed her neck and ears. By then the steam had filled the bathroom, but it was unclear how much they had generated with their passion and how much was caused by the hot water streaming down over their naked bodies like a summer rain.

As they stepped out together, Julie handed him a robe. "Don't put your clothes back on," she said with a smile. "Meet me in bed."

"I'm not sleepy now," Wayne said with a big grin.

"Neither am I," she said before disappearing out of the room.

Wayne lay back on the bed, soaking up the romantic atmosphere. *Candles, soft music, fluffy pillows and my gorgeous wife. What more could a man ask for?* he thought contentedly as he closed his eyes.

Just then, he heard a pop. Julie had reappeared with a chilled bottle of champagne and two glasses.

"If I'm dreaming, I hope nobody wakes me," Wayne said, admiring his wife.

"It's not a dream," Julie said. "It's just a small taste of our new life together."

"I love it already."

She poured the champagne and they toasted to each other. Then she got into bed. For the rest of the night, a sheet of paper couldn't have fit between the two of them. They made love, then fell asleep and woke up to begin again. Wayne vowed that their love would continue forever and that he'd never let that magic go as long as he lived.

"How long do you think that will be?" Julie asked, running her finger back and forth across her husband's bare chest.

"I don't know how long I'll live, but I can tell you how long I *want* to," he said.

Julie looked at him with a curious smile, awaiting his answer.

"I don't know the author of this quote but he said exactly what I feel: 'I want to die exactly one day before you do because I won't be able to live a single day without you.'"

Chapter Seven

Court is in Session

*If you limit your choices only to what seems possible
or reasonable, you disconnect yourself from what you
truly want, and all that is left is a compromise.*
—Robert Fritz

On Monday, at 5:00 a.m., Wayne woke up at his in-laws' house in Oxford. Julie had already put her plan into motion and had begun house hunting in the area and registering for classes. She wasn't the kind to waste any time—especially when it came to what was best for her family.

For his part, Wayne was happy to be closer to Stonewall County that particular morning. He had an appointment to meet Jack Burchfield for coffee before court began—but his friend insisted that they meet by eight at the latest, stipulating that they had to be in the courtroom before nine.

As Wayne entered the still-sleepy town square of Puknik, there were few cars parked in front of the courthouse. He pulled up by the coffee shop across the street, walked in and saw Jack chatting with a lady.

"Wayne, this is Patty Franklin. She owns the local newspaper," Jack said.

"What's *left* of it, thanks to the county supervisors and their business associates," she said, looking over at Jack.

Jack bowed his head slightly and started rubbing his forehead as he grinned sheepishly.

"Nice to meet you, Wayne," Patty said, then excused herself. "I'll leave you two gentlemen to enjoy your coffee—that is, if you ever get somebody to wait on you here."

"What was that all about?" Wayne asked as he lightly grabbed a passing waiter by the arm, then asked him to bring two cups of coffee.

"Patty's a nice lady but personally, I try to stay out of it. She blames the supervisors for disliking her paper—*and* for their connections. She's going bankrupt because so many business owners have pulled their ads, and she can't keep the paper going by selling copies alone."

"That's too bad," Wayne said, sipping the still-hot coffee he'd ordered. "Sounds like typical small-town politics."

"Tell me about it," Jack agreed.

"So, why was it so all-fired important for me to get here this early?" Wayne asked, focusing on the trial ahead.

"'Cause I have no intention of going back to jail," Jack said, checking his watch nervously.

"What do you mean?"

"What I mean is Judge Cates watches his clock like a hawk. If anybody who's supposed to be in his courtroom is late, even by one minute, he has the bailiff lock them up in a holding cell."

"You mean he locked you up?" Wayne asked with a surprised look.

"Hell yes. For being two minutes late. I was trying the case then, but the boss is trying this one, unless he's sick or something. Either way, I ain't takin' no chances," Jack said, putting down money before the check even arrived. He stood to leave. Wayne was only halfway through his first cup of coffee, but he left it behind.

"That's hilarious. How long did he leave you in jail?" Wayne asked as they quickly made their way across the street and into the back door of the old courthouse.

"All day, until court was over. That old man is crazy," Jack said as they reached the top of the stairs and opened the door behind the judge's bench.

"Who's crazy?" Judge Cates asked, surprisingly stumbling upon the duo as he made his way to his chamber.

"Oh, sir, I was just talking about an old college professor," Jack fumbled with fear in his now-trembling voice. "By the way, this is Wayne Lott, an AUSA from Jackson." He hoped the introduction would divert the judge's attention as he tried to recover.

"What are you doing up here, young man? Making sure I run my court correctly?" the old judge scoffed loudly, then mumbled something that sounded like "damn feds."

"No, sir, absolutely not," Wayne said, flustered. "I'm just here to learn from your DA and visit my old law school buddy, Jack."

"Jack's a good boy...but don't set your watch by his," the judge warned sternly, walking away abruptly with a straight face.

Jack took that as a sign that attendance was about to be taken, so he and Wayne hurried into the front of the courtroom through the small, wooden swinging gate and found their seats. They sat quietly, like two schoolboys awaiting the teacher's appearance, hands folded on their laps.

However, it appeared that—on that day, at least—court wouldn't be starting on time due to some negotiations between lawyers and adjustments to the docket. Just as Chastain had predicted the week before, the drug defendant's lawyers were in the chamber with the judge, discussing a plea deal.

It was almost 9:40 a.m. before the judge, dressed in his robe, appeared through the back door. Apparently he was the only one who could keep people waiting.

"All rise. The circuit court of the twenty-third district of the State of Mississippi is now in session. Judge Albert Cates presiding," the old bailiff, wearing a khaki deputy's uniform, announced in a loud, commanding voice, his right hand resting precariously on his gun.

He might have shot somebody if they failed to rise on command, Wayne thought, looking around at all the people standing at attention. *Hell, if he hadn't, the old judge might have locked him up, too.*

The case called for trial was that of Bobby Dilworth, who was charged with arson. As Wayne reached for the file that Chastain had given him to read, a hand suddenly appeared and grabbed it from him.

"So, what did you think?" Chastain asked, smiling and tapping the folder against his hand.

"Frankly, sir, I didn't have much time to look at it due to some family issues," Wayne said with some embarrassment.

"That's okay, Wayne," Chastain replied playfully. "Just watch and learn."

———

The trial began with an opening statement from Dilworth's high-class lawyers: the Falconi brothers—and their father—from a nearby county. The whole family law firm showed up and all three members sat at the lawyers' table in their $3,000, custom-made, Italian suits. It looked like the front pew at a mobster's funeral.

The fireworks really began to go off when the DA got up to question the first witness. Chastain couldn't open his mouth without the old-man lawyer or one of his two spoiled sons objecting. It didn't matter what it was about; they would have objected to the DA saying what nice weather they were having. The judge was more tolerable than one would have expected, but even he was getting fed up.

After one more objection—this time shouted out simultaneously by all three of them—Judge Cates slammed down his gavel.

"Mr. Falconi, as one old buzzard to another, I'm going to tell you something—and I want your boys to listen, too. You may run the courtroom in your home county, and you may get away with it over there. But it will be a cold day in hell before you run *my* courtroom. Now, we are going to get something straight right now. You can all represent this client if you want to, but all of you are *not* going to address this court. I have heard enough objections to last me through the end of this trial and I may hear more…but I'd better not hear them from more than one of you. Now, you three decide among yourselves who's gonna do the talking for all of you. Do you understand me, sir?" At that point the judge was pointing the gavel at the elder defense lawyer like a pistol.

"Yes, your honor. Please accept our apologies. My oldest son will represent our client."

"Your honor, I echo my dad's sentiments, sir. Please accept our apologies," the older son repeated.

"I apologize, too, sir," the younger one chimed in.

Judge Cates could do nothing but roll his eyes and motion for the DA to continue.

Chastain looked at the jury with what was known in Mississippi as a "shit-eating grin," then expertly picked up his line of questioning where he had left off.

The trial went on throughout the day with much-better behavior by the defense team, though close observers, like Wayne, could see the other two Falconis practically bursting from holding in their objections.

By the time court recessed at 5:00 p.m., however, Wayne had forgotten about the defense team altogether. He was entirely enthralled by Chastain's rapport with—and power over—the jurors. He couldn't wait to see what the DA had in store for the next day.

The following morning, before most of the jurors were done digesting their breakfasts, Chastain had somehow managed, in short order, to make the accused arsonist appear to be worse than Osama bin Laden, just like he had with the drug defendant the week before. This guy was charged only with burning down a vacant house, not destroying two fully occupied towers, but he looked so bad by the time both defense and prosecution had finished questioning the witnesses that, against their better judgment, the Falconis decided to put Dilworth on the stand. It was a mistake they would not soon forget.

The accused started off well enough, talking about how he had taught Sunday school and done a lot of other good things in his life. In fact, for a while, the jurors seemed to be eating it up. That was, until Chastain got his shot at the guy.

"Mr. Dilworth, according to testimony given here today, by your own admission, you were at the house in question earlier that day, is that correct?" Chastain asked innocently enough.

"Yes, sir, but that was about six p.m. and it was later that night that the fire department was called. I was nowhere near the house when it caught on fire. I had only been there to check to see what work the crew would need to do on it the next day," Dilworth said.

The defense attorneys were livid. They had told their idiot client to answer only the questions and not expound on the subjects. Apparently he was as dumb as a witness as he was an arsonist.

Chastain nodded his head in consideration. He asked a few more questions, most of which seemed pretty innocuous. From his seat, Wayne actually was surprised that the DA wasn't tearing into the accused more, now that he had the chance. Dilworth was clearly already rattled but Chastain was sedate, seeming to be saving his harshest words for the jury.

After the defense made its final, whining plea, it was Chastain's turn to address his audience—the jurors.

He took the floor like a Shakespearean actor stepping on stage. "Ladies and gentlemen, the defense would have you believe that this three-thousand-square-foot house, which was eighty-percent complete, with no electricity, gas or other combustibles, just somehow caught fire on its own and burned up. They would also like you to believe that Mr. Dilworth had no reason to burn the house himself and further that he was nowhere near the house when it caught fire. He has painted himself as a Sunday-school teacher, a respectable businessman and a responsible father of two. But it is *my* job and obligation to show that he had the means, the motive and the opportunity to carry out this crime."

Wayne sat forward in his seat. He knew that the *real* show was about to begin.

Chastain continued. "You have heard the fire marshal explain a fire triangle, which requires all three sides to be met before a fire is possible. There must be oxygen, fuel and heat." The DA ticked off each item on his fingers. "We have proven here today that the defendant brought two of those things to the scene with him. His credit card records and the store video show that a half hour before he was seen at the house by a neighbor, he stopped at a Home Depot eight miles away and bought a large can of plumber's glue and a grill lighter. Now, those are some pretty odd things to bring to a barbecue, don't you think?"

The jurors laughed. It was the exact response that Chastain had intended.

"Mr. Dilworth here may not seem so smart, but he knew he couldn't introduce some accelerant to the scene that shouldn't be there, such as gasoline. Besides, that would have burned too fast and wouldn't have given him enough time to get away. So he put the can of plumber's glue under the sink, next to some papers and pressed board, then removed the top, which he placed next to the can, and lit it. Don't forget, he'd been a plumber himself before becoming a building contractor, so he knew that the glue had a slow burn rate.

"You also watched the fire marshal's demonstration with a much-smaller can of plumber's glue when he came in this morning. He lit that in the metal pan over there across the courtroom and, as you can see, it's still burning. That was four hours ago, ladies and gentlemen. So it was only a matter of time before that large can, confined under the sink in the cabinet with paper and particle board, went up in flames."

Wayne glanced quickly at the jurors to assess their moods. He could practically see the word "guilty" written on each face.

Chastain continued to paint an image with words, taking the

members of the jury into the burning house with him. "Imagine, if you will, that plumber's glue smoldering and burning for hours before nearby articles started to catch on fire. It gave Mr. Dilworth plenty of time to get somewhere else so he'd have an alibi."

The DA paused dramatically, shaking his head in disapproval. "As you'll recall, the fire marshal testified that the fire started in the bathroom, where the burnt can was found. You also saw that for yourself in the crime scene photos. Now, think of those pictures together with the federal-court records showing that Mr. Dilworth had filed recently for bankruptcy, and it's like adding two plus two. Due to the recession and the bottom falling out of the real estate market, he couldn't complete the building of the homes that he had under construction. The bank had refused him any more construction advances. We can all understand that, can't we, folks?" Chastain said quietly to the jury. "I mean, we've all been affected by the recession in one way or another."

The jury members nodded their heads solemnly.

"But what we *haven't* done is gone around burning houses, have we? Destroying property? Putting people's lives at risk?"

Chastain took a few steps toward the defendant. "Means!" he screamed loudly. "He brought accelerants to the scene, thinking he could use them to fool our fine investigators. At the same time, he brought a lighter, ladies and gentlemen—the very same charred lighter you saw with your own eyes lying next to the burnt can in the photos."

Jabbing his index finger into the air, Chastain yelled even more loudly, "Motive!" He looked accusingly at the defendant, then back into the eyes of the jurors. "Mr. Dilworth was broke and couldn't finish the house for the buyers. He needed the insurance money," he sneered, "and saw an easy way to get it. The rest of us? We have to work hard for our money. We don't just go around *breaking laws.*"

At that point, the jury was glaring menacingly at the defendant, who seemed to shrink behind his three stocky lawyers. By then, they looked more like bodyguards.

"Opportunity!" It was the DA's loudest appeal to the jury yet. "Mr. Dilworth had not only the opportunity to set the fire but also to create his own alibi by using a slow-burning glue that would give him plenty of time to flee the scene and be long gone when the house caught fire."

There was another long pause as Chastain turned and looked directly at the defendant. His words, however, were meant for the jurors' ears alone. "Not only is this man an arsonist, he is attempting to commit insurance fraud…"

The defendant looked anxiously at his lawyers and blurted out, "I didn't tell him about the claim."

"Objection, your honor," the older Falconi son interrupted. "May I approach the bench?"

Judge Cates nodded, and both the defense and the DA stepped closer.

"Your honor, the district attorney provided us with no evidence in discovery that our client had filed an insurance claim. I insist you instruct the jury to disregard that comment," the defense lawyer said.

"I didn't *know* he filed a claim, Counselor," Chastain replied innocently. "Your objection interrupted me. I was about to say, 'He is attempting to commit insurance fraud…*I believe.*'"

Falconi stared at him, his eyes bulging out.

"Of course, he just confirmed my suspicion with his spontaneous admission, and that makes the motive even stronger," Chastain said, smiling. "May even make it a new charge of insurance fraud." He shrugged. "It's not my fault your client didn't tell you everything."

"Overruled," Judge Cates said, clearly impressed. "Continue with the argument."

The two attorneys stepped back. Falconi was sweating visibly, like he was about to stand on the wrong side of a firing squad.

Chastain, on the other hand, looked like the poster boy for Degree antiperspirant. He was confident that he had the jurors eating out of his hands. And, just like the week before, it didn't take them long to find this guy guilty.

Chapter Eight

The Reporter

Sure, there are dishonest men
in local government. But there are dishonest
men in national government, too.
—Richard M. Nixon

Wayne left the court in awe, seeing Chastain as some kind of superstar no matter what type of case was thrown at him. That was the style of prosecutor he wanted to be: fearless and uncompromising.

When Jack left to go back to his office, Wayne walked around the town square a bit, reflecting on what he had just witnessed: justice, pure and simple. As he was strolling, he picked up an issue of the Stonewall County paper; he'd seen Chinese take-out menus with more pages.

There has to be two sides to this story, he thought to himself, remembering what Jack had told him about that woman in the coffee shop. *After all, Stonewall County seems like a nice place. I can't imagine the county supervisors are all that bad. Then again...*

Wayne was no stranger to corruption, strong-arming and manipulation. After his entanglement with extortion and murder among members of the legislature, he really couldn't put anything past *any* politicians, no matter how small-time they might have seemed.

Right then, Wayne decided to follow in the footsteps of Chastain.

Stifling freedom of the press was not something to take lightly, and since he'd be spending so much time in Stonewall anyway, he would get to the bottom of what was going on in that county. He'd bring the truth to light—and make his mentor proud.

———

It didn't take Wayne more than five minutes to find the newspaper office. It was near the town square, conveniently located by the coffee shop where, he imagined, Patty went frequently for her caffeine fix. She looked a bit disheveled, like someone addicted to double espressos.

That's what deadlines will do to you, he figured.

Wayne opened the front door, letting a stream of light into what was otherwise a cramped and rather musty-smelling office. With so many stacks of old, yellowing newspapers lying around, it certainly wasn't the place for anyone who suffered from claustrophobia—or who was careless with matches.

"Hello?" Wayne called out, standing near the unoccupied receptionist's desk out front.

Patty poked her head out of a back room, seeming surprised to hear a human voice.

"Hi, Patty. Remember me? Wayne Lott..." he said.

"Oh, sure. You're Jack's friend...from yesterday." She stepped into the front room, wiping what appeared to be newspaper ink off her face. However, since there was more black ink on the back of her hand, she succeeded only in smudging it more.

"So, what can I do for you?" she asked, smiling. "Sure hope you didn't come about a job. As you can see, we have a lot of vacancies." She waved her arms around the empty office. "But they're not exactly paid positions."

"Nah, my days as a newspaper delivery boy put me off to the world of publishing completely," Wayne joked. "Besides, I'm pretty busy at the moment—apprenticing under John Chastain."

"Hmm, then you *must* be busy," Patty said. "That man makes more court appearances than Roger Federer." She laughed.

"Yeah. Who knows where he finds so many criminals to prosecute? I mean, Stonewall County seems like an ideal Southern setting to me."

"Does it, now?" Patty asked, raising her eyebrows. "Well, Wayne, just goes to show you haven't been in town all that long."

"What do you mean?" he asked curiously, knowing she would lead him to the information he was seeking.

"Wait here. I'll be right back." Patty disappeared back into her office. She pushed her way quickly through the door; it wouldn't open all the way due to the disorganized stacks of newspapers crammed into every corner of her small room, which she had clearly outgrown three years earlier.

Miraculously, she came back through the door in mere moments, with an armful of newspapers that dated back a couple of years. Only she could have known where they were and gone directly to them.

Patty blew some strands of hair out of her face and handed the stack of papers to Wayne. "When you get the time, read through these. They'll give you a more-complete history of this place."

"I don't know that I'll *ever* have enough time," Wayne said, weighing the heavy stack in his hands.

"It won't take you too long to start to see a few connections," she said. "The supervisors run this county and call all the shots. If anybody opposes them, they use their positions in the chamber of commerce and their connections at the Consumer Bank to close down businesses. That's what they did to me. Now I'll probably have to move back by my family in Florida in order to survive."

"Are you sure about your accusations?" Wayne asked. "As a news professional, you know that such unsubstantiated talk can amount to slander."

"Oh, so let them sue me," she said. "I didn't print it, so it's not libel. Anyway, what have I got to lose at this point? The paper's closing down in a few months, and no one seems to get it—not even your friend

Jack. You seem a little sharper, though." She studied Wayne closely for a moment. "I figure maybe if I tell enough people, something will be done about these crooks someday. They're not the people you think they are."

"I don't know. Most county supervisors are sharp, hard-working people… But you never know how power can corrupt someone. I have a little experience in that area myself, so I'll keep it in mind as I do a little light reading," Wayne said, nodding toward the heavy pile of papers in his arms.

"Oh, yeah, they're sharp and hard-working, all right," Patty replied sarcastically. "They work very hard to steal all they can and they've been sharp enough not to get caught." She paused, suddenly getting serious. "Look, Wayne, I hope after you've done some research you can feel comfortable enough to take this issue back to the US attorney's office and get something done up here. What they're doing is criminal," she concluded.

"Criminal, huh?" Wayne echoed. "You think they take bribes?"

"I wish I knew. If I could spend a few more months here and had the right investigative reporter, I'm sure I could uncover something," she said wistfully, looking around her empty offices again. "If anybody could find evidence of criminal malfeasance here it would be the county investigator, Randy Wood. He knows about every criminal in this area and has developed a lot of informants. But what good would it do me now? And who would prosecute the case if he ever found anything?" Patty asked despondently.

"You never know, Patty. There are still some good guys left in the legal profession," Wayne said, thinking specifically of Chastain.

"Now *that* would be front-page news," she said. "Anyway, you really should meet Randy if you're looking for a mentor. He could teach anyone a thing or two—even Sheriff 'Doc' Sanders."

"Not exactly the long arm of the law?" Wayne asked.

"The only thing long about Doc is the afternoon nap he takes each day." Patty laughed. "He's a little, old man in his mid-sixties with thinning, gray hair, glasses and a big, old Masonic ring—not exactly intimidating, but a true Southern gentleman. He's fair, has a sense of humor and always sees the good in everyone."

"Well, that doesn't sound so bad," Wayne said.

"In case you haven't noticed, most cops wear reflective Aviators, not rose-colored glasses. Those don't usually work in law enforcement."

"I see what you mean," Wayne said, thinking of his father, who was fair but a far cry from naïve.

"Well, I'm sure you'll meet everyone in the sheriff's office eventually," Patty said.

"I look forward to it."

Patty opened the door for Wayne to walk out. Carrying his load of newspapers in front of him, he couldn't manage the doorknob, let alone see over the stack. He bid her goodbye then walked directly to his car to drop off his bounty. He was intrigued by what Patty had told him and was looking forward to learning more about Stonewall County and its political situation. But there was one more place he wanted to stop first.

Wayne started the short walk over to the sheriff's office. He figured now would be a good time to meet this Randy Wood one on one.

Chapter Nine

The Investigator

Seize the moment of excited curiosity
on any subject to solve your doubts; for if
you let it pass, the desire may never return,
and you may remain in ignorance.
—William Wirt

Wayne walked into the sheriff's office—a small, unimposing, brick building that didn't look any less cluttered inside than Patty's workplace.

Must have the same interior decorator, Wayne mused.

There were two or three people chatting around the water cooler and one man hard at work at his desk. From what he'd heard, Wayne assumed that the man working must have been Randy Wood.

"Excuse me... I'm Wayne Lott, AUSA from Jackson. Patty Franklin told me I could find County Investigator Wood here."

"Find him you did," Wood said, looking up from his work. "Sure *you're* not an investigator?"

Wayne smiled. "I'm sure. At most, I'm a wannabe prosecutor."

Wood, a bit disheveled from running his fingers through his hair while working, studied the man standing in front of him for a few seconds. "Wayne Lott, huh? I've heard that name before. You did some informant work for special agents down in Jackson. You know, with that kind of background, you probably *could* make a good county investigator. I mean, if you weren't a lawyer and all."

Wood glanced up at the clock hanging on the wall and looked surprised. "Seems my day ended thirty minutes ago. You saved me from more unpaid overtime, Wayne. What do you say I buy you a beer?"

"You mean you have bars here in this little country town?" Wayne asked.

"Well, not exactly. A lot of the folks around here haven't heard that they've repealed Prohibition. But we can get a small pitcher of beer over at the Pizza Cellar behind the square. It's just a short walk," Randy said.

"Is anything in this town a *long* walk?" Wayne laughed.

"Nope. But some days the walk to that ice-cold pitcher sure *feels* long enough."

"Sounds good to me," Wayne said.

Upon their arrival at the bustling pizza joint Randy chose a seat hidden away in a rear corner with his back against the wall. He could see the front door and any customers coming in. It was the spot that two opposing types would take: outlaws or law-enforcement officials. Wayne wondered what the investigator was looking for—or trying to conceal.

"We'd like a pitcher of Miller Lite draft with two cold mugs," Randy told the waiter when he came around.

"So what kind of cases do you work on over there?" Wayne asked.

"You name it, we work on it. Whatever comes up: drugs, murder, robbery and more burglaries than I can count."

"Which ones do you prefer?"

"Drug cases, without a doubt," Wood said. "I worked as an undercover drug agent before I came here and I know most of the dopers and their habits. Made fifty-five cases on twenty-two defendants in an undercover sting bar before taking this job. Some are in prison now, some are awaiting trial and some are still waiting to get caught."

"That's some record," Wayne said, impressed. "Well, you certainly have a great DA here to prosecute drug cases. Seems those just might be his favorite, too."

"You mean Chastain, the people's champion…" Wood began. Before he could continue, the waiter returned.

"Here's your beer, guys. Having any pizza this evening?"

Wayne and Randy looked at each other, debating.

"Why not, Randy? You pick one. I like them all…and I'm buying," Wayne answered.

After placing the order for a small cheese pizza, Wood said, "I hope I'm wrong, Wayne, but there are some things here that concern me sometimes."

"What kind of things?" Wayne asked.

"Well, I'm telling you this because I know I can trust you…with your background and all," Wood said, looking around stealthily. "It's just that there are some people who never go to trial and I don't know where the ball gets dropped. Problem is, working for the county, I can't look into it myself. Could be somebody in the DA's office protecting criminals from having to face Chastain's wrath. Could also be in the circuit clerk's office or even the circuit judge himself. I just don't know."

"I see," Wayne said soberly.

"Did you meet the lawyers next door to the DA?" Wood asked.

"No, I didn't. Who are they?"

"The Tucker and Tatum Law Firm. Let's just say I have a hunch that they're somehow involved," Wood said as he drained his beer mug. "Billy Tucker and Royce Tatum run the firm—just penny-ante stuff, you know. But they do represent a lot of the locals on felony charges."

"Disappearing cases doesn't sound good," Wayne said. "Does Jack Burchfield know about this?"

"I've tried to talk to him about it before but he kind of brushed me off. I think he's a good guy but he doesn't seem to want to get involved in anything too political. Probably just trying to save his job...just like I've been doing up to this point."

Wayne thought about that description of Jack and realized it made sense. His friend never had been one to stick his neck out on principle—especially when he could get his head handed to him—but he was a good man.

The pizza arrived, nice and hot, and Wood waited until the waiter left to continue the conversation.

"I'll be honest with you, Wayne," he continued in a conspiratorial tone. "I've just about had it with the politics around here and may very well move on, so I don't really have anything to lose by telling you this. Since I know you have a reputation for going after corruption and not backing down, maybe you can do something about the situation."

Wayne considered it as he slowly chewed on his slice of pizza. He wasn't quite sure what to say. First, there'd been Patty and her belief in a conspiracy against the newspaper. Now, there was the county investigator with his suspicion of missing cases. If both theories were true—and possibly related—it could have been more than Wayne was prepared to tackle. It also could have gotten him embroiled back in the world of political corruption from which he'd fought so hard to free himself.

On one hand, he was a stranger in a tight-knit town. On the other, this way a sure-fire way to distinguish himself to his mentor.

"Hey, I didn't realize the time," Wood said, glancing at his watch. "I'm not expecting any answers from you right away, Wayne. In fact, I'd like to discuss this issue with you in more depth. But I'd better be going now. My wife's getting tired of me coming home late for dinner, and here I am eating pizza."

"Okay, Randy," Wayne said, glad to be off the hook for the time being. "We'll definitely talk soon."

As the county investigator was leaving the restaurant, he received a call on his cell phone. He assumed it was his wife, ready to give him hell about another ruined dinner.

It turned out to be much worse.

Chapter Ten

The Missing Man

*Reality is that which, when you stop
believing in it, doesn't go away.*
—Philip K. Dick

Chastain was on the other end of the line, screaming bloody murder. To the county investigator, it was the usual reaction of a megalomaniacal man who wasn't used to *not* getting his way.

"Randy, where the hell are you? I've been trying to get you at the office for almost an hour."

"What is it you need?" Wood asked calmly.

"Do you have any contacts with the DEA?" Chastain barked more than asked.

"Yes. Why? What's going on?"

"There's a guy named Buford Lancaster—a wealthy businessman in the county who's making my life miserable."

"What's his story?" Wood asked, unfamiliar with the name.

"He's kind of a loner, not well known in the area. Keeps most of his assets in Memphis and Miami. This guy's a skilled pilot who owns several airplanes but one of them has been missing for over a year—along with Lancaster himself. It was a big deal when it first happened, before you got here, but then the trail went cold and the case kind of went quiet."

"Let me guess. You assume he might be involved in drug trafficking and our gifted DA is desperate to crack such a potentially explosive and high-profile case…just in time for congressional elections." Wood laughed.

"With your help, of course," Chastain said humbly, clearly having calmed down.

"Well, you're in luck," Wood said. "I just talked to my DEA contact a few hours ago and he was planning to be in his office tonight. I'll run back to my desk and give him a call to see if he's got any information on this small-town Scarface of yours."

"Thanks, Randy. I knew I could count on you," Chastain said with a sigh of relief. "I think this case could be pretty hot, so can you make sure to get back in touch with me tonight?"

Randy did believe that Chastain served the public as best he could, with a side of self-serving thrown in. So he could forgive him his occasional outbursts and overzealousness.

"Sure," Wood said. "I'll get on it right now and get back to you soon."

As Randy went back to his office instead of heading home, he wondered how much longer his wife would understand and accept his unwavering interest in the public good before tossing him out on his ass altogether. Sure, his desk was well worn and comfortable. But he'd never had to try using it as a bed before.

~~~

Back at the sheriff's office, which was beginning to feel like a first rather than second home to him, Wood let out a deep sigh and dialed his DEA contact.

"Mack, how are you, buddy?" he asked the familiar voice on the other end.

"Randy! You still working or is this a social call for a beer run?" Mack asked, seeming eager for it to be the latter.

"Don't I wish," Wood responded. "I'm at the office and have a favor to ask you for our DA."

"Shoot," Mack said.

"You know anything about a man named Buford Lancaster? He's supposed to have gone missing from Stonewall County over a year ago… Might have been flying a plane around the islands off the southeast coast of Florida."

"Doesn't ring a bell," Mack said after thinking for a few moments. "But I can run him through my system. You have his date of birth?"

"No, but I know he's a white male in his mid- to late forties who should have several planes registered to him," Wood said, checking the email Chastain had sent him.

"Okay, that should do it. I'll check the FAA records, too. Can I call you back in a few?" Mack asked.

"Sure. I'll be in my office, as usual," Randy replied, hanging up wearily.

He spent about thirty long minutes staring steadily up at the clock on the wall. The minute hand barely seemed to be moving and he was just about to get up to make sure the old timepiece was still working right when the phone rang. It was Mack.

"Randy, sorry it took so long but there was a good bit of activity with this Lancaster guy to sort through—up until about a year and a half ago, that is. We have some intel reports, most of which deal with his jumping in and out of the Turks and Caicos Islands, as well as the Caymans and Bahamas. He got caught one time with a large amount of cash he didn't declare and British customs seized it."

"Really?" Wood asked, suddenly seeing what had piqued the DA's interest. "Do you know how much?"

"All the report shows is that it was over a hundred thousand dollars. But that's just a checkmark in a box. It could've been considerably more. To tell you the truth, Randy, I'm not sure why we weren't looking at this guy more closely. The Miami office should have done it, but they're always swamped."

"Some of these guys have a way of staying under the radar," Wood agreed.

"Tell you what," Mack said. "I'm going to fax you what I have and maybe I can get some more information tomorrow. You know, most of our guys don't work late hours like you and me."

Wood managed a smile and a small laugh; he was too tired for anything more. "If I don't hear back from you, I'll assume there wasn't more info," he said.

"All right, buddy. Take care...and don't work too hard," Mack added.

"Thanks."

Less than two minutes after hanging up, Randy retrieved the information from the fax machine and reviewed it before going back to the DA's office.

The office was mostly dark except for the energy-saving lamp illuminating the papers strewn all over Chastain's desk. The DA himself was pushed back in his chair, sitting in the shadows. All Wood could make out was the burning tip of a cigar. He knew this position, though. It meant Chastain was lost in thought.

"Mr. Chastain," Wood said, clearing his throat. "It's after nine and my wife is going to shoot me if I don't get home soon."

"I appreciate your dedication, Randy," Chastain said, flicking on the overhead light switch behind him. "But as you know, the bad guys don't rest."

"Neither do we," Wood muttered. "I got some information on that Lancaster guy. Seems the DEA had some suspicious-activity reports filed on him but they didn't really have much on him as far as being a drug suspect. In fact, they don't have anything on him at all for the last year and a half, since he's been missing."

"Let me look at what you have," Chastain said, reaching for the stack of faxed papers Randy held in his hand. After studying them for a few moments, he said, half-aloud, "This coincides somewhat with what she said."

"What *who* said?" Randy asked.

Chastain looked up as if he'd forgotten the other man was there. "Lancaster's wife, Sheila. We go to the same church." He let out a long breath. "The poor woman's gone through all types of emotions. At first, she frantically reported him missing along with one of his larger single-engine airplanes, a Cherokee Six. Later, she found love letters from some girlfriend he had in the Grand Cayman Islands—the vice president of a bank there. Sheila discovered information on accounts she didn't even know he had."

Wood shook his head, thinking of his own wife waiting for him at home.

Chastain went on. "People who Sheila didn't even know started calling and asking about her husband. She said some of them were international callers with foreign accents, some Hispanic, some British. She knew Buford was doing well as a businessman in Memphis and it seemed like the more he traveled, the more money he made. His wife really is a sweet, naïve person, but I know better. I think this guy was involved in major drug smuggling throughout the Caribbean using his aircraft."

"So what do you think happened to him?" Wood asked.

"Well, if you had asked me that exact question yesterday, I would have told you the same thing everybody else thinks: That he probably crashed in the ocean somewhere in the Caribbean or South Atlantic. Hell, maybe that he even disappeared in the Bermuda Triangle. He frequented that area enough." Now it was Chastain's turn to shake his head in disbelief. "It's weird, Randy. It's like this guy just vanished from everyone's mind after a while. Even the FBI was working on his case, but nobody has heard anything until now."

"That tells me a lot. The FBI and DEA still aren't sharing information, even after September eleventh. My DEA contact said they had nothing on the guy at first. So what happened now?" Randy asked, brimming with curiosity.

"This," Chastain said, handing the county investigator a credit-card bill.

"This only has one charge on it for the whole month—for aviation fuel in Jamaica," Wood said, staring down at the document.

"That's right. It's Lancaster's card...and it hasn't had a charge on it in eighteen months," Chastain said.

"Now, that *is* interesting," Wood mused, never one to let a good mystery go cold, even though that was exactly what the dinner his wife had prepared was doing at the moment. "That means either he's still alive and has been hiding out all this time but screwed up by using an old card..."

"Sheila said the last time she saw him, he had a lot of cash on him. Maybe it's running out," Chastain prodded.

"Or he crashed on land somewhere and some scavenger got to his credit card," Wood said, finishing his thoughts.

"Randy, I think you're on the right track with this thing," Chastain said, standing up excitedly. "His wife now seems to think he was involved with somebody else pretty big around here...someone with a lot of money who was up to his neck in planeloads of dope."

The picture crystallized pretty quickly in Wood's mind. This case really was a big deal—one that the DA, a congressional hopeful, could have a chance at solving.

"Because of the suspicion surrounding his disappearance," Chastain continued, "the insurance company hasn't paid the death claim on him yet. Not only that, but if it's proven that he is in fact dead, and that he died as a result of an accident, they have to shell out twice the amount because he had a double-indemnity life-insurance policy payable to his wife…and Sheila really could use the money. She's been in a bad way, understandably," the DA concluded sympathetically.

For a moment, Wood couldn't shake the feeling that he was sitting in a juror's box in court. Chastain was *that* good.

"You know, Mr. Chastain, this case might involve intelligence and investigative information from a number of federal agencies, especially since the DEA really had no great suspicion of drug smuggling about him. Money laundering and hiding cash in the Grand Cayman banks is probably more like it, especially since his girlfriend was VP of a bank there," Randy said, hooked on the case by then.

"What are you getting at?" the DA asked, knowing that Wood never made a comment without significance.

"Well, we have the FAA involved with the plane, US customs involved with his movements, British customs regarding his funds seizure, the DEA, probably the FBI." Wood ticked each one off on a separate finger. "And, as I said before, you know the FBI's reputation for not often sharing information with other federal agencies. But they do have to talk to US attorneys."

Something was starting to click in Chastain's mind.

"I was just figuring that maybe we could use the help of that new assistant US attorney hanging around here… You know, Wayne Lott," Wood said. "He seems just as interested in drug cases as you and I are."

"That's a great idea, Randy," Chastain said enthusiastically. "Why don't we give him a call right now?"

"Why don't I get on it first thing in the morning instead?" Randy asked evenly. "You know, he does have a family."

"Yeah, yeah, you're right. And you really should go on home to your wife, Randy," Chastain said, finally taking the hint. "We don't want you to come up missing, too."

"Ah, she's not really likely to commit murder and dump my body somewhere. Worst-case scenario, I might get hit with the skillet she fried the chicken in hours ago…but at least it won't be hot."

Chastain thanked the county investigator and wished him a good night. Then he sat in his office, just meditating silently.

After an hour had gone by he got up and pulled a picture off the wall near his desk. It was a photo of himself dressed in his flight suit, standing by one of the few dual-engine propeller reconnaissance planes left in service; he had flown it in the Gulf War as a Marine-reserve pilot.

All the talk about the missing plane brought back his days of looking for downed pilots as well as the enemy, and Chastain started to catch airplane fever all over again. It was in his blood, something always boiling near the surface. And now, as he stared at the picture in his hands longingly and intently, he convinced himself that he could justify buying a plane to use in his race for the Senate.

Hell, he even thought about going down and searching for Sheila's husband himself.

Chapter Eleven

Wayne's Reassignment

*There is nothing like returning to a place that remains
unchanged to find the ways in which
you yourself have altered.*
—Nelson Mandela

"Good morning," Wayne practically sang out to the receptionist
at the front desk of the US attorney's office in Oxford. "I'm
Wayne Lott, your new assistant US attorney. I've just been reassigned
from Jackson, thanks to Special Agent Tischner, and I decided to
stop by a day early on my way to Stonewall County."

"Well, welcome, Mr. Lott," the receptionist said with a cheerful
smile. "I do believe you're going to be very popular around here."

"Why do you say that?" Wayne asked with a curious look on his
face.

"It's not even time for you to begin work yet and you already have
three phone messages," she said. "One from the DA in Stonewall
County, one from an investigator in the same county, and one from
Agent Wallace Tischner himself, who wants you to come downstairs
before you check in."

"Guess he knew I'd be overeager to start," Wayne said sheepishly.

"He does have great intuitive powers," she agreed conspiratorially.
"He *is* a special agent in charge, after all."

Wayne thanked the secretary and went on his way, wondering

what Chastain and Wood could possibly want that couldn't wait another hour or so for his arrival.

First things first, though, he thought, heading down to Tischner's office. After all, this was going to be his job. His position in the Stonewall County courtroom was merely as a spectator.

"Special Agent Tischner, sir? Wayne Lott reporting for duty as ordered," he announced, poking his head into the office.

"Well, hello there, my long-lost friend. Haven't seen hide or hair of you in the neighborhood yet. Are you ready to go to work?" Tischner asked expectantly.

"Can't wait. That's why I'm here early," Wayne said with a great deal of vigor.

"Glad to hear it. I know you don't officially start until tomorrow, but it couldn't hurt for you to meet the boss now."

"I thought *you* were the boss," Wayne said with a laugh.

"Well, I want you to keep that in mind. But I'd like to introduce you to the man with the actual title—the northern district US attorney," Tischner said authoritatively, as if he really were the boss.

They walked down the hallway and stopped in front of US Attorney Spillers' door.

After one brief knock, Tischner opened the door and announced proudly, "Boss, I'd like you to meet our new hired hand, Wayne Lott."

"Come on in, guys," Donald Spillers said without any air of pomposity, which was a rarity for someone in his position. "Wayne, it's a pleasure to meet you. Once you get settled in, let me know if there's anything you might need. My door is always open."

"Boss, he ain't got time to settle in. I'll get him initiated eventually, but we gotta get started pronto. There's plenty of work to do—and he should have been here last week instead of sauntering in today," Tischner practically barked.

Wayne decided that now was not the time to remind him that he wasn't even supposed to be there that day.

"Okay," Spillers said jovially. "You two get to work and I'll see you guys later. Welcome aboard, Wayne."

"Thank you, sir," Wayne managed to say before Tischner nearly dragged him out the door.

"Now, Wayne, the first thing I want to ask you is how your relationship with Chastain is going," Tischner said, sounding all business.

"Great," Wayne said, furtively checking his watch. He knew he'd be late for court in Stonewall County—and felt it would be better not to incur Judge Cates' wrath against the prosecution on his behalf. There was nothing he could do about it now but relax and ride the rest of the day out in Oxford.

"Chastain is one hell of a smart prosecutor and I admire his dedication," Wayne elaborated. "I learned a lot from him in the short time I was up there. I owe him a lot, like you."

"I'm glad to hear you two hit it off so well," Tischner said. "But I wasn't asking out of jealousy. Fact is, we're getting a lot of undesirable intel about supervisors in that county and we might just need his help. Think you can count on him?"

"Well, I don't know how he feels about pursuing county supervisors, but I can tell you for sure that he loves to prosecute drug cases and is always looking for bigger and better ones," Wayne said. "That makes me think he'll do anything to help clean up the county."

"Good," Tischner said. "I'll brief you more about our intelligence later, but you should know we have more going on in that particular county than anyplace else. The whole damn board of supervisors appears to be corrupt and might be involved in a single conspiracy with banks, newspaper editors and lawyers."

"What kind of conspiracy?" Wayne asked when they got back to Tischner's office, closing the door securely behind him.

"Right now, we're watching a civil suit and listening to testimony that we may be able to use down the road in a criminal case," Tischner said, taking a seat. "When your daddy, Will, was in this business over thirty years ago, we had a big operation to target county supervisors and we snagged a few other corrupt officials in the process. We called it 'Operation Pretense,'" he said nostalgically. "Fortunately, politicians forget easily—everything *including* their campaign promises—and more so as the years pass. So we've started a new operation of the exact same type, only now we're calling it 'Operation Boomerang' because the damn thing has come back to us yet again."

Wayne listened with mixed emotions. On one hand, he was immensely proud to be involved in any operation similar to one in which his father had taken part. On the other hand, he was sorry to hear it was happening in Stonewall County.

"Problem is," Tischner continued, "there's so much corruption in that one county alone that we may have bitten off more than we can chew. That's why I needed your help."

"Well, I'm more than ready. Heck, I've already got two years' worth of newspapers reporting on those same supervisors, I believe."

"What?" a stunned Tischner asked. "How did you know—"

"I didn't," Wayne replied. "I just happened to meet the newspaper editor… The one who most likely filed the civil suit you're talking about—Patty Franklin. She isn't involved with the supervisors, is she?"

"Oh, no, she's definitely not," Tischner said. "I'm impressed. Your first day on the job to boot."

"Don't be too impressed," Wayne replied. "I haven't had the chance to read even one article yet."

"I'll save you the trouble," Tischner said, putting his feet up on his desk. "Here's the brief on our end: Our operation started covertly over a year ago. But as we got more involved in these things and started retrieving records before they began to disappear, word got out. So we've been working *overtly* there for the last few months."

Sitting across from the special agent's desk, Wayne nodded and pulled out a pad to take notes. It was a habit he had developed the last time he'd worked with Tischner, who was a notoriously rapid-fire speaker.

"We weren't ready to present our cases to the grand jury yet but one of those asshole supervisors jumped one of our agents in the clerk's office at a board meeting," Tischner went on. "We arrested him and charged him with assault on a federal officer. Any cover we might have had was blown at that point. That's okay, though. We're at the stage of gathering records, conducting interviews and developing informants. You with me so far?"

"Sure," Wayne said, scribbling furiously in his notepad.

"Okay, so then the owner of the only newspaper in town starts writing derogatory stories about the supervisors. They, in turn, get pissed off at her and, through their network with the chamber of commerce, other newspapers in different towns and the Consumer Bank, start putting the squeeze on her businesses. Next thing you know, the county notices are up for bid and the supervisors pursue the other paper on the other side of the county, looking to take control of the news themselves."

Wayne stopped writing for one brief second, realizing how right Patty had been about everything she'd told him.

"So this Patty Franklin woman sues them, saying the other newspaper is not qualified because it doesn't provide service throughout the county since it's only a town paper. Then the political machine goes to work with their contacts at the Consumer Bank in an attempt to put even more pressure on Patty," Tischner said all in one breath.

"What makes the Consumer Bank so powerful and attractive to the supervisors?" Wayne asked, massaging his writing hand.

"Good question—and one that you'll hopefully be answering yourself. That's something we need you to find out. But we know they hate Patty and her paper because she named the bank in an antitrust suit. With the proof required in the suit, though, Patty didn't stand a chance. Seems that she just got on the wrong side of the supervisors and the bank, stepped on their toes, and they paid her back."

Tischner took an uncharacteristic pause. "Funny thing is that the competitor newspaper won't print a derogatory statement about any county official no matter how true it is or how much the public has a right to know. I thought at first the editor had no balls, then I found out he had an agenda. Patty might have been too editorial but at least she exercised her First Amendment rights. This new rag, though, is just a convenient way of covering up the real news." He sighed. "I don't know what this country is coming to."

"This goes pretty deep, then," Wayne observed.

"Well, that's it as far as the supervisors, bank and competitor newspaper go, but if you ask me, we haven't even scratched the surface," Tischner said. "It will all make a lot more sense to you when we start putting together the conspiracy charts. Sadly, you'll probably have a lawyer or two in the mix."

Wayne grinned. He had almost managed to forget all about the conspiracy charts that were a constant part of working with Tischner. He imagined that if some kid working at a fast-food drive-through forgot to include the fries in his order, Tischner would pull over immediately and begin sketching out an elaborate diagram to explain the anti-federal-agent French-fry conspiracy.

Tischner caught Wayne's amused look but couldn't comprehend its meaning. "Wanna take a break for lunch?" he asked.

"Wow, you *are* intuitive," Wayne said, remembering what the secretary had told him. He hadn't remembered, however, to call back Chastain or Wood.

Chapter Twelve

The Bank Deal

*One's first step in wisdom
is to question everything—and one's last
is to come to terms with everything.*
—Georg Christoph Lichtenberg

Early that afternoon, Johnny Chastain paced his office like a man possessed. He was sure he could get Wayne's help on the Lancaster case, but the fact that his self-appointed apprentice hadn't called him back or showed up in court that morning wasn't what bothered him. He had even put Mrs. Lancaster's problems on the back burner for the time being. What had gotten under his skin was the need to take to the skies.

Chastain couldn't stand it anymore. He practically blew past Betty Sue on his way out the door. She called after him, "Taking an early lunch today?" but got no response.

The DA walked briskly toward the Consumer Bank on Puknik's square to see the bank president.

"Beautiful day out, isn't it, Mr. Chastain?" the bank receptionist greeted him.

"Why, yes... Yes, it is, Mrs. Swindol," he answered. "In fact, it's a perfect day for flying in that clear sky."

The woman smiled uncertainly, unsure of what he meant. "Do you need to see Mr. Buchanan?" she asked.

"Sure do. Is he in?" Chastain asked hopefully.

"Yes, sir, he is, but he just went into a meeting with Mr. Jackson from the hardware store. I can get you in to see his new assistant, Forrest Musgrove, if you want," she said cheerfully.

"No, that's okay. I'll wait for Mr. Buchanan himself," Chastain replied, fiddling with the copy of *USA Today* that was sitting on a small table in the lobby. "Don't you worry about me. I'll just catch up on the news here while you go on about your business." He forced a smile and sat down, checking his watch and barely able to keep his mind on the paper in front of him.

Over half an hour passed by excruciatingly as Chastain watched cars drive past on the street through the smoke-tinted windows of the nice, new bank building. It was meant to be a distraction, but each time the secretary moved or another customer walked in, he snapped his head up like an expectant father.

Finally, the bank manager emerged from his office. It took all of Chastain's will power not to leap from his chair at the sight of the man.

"Johnny, come on in," Buchanan said jovially as he reached out his hand to Chastain. "I'm so sorry to have kept you waiting. Whatcha got on your mind today?"

"Well, it's kinda complicated, Billy," Chastain said, entering the office. He didn't take a seat since sitting down and relaxing seemed out of the question. "You know I flew dual-engine propeller planes during the Gulf War, right?"

"Sure I do," Buchanan said, not quite seeing where the question was leading. "Heard you were a damn good pilot, too."

"Well, if I wasn't when I flew those recon missions, I sure wouldn't be sitting here talking to you right now," Chastain said.

"You're not thinking about going back in the service, are you, Johnny?" Buchanan asked with some concern. He wasn't used to seeing the self-controlled DA seem so out of sorts.

"No, Billy. That's not it." Chastain took a seat and leaned forward, staring intensely into the bank manager's eyes. He was back to his old form again—half attorney, half hypnotist. "I'm running for the US Senate, Billy, and I'm confident I'm going to win. But, as you know, this is a pretty big congressional district and it takes time to get from point A to point B. I've had a lot on my mind about airplanes lately and I've been thinking about it a great deal… I want to buy one."

"An airplane?" Buchanan asked with a puzzled expression.

"That's right," Chastain answered assuredly.

"And you need the bank to finance it for you?" Buchanan ventured.

"Sure do."

"Well, now, wait a minute, Johnny. You know you are just about maxed out on your credit line already," the bank manager said. Now he was the one up and out of his chair, pacing around his office. "Besides that, the only planes this bank has ever financed were a few crop dusters here and there. You ain't talking about a crop duster, are you?" Buchanan asked, pulling on his suspenders nervously.

"Hell naw, Billy. I ain't talking about no damn crop duster. I'm talking about a very-sophisticated airplane with two engines. A plane that—once I get elected—I can fly back home from Washington regularly without having to waste time or taxpayers' money on commercial flights," Chastain replied with some degree of frustration.

"Well, just how much would a plane like that cost, Johnny?" Buchanan stammered. "Have you found one yet?"

"Sure have. It's a nineteen eighty-five Beech Queen Air. Here's a picture of it that I found in a magazine," Chastain said, showing the photo proudly. "It's already up in Memphis just waiting for me."

"Yeah, that's a nice-looking plane," Buchanan said, staring down at the picture. "But it doesn't tell the price."

"The price is only three hundred forty thousand dollars," Chastain said with a smile.

"Holy crap! For a nineteen eighty-five model?" the bank manager asked in disbelief.

"You can't pay any attention to the model years of aircraft, Billy. Don't you know that? You have to look at the total time on the frame and the total time on the engines, as well as when the last annual inspection was done. You also have to consider the avionics and radios, along with all the other special features. It has autopilot, too, and is totally configured for IFR—you know, instrument flying in bad weather."

It was clear that Chastain had done his homework. Buchanan got the sick feeling that he was in for quite a fight.

"Johnny, I'm going to have to check on this and talk to some of the board members. Can you come back tomorrow afternoon?"

"Billy, my daddy never walked out of this bank without money when he needed it—and I never have either until now. Next thing you know, you'll probably want me to fill out an application or something. What's this place coming to?" Chastain asked, offended.

"Johnny, I hear what you're saying, believe me. But times are tough and money is tight. This is a third of a million dollars we're talking about here, probably half a million with interest, depending on how long it's financed," the bank manager said, practically pleading with the powerful and intimidating DA to understand. "We don't usually finance fancy airplanes…and you know your income-to-debt ratio isn't that good. If your daddy were still living, he'd probably talk you out of this."

"Well, he ain't," Chastain said, getting up to go. "I'll be back tomorrow, Billy, but don't waste my time. I'm going to be your next US Senator, and I'm telling you I *need* that airplane."

———

The next day, it was Chastain's turn to blow off court. He left Jack Burchfield to take over and left word for Wayne to meet him in his office afterward. The DA was in such a rush that he was already settled in the bank's lobby long before the startled manager reported to work.

Buchanan's first reaction was to glance over at his secretary, who gave a silent shrug and pointed to her watch, indicating that Chastain had been waiting outside when she had gotten there.

The bank manager looked over at the DA, put aside his annoyance and smiled. "Why don't you come on in my office, Johnny? I believe I have some good news for you."

Chastain practically sprang inside. "You mean the bank's going to give me the money for the plane?" he asked excitedly.

"Well, yes, Johnny, we can do that. I talked to the board members… But I'm going to have to warn you that there are some stipulations," Buchanan said seriously.

"Like what?"

Buchanan cleared his throat. He hadn't even had his first cup of coffee and already had to deal with this. "Well, we checked on the value of the plane and, according to our sources, it's probably only worth about two hundred fifty thousand dollars tops."

"Not with all those avionics and radios," Chastain said, raising his voice. "Hell, they're worth ninety to a hundred thousand by themselves."

"Johnny, we can't sell the board on that," Buchanan said, using his most pacifying tone. "It is simply out of our league. However, we have come up with a way for you to get what you want." The manager stepped over toward Chastain and put a hand on his shoulder. "All we need is some collateral. You'll have to put up those one hundred acres of land your daddy left you with all them cows on it."

"What?" Chastain yelled, pulling away from his grasp. "There's development going on all around me. You know that land will be worth a hell of a lot more than that airplane when it's split into developed housing lots."

"That might be so, Johnny. But it isn't split up yet—and the board has spoken. I can have Mrs. Swindol draw up the papers right now if you want and we can get you out of here and into your plane," Buchanan said. "Or, if you don't want—"

"I'll do it," Chastain interrupted. "I'll do it but I damn sure don't like it. My daddy never had to put up land. His word was his collateral."

"Times have changed, Johnny. You know that. And my hands are tied," Buchanan said apologetically.

"I know that, Billy," Chastain said, struggling to calm down. A million thoughts were going through his head at once, competing for attention. He thought about the possibility of losing his father's land, of giving up his dream to fly again... But the thought he heard above them all was, *I can lease the plane back to my campaign and my supporters will be the ones paying for it...*

"I understand the bank's position," the DA said finally.

"Good," Buchanan replied with a slight smile. Then his expression suddenly became stark and his voice lowered. "Johnny, you've got to know that the feds are in town. We're the second bank they're looking at. You know about the other bank down the street, don't you? Hell, the old man who served as president died and his subordinate's about to start serving time." He shook his head and a shiver seemed to go through his large frame. "The auditors now require us to take applications on everybody—including wealthy farmers."

"Well, I guess the DA is last to know anything," Chastain said with a friendly smile.

"Johnny, this is a federal case going on here. Those people don't talk to anybody. If you don't have a need to know, they just don't tell you."

"It just seems like the whole county has become the subject of investigation for the federal government," Chastain said, looking down in disgust. Then he thought about his plane and his eyes brightened up. He slapped the bank manager on the back with assurance and said, "I'm gonna go find out if they think we can't do our jobs around here. Talk to you later, Billy."

"Johnny, don't you want to read through those papers now?" Buchanan asked.

"Consider them signed, Billy. I'll stop by Mrs. Swindol's desk on my way out. But I don't have my magnifying glass with me now to read through all the fine print—don't have the time, neither. Got a young fed waiting for me in my office."

"You mean FBI?" Buchanan asked, shocked.

"No, an assistant US attorney from Oxford," Chastain said, walking away. He turned around and added with a wink, "Believe it or not, I've got to talk to him about an airplane issue, too."

Chapter Thirteen

The Handoff

Ninety percent of the politicians
give the other ten percent a bad reputation.
—Henry Kissinger

Chastain walked back to his office, clearly in high spirits. He wouldn't let a few hassles with the bank or some federal investigations get in the way of his dream.

Hell, once I become a senator I'll have all the problems in this county sorted out, he thought. *And I'll have enough money to pay off the loan and buy a few bulls for those long-suffering cows of mine.* He chuckled to himself.

He opened the door and smiled at the sound of the cowbell. "Hello, Betty Sue," he called. "And Wayne! How are you?"

Wayne stood up with a goofy smile. "Fine, just fine. Good to see you again, John."

"You too. Sorry I missed you this morning. How did things go?" Chastain asked, ushering Wayne into his office.

"Jack did a great job. You'd be impressed," Wayne said. "But I was sorry to miss you in action on my last day here, not to mention yesterday—"

Chastain cut him off with a friendly wave of his hand. "Please, I understand you must be really busy. After all, you're not getting paid to be in court like me and Jack—though Jack isn't getting much pay, either." He laughed.

"Thanks for understanding," Wayne said, continuing to explain. "I'm just getting moved into my new office in Oxford, and my wife and I are trying to buy a house. I know that's no excuse for not returning your call the other day, but I figured we'd have a chance to discuss it face to face."

"Ahh, that's okay," Chastain said. "But I'm glad you're here now. I want to get Randy Wood from the sheriff's office over to talk with us, too."

He stuck his head out the office door and shouted, "Betty Sue, call over to the sheriff's office and get Randy to come over right away…and tell him to bring the airplane paperwork."

"Sure," Betty Sue replied, putting down her nail file and picking up the phone.

"Airplane paperwork?" Wayne asked, looking at Chastain with a curious expression.

The DA gave him a Cheshire-cat smile. "Just wait a few minutes, Wayne. It'll all be explained."

Not more than five minutes later, Randy arrived somewhat sweaty and out of breath. He was carrying a huge stack of paperwork.

"Wayne, how are you? I tried to call you a couple of times yesterday but missed you," he said.

"Yes, I know. I'm so sorry about that, Randy. I was just getting checked into work and planned to call you back…but the time just slipped away from me."

"You don't have to tell me about that," Wood said. "I know all about it."

"I knew I'd be coming up here today and planned to come see you. I hope whatever you needed could wait," Wayne added apologetically.

"Actually, Wayne, I think Randy and I are both interested in talking with you about the same subject," Chastain said. "I seem to have airplanes coming out of my ears lately."

Wayne gave Randy a quizzical look, hoping he could explain.

Chastain laughed and said, "Randy and I were just talking about airplanes the other day and it reminded me of my time spent flying in the Gulf War. So guess what I did?"

"Booked a first-class flight to Iraq?" Wayne asked.

"No, not hardly," Chastain said with an irrepressible smirk. "I'm going back to flying! I just came back from the bank, where I asked for the money to buy a plane for my upcoming Senate race."

"Wow, I didn't know you were doing that," Wood interjected.

"Neither did I." Chastain laughed. "It was a spur-of-the-moment thing. After you and I talked about that missing plane I just couldn't resist or put it off any longer. I had the fever."

"Good for you. Congratulations," Wayne said.

"Thanks. I'm gonna also make a few Ole Miss away games in it. You're both welcome to come along," Chastain said cheerfully.

"I might just take you up on that sometime," Wayne responded. "But until then, what can I do for you fine, upstanding gentlemen today?"

"Oh, sorry to hold you up like that, Wayne," Chastain said, suddenly remembering the real reason why they were all there. "It's just that Randy and I are looking into an old case… Well, it's only a year and a half old, but it's going to involve multiple federal agencies and we think we need a good person like you to help us coordinate it."

"Me?" Wayne questioned, honored that Chastain would ask for his help.

"Yep. I think it's going to turn out to be a big drug case, and you know how I feel about that," Chastain said. "However, I'm about to start spending a lot of time getting my physical for flying, checking out my new plane, campaigning for the Senate and so on. So I'm asking that you work with Randy for now and if we do end up with a big drug angle for my county, I'll step in and prosecute." He smiled sheepishly. "That kind of publicity could help with the Senate race."

Wood rolled his eyes, used to the fact that the DA's passions were split between aiding justice and helping himself in the process.

"I'd be glad to help," Wayne spoke up, realizing that Chastain wouldn't be much assistance to the FBI corruption investigations if he was too busy to even follow up on one case. "Where do we start?"

"Well, I was actually waiting for a return call from another agency when I got called over here," Wood said pointedly. "If you just want Wayne and me to work together, Mr. Chastain, do you mind if we go back to my office? I'll brief him there."

"That's fine with me, Randy. Wherever you're most comfortable." Chastain laughed. "I know how you hate to be out of your office for too long. Y'all just let me know if you need any help."

Wayne and Randy went back to the sheriff's office and rolled up their sleeves, ready to start wading through mounds of paperwork, including newspaper clippings, bank statements, fax reports and the like.

Wood let out a long sigh and said, "Wayne, I want you to know that this incident happened before I came here, so I really didn't know anything about it until the DA brought it to my attention. But, as you've just heard, he's interested in it for obvious reasons—plus some new information has just come up."

"Okay," Wayne said agreeably. "What do you want me to do first to help?"

Wood launched into the story about Lancaster, the missing airplane and Chastain's drug theory. Then he added, "The latest thing we have is a statement showing that his credit card was used to purchase aviation fuel in the Caribbean last month. The credit-card company is out of state, so I need federal assistance in getting the actual fuel receipt that the user—whoever it may have been—might have signed."

"No problem. I can get Special Agent Tischner to help with that," Wayne said.

"Great. I also want to get the phone toll records for his cell phone.

We can do that here but I just have to get a *subpoena duces teacum* to deliver to the phone company. I want to see who he was calling before he came up missing and if any calls were made after that," Wood explained.

"Good idea. Anything else you need from the federal side?" Wayne asked.

"Now that you mention it, yeah. As I understand it, every time this guy flew or took any other means of transportation to the various islands he had to clear customs and fill out a declaration form. At one point, British customs seized over a hundred thousand dollars from him for not declaring it. I'd really like to see that report."

"Okay," Wayne said.

"I'd also like to know if there has been any FAA activity on the airplane that went missing at the same time he did. I want to find out which airport he last filed a flight plan with and how many people he declared onboard. I'd also like to know if he had any bank accounts other than the ones his wife has provided, and I need a complete criminal history on him," Randy concluded.

"Anything else?" Wayne laughed.

"Nope. That should just about do it."

"Good. I was worried you were going to ask me to find out what he had for breakfast the morning he went missing," Wayne joked.

"Funny," Wood said. "Just don't mention that to Chastain. He'll have us calling every IHOP in the country."

Wayne laughed. "It's not a problem, Randy. I'll get on everything you asked."

"Thank you," Wood replied with considerable relief.

"I'll get Tischner to contact you with some of this," Wayne said, "but I've got to warn you that the wheels turn slowly at the federal level. Football season could be over by the time this info comes in."

"It's not like I'm going anywhere just yet," Wood said, digging into the pile of paperwork in front of him.

Chapter Fourteen

Football Season

*I've arrived at this outermost edge of my life
by my own actions. Where I am is thoroughly
unacceptable. Therefore, I must stop
doing what I've been doing.*
—Alice Koller

By mid-August, Wayne and Julie were settled into their new house—right next to their new neighbors, the Tischners. It had everything Wallace had prescribed for the family: a wading pool, a swing set and a fence. Much to Wayne and Julie's delight, it also had four bedrooms, just in case one of them needed to be turned into a nursery soon.

While the rest of Wayne's life was falling into place, however, there had been little progress in the case of the missing man, despite the fact that Wayne, Randy and Tischner were working on it day and night.

Someone else seemed to be missing, too. Chastain was spending less and less time in his office as he was out campaigning. It had been months since Wayne had last seen his ex-mentor.

News from the campaign trail didn't sound so promising. Although there was only one person running against Chastain his opponent was strong and had huge name recognition in the state thanks to his grandfather's thirty years in the Senate. John A. Stoddard III would be a shoo-in, so everyone thought. But Chastain didn't let that bother him. He had a top-notch media firm and would often fly his plane from one end of the district to the other in order to squeeze in three speeches a day.

He would land and get out of the plane with speech in hand, vowing to all assembled in order to get congressional funds for expansion and business development. His advance teams had already arrived in cars with loudspeakers attached to announce the arrival of the next US Senator from Mississippi. It was a photo op like no other and Chastain managed to get his face splashed across countless newspapers. That was the only way Wayne was still able to see him.

In early September, Chastain changed tactics, slowing the pace down by going exclusively to all the political hotspots within his district. He kissed babies, worked on assembly lines in factories for an hour at a time and rode bulldozers on construction sites wearing a hard-hat bearing the words "Chastain for Senate."

His intention, as he made clear at these events, was "to help everybody with new federal laws that protect children, to improve labor laws and raise minimum wages, to offer stipends to construction workers laid off during bad weather and to vote against congressional raises in my first term." It was a tall order but he said all the right things—even going so far as to bash illegal immigrants who were taking "American jobs." Chastain didn't care how the immigrant community felt about that since he knew that only a handful had the right to vote.

Even those who didn't share his views had to admit that this guy was as polished as he was aggressive. And that impressed a hell of a lot of potential voters—particularly Ole Miss graduates like himself.

Chastain didn't keep it a secret that he was an SEC madman, often stepping off his plane in a well-cut suit and a well-worn Ole Miss cap. His staunchest supporters were the same way, including his oldest buddies in the county.

With football season upon them, the mouths of these loyal fans and friends—some former players themselves, and all of whom had season tickets—drooled when they heard that their good buddy had a plane that could take them to all the away games.

Late one night, exhausted from a hard day of stumping, Chastain got a call from one of these friends.

"Hey, Johnny boy. Rebel Rouser here. How have you been, man?"

Chastain smiled wearily on his end, glad to hear a familiar voice after a full day of shaking strangers' hands. "Well, Reb, to be honest with you, I've been busy as hell."

"I heard you have, Johnny, and that's why I'm calling. Now, listen… I've got a great proposal for you that'll allow you to take some much-needed time off. I've managed to round up two well-known businessmen from the district who are just loaded with money—and they want nothing more than to have chartered trips to the games…*in your private plane*. What do you say, bubba?" Rebel Rouser asked enthusiastically.

Chastain was so burnt out he could hardly register the words. "What do you mean *in my plane?*"

"Johnny, man, what I mean is I've got the goods, you've got the means of delivery." Reb laughed long and loud. "Now don't tell me that with all the campaigning you've been doing you couldn't use some more cash."

Chastain rubbed the bridge of his nose between his eyes and let the proposal sink in. Those two things certainly were true: He could use more money and some time off.

"What the hell, Reb, I'll do it!" he whooped. The idea was starting to appeal to him and he built up a head of steam. "I might even take my assistant, Jack Burchfield, along for the first few trips. He's going to be running the grand jury for me for the next session and I can't think of a better way to thank him."

"Hell, bring whoever you want," Reb said. "It's your plane. You can stuff it full of your fancy politician pals and whichever supporters have the fattest wallets. The more the merrier." In the middle of his patented good ol' boy guffaw, Reb suddenly stopped and became serious. "As long as they're all Ole Miss fans."

———————

The private-plane proposition was showing all likelihood of becoming a success. Chastain was promised loads of campaign donations in return and most of them came through as he and his passengers flew from Vanderbilt to Auburn then to South Carolina, partying all the way there. With drinks pouring around the plane like water, even Chastain would partake but was confident that he knew his limit.

Coming into the approach at South Carolina one late September day, everything was going smoothly as usual, including the Southern Comfort on its way down the partiers' throats.

"Hey, Johnny," Rebel Rouser called up front to the cockpit. "What do you say, man? Is Ole Miss gonna kick some ass or what?"

The group of four businessmen—and newly confirmed Chastain supporters—in the back heartily yelled their support.

Chastain just smiled and shook his head. He was used to Rebel's rousing and this kind of thing before each game was becoming routine. Then something went terribly wrong.

As Chastain lowered the landing gear for touch down, a loud noise rang out through the cabin. The landing-gear-lock indicator wasn't illuminated.

All of the drunk passengers who previously had been laughing and living it up were now frantic and devoutly religious, saying their prayers like Sunday-school students.

"Johnny, what's wrong? Are we gonna die? Are we all gonna die?" Rebel Rouser squealed.

"I've got a baby on the way, Johnny. Please don't let me die," Pete Chaney pleaded. He was another of Chastain's old buddies along for the ride. "Shit, man, I don't even have a will. I never should have come on this trip. I told my wife it was for business. Now she's gonna know. And if I don't die, she's gonna kill me."

"Shut up, man. Y'all be quiet," Chastain said, cutting off their rambling. "I have to call the tower."

He radioed in as the passengers held their breath. "Beech Craft November one six seven eight five four… Columbia tower, inbound on final. Having gear trouble," Chastain said nervously.

"Are you declaring an emergency?"

"Not yet. Don't want my plane soaked down with foam by a bunch of hose-happy firemen unless it's absolutely necessary," Chastain said, trying to make a joke. But his mouth was too dry even to crack a smile.

"Roger, Beech Craft November one six seven eight five four. Conduct flyover at or below five hundred feet for control tower visual on landing gear. Reenter pattern and do a go-around while we clear traffic," the controller said calmly.

"I'd be glad to, sir, but it isn't just the light. There was a loud bang that sounded like it was on the starboard side when I lowered the gear," Chastain said, trying to keep the panic out of his voice.

In the back, businessman Bobby Bradshaw started swigging down a fifth of Southern Comfort as if he were taking his last drink. He spilled it all over his stiffly starched white shirt, which had his initials embroidered on the cuffs. Normally, a stain on one of his fine garments would've ruined the rest of his day. Now, however, he had bigger problems.

Bobby fumbled for his cell phone and hit the first number on speed dial. It was his girlfriend.

"Listen, honey," he said quickly, getting his affairs in order. "If in the next few days you happen to hear something about my marriage, don't believe what my wife says. We really have been separated a long time. And if I don't get back to you soon, call my secretary about the condo rent but never discuss it with anyone else."

He hung up as soon as he heard the tower controller come back over the radio speaker up front. "Roger, we have confirmed visual, but it isn't your starboard gear. You have no nose wheel extended."

The passengers stared at each other, not knowing if that was good or bad news.

"Runway twenty-three is under construction," the controller continued. "I need you to attempt an emergency landing on runway two-niner. Emergency vehicles are being dispatched."

That last part, they knew, wasn't good. So Bobby and the boys started passing around the bottle.

"Damn, get that booze back in the bags now, you stupid bastards," Chastain called to them. "I'm going to land this plane and it's going to sustain some damage, but I don't need any bad press to make things worse. Just shut up and do as you're told and we'll be all right. Shift all the weight to the back and get your seatbelts on NOW!"

Two seats were still empty in the far back of the plane. There were just discarded bags from the liquor store lying on them. Jeff Finch, an obese banking major from Ole Miss—but at one time a hell of a line-backer—sat in one of them quietly, hoping to act as ballast. He was turning green from a dip of Skoal he'd accidentally swallowed and looked as though he would pass out at any minute, which would've been fine as far as Chastain was concerned. Dead weight was as good as any.

The rest of the passengers also shifted back for fear that the plane's nose would hit the ground and the entire aircraft would flip over on its top.

Chastain was occupied in the cockpit, trying to go over emergency procedures. "Beech Craft November one six seven eight five four to Columbia tower," he radioed in.

"Go ahead, sir," the tower controller patiently replied.

"I've got five passengers and half a tank of fuel onboard. I'm going to have to fly the pattern and burn some off before I feel comfortable doing this emergency landing," Chastain reasoned.

"Maintain pattern, sir, and stand by."

The controller switched off the receiver with a worried look on his face and went to update his supervisor.

"We'll have no way of telling how many aircraft will be stacked up before he burns off that much fuel," the supervisor said. "Vector him southeast to Charleston and notify their tower to take control. He can fly over the water there and burn off fuel, giving them plenty of time to deal with inbound traffic."

The tower controller did as he was told. "Columbia tower to Beech Craft November one six seven eight five four… Request you maintain a heading of one three five, climb to three thousand feet and redirect to Charleston Airport approximately nine-zero nautical miles at lat north three two five three point nine, long west zero eight zero zero two point four, elevation forty-six feet, winds currently variable at plus-five knots. You will be directed to a heading for burning fuel over water and emergency landing there. Do you copy?"

"Roger, Columbia tower. Turning right to heading one three five," Chastain said.

"Contact Charleston tower on frequency one twenty six point zero. You will have an inbound nine-thousand-foot runway, two hundred feet wide at runway number three-three-zero, inbound from the ocean when your fuel is burned off," the tower controller said. "Got all that?"

"Sure do," Chastain replied. "Anything else?"

"One more thing," the controller added. "Good luck, sir."

Chapter Fifteen

Declared Emergency

*Perhaps the most valuable result of all education is
the ability to make yourself do the thing you have to
do, when it ought to be done, whether you like it or
not; it is the first lesson that ought to be learned; and
however early a man's training begins, it is probably
the last lesson that he learns thoroughly.*
—Thomas H. Huxley

While Chastain's plane was passing through Charleston airspace and flying off the East Coast, Jeff Finch, the biggest passenger—who had also been the biggest eater and biggest drinker on board—blew his groceries all over the back of the pilot.

The awful smell of vomit resulted in a chain reaction: Two others gagged intensely before also throwing up. As if they didn't have enough trouble to deal with, the plane was a complete mess.

As Chastain struggled to clean off the back of his neck and save one hand for steering, the tower controller at Charleston radioed in. "Charleston tower to Beech Craft November one six seven eight five four... Request you enter the pattern and let us get a closer look at your gear because of the discrepancy Columbia reported as to where the noise was heard."

"Roger, Charleston, on downwind... Stand by...on baseleg... Turning to final over runway nearing tower," Chastain said, focusing intently on the task at hand.

Seconds later, the controller said, "Charleston tower to Beech

Craft November one six seven eight five four... We have a visual. Climb back into pattern."

From the sound of his voice, no one on the plane could have guessed the danger they were in. But on the ground, it was a different story.

"Holy crap," the tower supervisor said, staring at the visual. "He's got more than nose-wheel trouble. That nose wheel must have come off in the turn at Columbia, flown to the side and struck the starboard wheel. That tire is busted." He looked over at the tower controller. "How much fuel has he got left?"

"Charleston tower to Beech Craft November one six seven eight five four... You have a busted tire on the starboard side in addition to the missing nose wheel. How much fuel do you have left?"

"Less than one-fourth of a tank," Chastain replied steadily. "But I'd like to burn off a little more."

"Roger, Beech Craft November one six seven eight five four. You are free to depart pattern and advise of intent to reenter. All emergency vehicles are on standby for runway three-three-zero. All traffic cleared," the controller stated.

"Johnny, what if we run out of gas out here over the ocean?" Rebel Rouser asked, his voice sounding ten octaves higher than normal. "I can't swim...even if we do land safely on the water."

"Don't worry. We're not going to run out of gas over the ocean and we're not landing in the water," Chastain said, gritting his teeth. "I only want enough fuel left onboard to give me three chances at the landing. If I don't feel comfortable, I'll pull up and go around, but I'll only head back to land when it feels right. I don't want any sparks to ignite a lot of fuel and turn this thing into a roman candle."

That last part did the trick. Not only did it shut up Rebel Rouser and the rest of the passengers, but it got them all silently praying.

By that time, the news media had gotten wind of the incident and recognized, from the flight plan they had gotten though sources, the name of the pilot as that of a senatorial candidate. A CNN helicopter was hovering just outside the emergency airspace; it had long-range photography and was broadcasting a live, minute-by-minute account of Chastain's plane approaching for the emergency landing. It made for gripping television but wasn't exactly the kind of coverage Chastain was after.

"Make sure your seatbelts are tight and bend forward with your hands clasped over the back of your head when we land," Chastain told his passengers.

Rebel Rouser mumbled, "Yeah, what that really means is 'bend over, put your head between your legs and kiss your ass goodbye.'"

Chastain continued with the emergency checklist: "Place a towel or piece of clothing in front of your face to lessen the impact..." The man they trusted and supported for the US Senate seat would now have to be trusted in the pilot's seat to keep them alive.

"Charleston tower to Beech Craft November one six seven eight five four... Are you prepared for landing?" the tower controller asked.

The atmosphere in the cabin was so tense that Chastain wondered if the occupants actually were holding their breath.

"Roger, Charleston, on final," Chastain replied, slowly dropping his altitude.

Suddenly, he could feel the plane rumble, and an alarm went off. Chastain shouted into the radio, "NEGATIVE! Negative, Charleston! Strong wind gusts, stall warning light and horn on. Passengers frantic, going around."

The pilot regained control of the plane and flew back over the coast. The stall light and horn were no longer a problem but the plane was configured with a low-fuel audible warning that was making a deafening, shrill sound. Chastain still believed he could land all right but thought it would be a miracle if none of his passengers died of a heart attack in the process.

"What the hell is that noise?" Bradshaw yelled from the back.

"It's the low-fuel indicator," Chastain said coolly. "I'm going back into the pattern. If we don't make it this time, we won't have enough fuel for another pass."

"Oh, my God," Rebel Rouser whispered. He couldn't be heard over the alarm's buzzing and the crying of his fellow passengers.

This time, Chastain was determined to pull out all the stops. There was no other choice. Killing the engines and shutting off all electrical power, he knew he would not be given another chance to rise back into the pattern for a third try. At least now all the gas was gone and with power off, there would be nothing to ignite what fumes remained. It was now or never. They had reached the point of no return.

As the plane circled around and then came in low, the passengers, plunged into darkness, saw their lives flash in front of them. All Chastain could see, however, was the looming runway, which was growing larger each second until...

BAM! The plane's screeching and the passengers' screams filled the air as the aircraft hit the runway.

"Help us, Jesus!" Pete Chaney screamed loudly.

Chastain was trying his best to keep the yoke back as far as possible, performing a maneuver known as a soft-field landing. This would keep the nose off the runway until the last possible moment, which would reduce the chances of the nose striking the runway and possibly flipping the plane over. He also was trying to maintain sideways control with the wheel so the aileron could keep some of the weight off the blown tire on the starboard side.

"I smell something burning," Chaney cried as the plane continued its skid.

"It's that blown tire. Don't worry," Chastain barked out as he fought the almost-uncontrollable aircraft. When he applied the brakes slightly they began to lose speed but sparks came flying from the right wheel where the tire had been.

In seconds, the rear of the aircraft lifted up with the nose beginning to point slightly downward. Chastain saw the white lines of the runway directly in front of his eyes.

"Hold on! I think we're gonna flip," he called out as a warning to his passengers. Chastain gripped the control panel tightly as the nose started digging into the runway.

At the last moment, though, the tail section settled down, rocking back and forth. Then the nose dropped softly to the runway like a child sitting on a seesaw, bringing the plane to a complete stop.

When all onboard managed to open their eyes, they could see the ambulances and fire trucks that had converged on the scene.

"Move out of my way," Jeff Finch said, unbuckling himself and pushing past the other passengers more quickly than they thought a man of his size could have. "I'm going to kiss the ground."

The door flew open and the traumatized passengers filed out one by one. Chastain was the last remaining. He sat in the pilot's seat a few seconds alone, numbly shaking his head.

Then he knew it was time to get out.

"Nose damage, nose gear missing, both props damaged, wheel and brake disk broken on starboard side. Looks like when that tire came off it hit the aileron, bending it, too," Chastain said to the emergency personnel, who were trying to hurry him away from the plane.

After a final look back, Chastain and his friends were taken to the terminal by service vehicles, all thankful to be alive.

When they arrived, a news reporter stepped in front of the shaken pilot. "Mr. Chastain, I'm Nancy Morgan from CNN. I'd like to talk to you about your heroic landing."

"I don't feel much like talking right now," Chastain replied.

"But, sir, you're a hero...and we understand you were a Gulf War hero, too. It's an amazing story that I'm sure our millions of viewers would like to know. Can we go live?"

Chastain thought for a second how this could help his campaign. "Sure. Why not?" he said, straightening his tie.

In a few minutes' time, Chastain's feat was broadcast live around the world, at least for the moment boosting him well past his opponent in terms of name recognition.

While he was being interviewed by CNN, Chastain's passengers were inside doing some answering of their own. FAA officials, as well as an investigator from the National Transportation Safety Board, met the quivering group in the terminal for questioning after they had rotated one by one to the restroom to clean off the vomit from the air sickness they had sustained in flight.

The smell of alcohol was strong on all of them, but nobody asked Chastain about any consumption on his part. He' done such a good job with the landing that he wasn't suspected of being under the influence. Besides, no one wanted to ruin the happy ending, which was so infrequent in news stories nowadays.

———

When Chastain and the entire group were flown back to Memphis later that evening on a commercial flight, they were greeted at the airport by a crowd of supporters, and the news cameras were there to capture it all.

Billy Buchanan, the bank president, was home watching TV when that footage came on, interspersed with images of the crash landing. He almost swallowed his false teeth when he saw it.

"Oh, my God," he mumbled to himself. "Johnny's already two payments behind on that damn plane—and now the bank's collateral is damaged. What the hell am I gonna do?"

Chapter Sixteen

After the Fall

It's choice—not chance—
that determines your destiny.
—Jean Nidetch

The following Monday morning, as the DA entered his office, Betty Sue had a stack of messages waiting for him. Most were from enthusiastic supporters and well-wishers. Several, however, were from the bank.

"John, Mr. Buchanan from the bank says he needs to talk to you right away—it's very urgent," the secretary called out as Chastain entered his office, closing the door behind him. "By the way, I heard about the plane crash. I'm glad you're okay."

"Didn't crash… Don't spread that rumor. Just an emergency landing," Chastain yelled back. "Where's Jack? I need to see him."

"I'll try his cell," Betty Sue responded, being uncharacteristically helpful. Just then, however, the cowbell rang and somebody came in through the door.

It wasn't the DA's assistant. In fact, it was the last person he wanted to see.

"Betty Sue, I need to see Johnny…now," Buchanan said as he

made his way to Chastain's door and quickly pushed it open without knocking.

The secretary stared at him wide-eyed, unused to such an act of bravado that was sure to bring the boss' wrath.

Buchanan shut the door and stood there studying Chastain silently. Then he said, "Johnny, you've got the board of directors all over my back. I don't know what to tell them. You're two payments behind on that damn plane. Now it's in pieces in another state and we never even received your insurance policy." He paused, letting his tone of voice soften. "I hope to hell you had that thing insured."

"Just relax, Billy," Chastain said, not getting up from his seat. "I have the insurance policy right here in my desk. Just haven't had the time to bring it by. I've already notified them about the accident and they're having a representative go by today to assess the damage. The mechanics are already working on it."

Buchanan studied him some more. "This policy says you have a five-thousand-dollar deductible, Johnny. You haven't even paid two of the notes due on the loan. How are you going to deal with this?"

"Listen, they're going to do emergency repairs and we're getting a ferry permit to bring it back to Memphis, where the dealership I bought it from will do all the cosmetic and final repairs. I'll talk to the campaign committee treasurer today and get lease funds transferred so we can catch up on the payments. Just give me a break, Billy," Chastain said, putting his fingers to the sides of his head to massage his temples. "I have a lot going on right now."

"Okay, Johnny," Buchanan said with a sigh. "But I think you made a bad mistake with this airplane. I hope it doesn't end up costing you your daddy's land." He stepped toward the door then turned back. "And I hope it doesn't end up costing me my job."

After the bank manager left, Chastain held his head wearily in his hands with his elbows propped up on the desk. But he sat up bolt straight when he heard a quiet rap on his door.

Jack Burchfield peeked in and said, "You needed to see me, boss?"

"Yes. I guess you heard about our trip."

"Sure did," Jack said, smiling. "No offense, boss, but I'm glad I didn't make that one."

Chastain smiled back but it disappeared in seconds and he turned deadly serious. "Jack, there's only a little more than a month left before the election. I had a very aggressive schedule of flying all over the district and to some photo ops in DC. I'm going to have to cancel most of those now, but I plan on driving to as many as I can. I need you to handle the special session of the grand jury next week by yourself."

"No problem," Jack said. "Just get as much done as you can and knock 'em dead out there. Don't worry about anything. It's all under control here."

Jack knew it was only part of the truth. But his boss didn't look in any condition to hear about Randy Wood's earlier call about "something urgent" he needed to discuss. Jack would handle that alone, too.

When Randy arrived at Jack's office later that afternoon he was very distraught. He acted like he had lost his best friend—and it turned out that he almost had.

"Jack, you knew about my getting the narcotics grant last month to hire an undercover agent, right?" Randy asked, skipping any preliminary greetings.

"Yeah, you told me about that. How's it going?"

"Not well at all," Randy said, pacing. "The sheriff gave me the latitude to hire whoever I wanted and let me handle the car purchase, the test kits and so on. It was completely *my thing*," the county investigator said, thumping his chest, "so nobody else would know anything about how it was done. No one even knew when it started. All the upfront costs—salary, vehicle purchase, even buy money—was paid for by the feds." He ran his hand through his thinning hair. "However, there was one small snag. Recurring costs like gasoline and vehicle maintenance were not part of the grant."

Jack interpreted his pause as a chance to jump in. "Is this something I can help you with as a prosecutor, Randy?"

"I'm sorry, Jack. I'm getting to that. It's just that you need to know everything from the beginning, so please bear with me."

Jack never had seen the county investigator worked up like that. Frankly, it intrigued him. "Okay, Randy, take your time. I'm listening." He leaned back in his chair and let Randy do the talking.

"Well, I hired an old friend of mine who I knew could do the job. He and I worked in a police department together a couple of years back. It was about three hundred miles away. Nobody here would know him." He stopped to stare at Jack intently. "I even got an undercover car tag from the narcotics bureau so nobody could check the registration of the car. The sheriff didn't even know the tag number and had never met the agent."

"Wow, that's pretty darn incognito," Jack said.

"Yeah, you'd think so. But the board of supervisors wouldn't give me a government credit card for him to buy gas with. They said he could get gas at their county barn, way out where he wouldn't be seen. I didn't like that idea at all and I argued against it. But as you might have guessed, I lost the argument," Randy said disgustedly.

"That's how it usually is with government finances," Jack replied, trying to show sympathy.

"Yeah, well, yesterday was his sixth day on the job. He hit the ground running. I had him teamed up with an informant who's been introducing him in to buy drugs. He's made several cases just in this one week alone," Randy said.

"So what's the problem? Sounds like it's going great."

"It was." Randy pulled up a seat, leaning in close to the assistant DA. "Last night, a couple of reserve deputies and I served a search warrant on a known cocaine dealer's house. A confidential informant said he'd seen cocaine there early in the evening and we have had the house under surveillance since then. When we got there to conduct the search, the dealer was gone but we searched the house anyway. We found a little coke and some weed… But that wasn't the big find."

"What was?" Jack asked, clearly curious.

"The mother lode was this guy's address book lying next to his living-room phone. As I thumbed through it, the names of known dope dealers popped out at me. But when I got to the back cover, I almost fell over," Randy said.

"Whose name was there?"

Randy didn't answer. Instead, he handed Jack a copy he'd made.

"W. Culpepper, five eleven, a hundred and eighty-five pounds, reddish-brown hair, orange Dodge Daytona, Leflore county tag LZZ nine eight nine," Jack read aloud. He looked up at Randy. "What does this mean? Who is this guy?"

"That's my undercover agent. He's only been here six days, Jack. Who would have known all that in such a short amount of time?"

"I don't know, Randy," Jack said thoughtfully. "Do you think the snitch burned him?"

"Of course not. He isn't even using his real name with the snitch. Besides, the snitch doesn't even know this coke dealer on this side of the county. I did my homework beforehand. It wasn't the snitch," Randy replied, too agitated to sit any longer.

"Well, who do you think it was, then?"

Randy ran his hand through his hair again and let out a sigh. "I think it was either the county supervisor or someone in his office." He paced around the office again, adding, "I called Culpepper last night and told him not to do any more drug deals for now, and asked him if he had signed his real name anywhere. He said the only time he could think of was when he went over to the country barn and bought gas. The gas ticket he had to sign was in a narrow book, not wide enough to fit his whole name, and he didn't want them to know it anyway, so he just used his first initial: W. Said he just dropped the ticket in the slot in the metal box next to the gas pump and left. He didn't see anybody… But he didn't go in the office, either. "

"So, where's the guy who owns the address book?" Jack asked.

"He's out of town 'til Sunday night—and you'd better believe I'll be waiting to lock his ass up after a lengthy prayer meeting with him about this information." Randy was standing still now, his hands firmly crossed in front of his chest.

"Think he'll talk?"

"Not willingly... That's why I wanted to talk to you."

"Okay. What's your plan?" Jack asked, motioning for Randy to take a seat.

Randy sat as nervously as a whore in church, with his leg moving up and down. "I want to arrest him Sunday night when he comes home. I'll ask the judge not to set bond until the following day, when you convene the grand jury, so we can present a case for conspiracy to obstruct justice by knowingly, intentionally and feloniously revealing my agent's identity as a John or Jane Doe case." His voice grew angry. "Damn it, Jack, Culpepper could've been killed if he'd gone in there to buy dope instead of letting me go in with a search warrant."

"You're right," Jack said. "We can amend the Doe indictment when we get the real name. The plan sounds good to me. Bring him down."

———

Randy and his men were waiting in the bushes of Charles Gaddy's secluded home when he arrived on Sunday night. There was some palpable tension since they were pretty certain the guy would be packing heat, but truth be told, it brought Randy a great amount of pleasure to hear the notorious drug dealer scream like a little girl when they popped out into the open and immediately took him into custody. The arrest went like clockwork and only lasted seconds. Randy was disappointed that Gaddy didn't try something stupid. Gaddy was transported to jail with instructions to the jailer that bond would not be set until the following day after lunch.

"You can't do this to me!" Gaddy called through the bars of his cell after Randy. "Don't you know who I am?"

"From the sound of it when we arrested you, I'd say you're the newest alto in the ladies' church choir. Am I close?" Randy asked, turning with a grin.

What Gaddy shouted afterward, however, certainly had never crossed the lips of any God-fearing member of the Stonewall County First Baptist Church's Singing Angels.

———

The next morning, Randy arrived at the jail to get Gaddy out of his cell and into the grand jury room where Jack was waiting to present the case. There was no tough-guy banter between them this time. This was all business.

"Ladies and gentlemen of the grand jury, because of the lengthy, multi-county drug roundup last month, we have kept you very busy. As you know, this is a special session of the grand jury to pick up the county cases and those presented by the seven towns within the county. However, we have a unique case to bring to you today," Jack began, standing in front of what looked like a normal conference room. This wasn't the usual court trial and the rules were more relaxed. "In most cases, you are empanelled to hear the facts against an alleged criminal and decide whether or not to issue an indictment. However, in this case, I'll explain the story to you then ask a few questions. You may do so as well."

The jury members exchanged glances, intrigued.

"This is an investigative inquiry meant to use this person as a witness to fry a bigger fish, you might say," Jack continued. "This witness, while under arrest for drug charges, is believed to have received confidential information about the identity and description of an undercover agent. What we want to elicit from him today is where he got that information and for what reason it was given to him so that we can pursue an indictment against the party—whomever it might be that was originally entrusted with those facts—for conspiracy to obstruct justice."

Jack turned to the defendant to start his questioning. "Sir, would you state your name?"

"My name's Charles Gaddy and I ain't sayin' nothin'. I plead the fifth."

"Mr. Gaddy, knowing who you are, I presumed that you would most likely take that stance. So I received an order signed by the circuit judge this morning giving you immunity from prosecution for your role in this conspiracy—so long as you tell us where you got the information and who else you have given it to."

Gaddy, being no stranger to court proceedings himself, said, "I know my rights. You can't trick me. I want a lawyer and I want to make bond."

"Mr. Wood, will you take Mr. Gaddy back over to the jail and enter a new charge of contempt of the grand jury on the jail docket, please?" Jack instructed Randy. "There will be no bond. We'll bring him back at the end of the week after he's had time to sit in his cell and discuss his fate with a lawyer, who'll explain to our aspiring attorney, Mr. Gaddy here, that he can continue to sit in jail without bond until the next session of the grand jury six months from now if he doesn't feel like cooperating by Friday."

Gaddy turned green. What he didn't know was that Jack had told the clerk already to call all the jurors in advance and inform them that they'd be reporting back for additional court presentations. He was that sure that this guy would spill his guts.

Chapter Seventeen

The Witness Returns

Crime butchers innocence to secure
a throne, and innocence struggles with all
its might against the attempts of crime.
—Maximilien Robespierre

On Thursday, Randy made a visit to the one person in the world he least wanted to see.

"Well, Mr. Gaddy, tomorrow's the last day of the grand-jury session. I assume you've had enough time to talk to a lawyer. Now, what do you say you talk to me?"

Although he'd spent less than a week behind bars, Gaddy was already looking the worse for wear, just like Randy had known he would. The drug dealers in the expensive houses became accustomed to a certain way of life and were always the ones to miss their creature comforts the most, no matter how tough they thought they were or how strong their reputations were on the streets.

Gaddy said nothing, though his eyes were practically pleading for release.

"Tell you what," Randy said. "I'll sweeten the deal. I'll call the assistant DA and see if we can get this thing over with this afternoon. You'll be free to celebrate tonight and keep it going through the weekend. What do you say? Just a little house party with a few of your closest friends?"

Just the thought of his home was enough to make Gaddy break. "I'll do it," he said.

Randy smiled and dialed Jack on his cell phone. "Jack, I was wondering if you could do me a little favor..."

It was all an act to try to get on Gaddy's good side. Burchfield had told Randy already that he'd run out of cases to present, and the jurors were getting restless. He wanted to bring Gaddy in front of them as soon as possible so that the foreman could sign the indictments and the jury could be let go no later than lunchtime.

The plan worked perfectly. Randy escorted Gaddy back to the grand-jury room, where he was ready to play nice this time.

"My name is Charles Thomas Gaddy. I swear to tell the truth, the whole truth and nothing but the truth," he proclaimed with his hand on the Bible.

With little prodding from Jack, Gaddy went on to sing like a bird. "A few days before I left for Florida I got a call from an old classmate of mine, Sarah McFails, who works for the county. Her boss told her an undercover agent would be getting gas at the barn, so she watched for him out the window. When he got gas and opened the lock box, she copied down his description and license-plate number and gave it to me."

"Why did she give it to you?" Jack asked.

"Because she knows I deal a little and didn't want me to get into any more trouble, so she said."

"Why?" one of the jurors sitting at the table asked.

Gaddy shot him a look and hissed, "Maybe she's more than a friend."

"And who have you passed this information to, Mr. Gaddy?" Jack asked. "Nobody. Like I said, I got the info right before I went to Florida and left it by my phone. When I came back, I was arrested before I even got into my house," Gaddy said, his stare throwing daggers at Randy, who was sitting across from him.

"What exactly did this woman say when she called you?" the foreman asked.

"She told me she had some hot info on a narc's ID and asked if I wanted it. Of course I said 'yeah.'"

"Have you ever sold her any dope?" a female juror asked.

"Not lately," Gaddy responded.

"But you *have* sold her drugs in the past?" Jack clarified.

"Yes, but I don't remember how long it's been."

A young, scruffy-looking juror made a wisecrack as if mocking Cheech and Chong: "Yeah, man, I heard that stuff really makes you forget things."

When the jurors laughed, Jack reminded them that they came from all walks of life. "Please remember that the witness is not on trial here, so it's not our right to judge his lifestyle. Thank you, Mr. Gaddy, for your cooperation. Investigator Wood will take you back to the sheriff's office for now and I'll be over to talk to you a little later."

Jack figured that a megalomaniac like Gaddy would respond well to having his ego stroked, which possibly could have gotten him to open up a bit more so he could continue being the center of attention.

"Mr. Burchfield, can I see you outside for just a minute?" Randy asked when the questioning came to a close.

"Sure," Jack said, stepping into the hall. He left the door open behind him so he could keep an eye on Gaddy.

"Jack," Randy whispered, "I want that indictment myself. I can't wait to put that bitch in jail. Maybe she'll flip on her boss and we can put that worthless, piece-of-shit politician away, too."

"Okay, I'll get the indictment out to you as soon as I can, but I still have some others to work on and it may take a few days. You'll get your chance, though. Don't worry."

"Great. Call me the minute you get it. I want her mug shot plastered on the front page of the paper and I want to send her fingerprints personally to the FBI." Randy flashed a cruel smile before heading back into the grand-jury room. "I'm really gonna enjoy this one."

Chapter Eighteen

The DA Returns

All truths are easy to understand once they are discovered; the point is to discover them.
—Galileo Galilei

After a few days, the DA finally made a guest appearance at his own office. "Jack, how did the grand jury go last week?" Chastain asked. He breezed in, still partially out of breath.

"Went great, boss. All true bills and finished a day early. Some of your favorites: drug dealers, an ongoing conspiracy investigation to obstruct justice in drug cases... Oh, and a simple felonious possession of a firearm by a convicted felon."

"Tell me about that," Chastain said, unwrapping his fast-food sausage sandwich and taking a big bite.

Jack wrinkled his nose in disgust, calculating that for breakfast, his boss was eating more than half of his recommended daily intake of calories.

"Well," he said with a shrug, "last Monday night, Randy was driving down Main Street in town and saw a Lincoln Continental with a switched plate. He knew that because the third digit was a number instead of a letter, which means it belongs on a truck. Randy figured he had a stolen vehicle on his hands."

Chastain nodded; his mouth was too full to make a comment.

"Randy ran a check on the license plate and it came back to an electrical supply company on the east side of the county, and it should have been displayed on a van. When he stopped the vehicle, he recognized the driver as Dennis Riley, who had just gotten out of prison on a manslaughter charge."

"I remember Riley," Chastain said, swallowing his last bite of the sandwich. "He was a nickel-and-dime dope dealer who also dabbled in diamonds and furs before doing time."

"Right," Jack said. "He was also known back then to carry a gun. So Randy patted him down and felt a small pistol in his right front pocket. He advised him of his rights and asked him where he got the gun. Like an idiot, the guy told him he'd bought it at Joe's Gun and Pawn, so Randy arrested him on the spot."

"Any felon worth their salt should know state and federal statutes prevent them from possessing firearms," Chastain said, rolling his eyes. "Fill me in on the conspiracy investigation to obstruct drug charges." He opened his desk drawer, found a pack of Tumsand popped two into his mouth.

Jack recounted the whole story of Charles Gaddy and how he had gotten the information on Randy's undercover agent.

"Seems like you got a great case. That would be some good publicity," Chastain said, sounding impressed.

"Yes, sir," Jack said, shaking his head at his boss' one-track mind.

"I've got to hand it to you, Jack—seems like you really have things under control."

"Thanks, John," the assistant DA said, turning to leave.

"Uh…by the way, Jack, before you go, I understand Wayne Lott's father-in-law is a retired judge in the Oxford area," Chastain said.

"That's right."

"His influence probably helped a bit in getting Wayne elected to the state legislature a few years ago."

"It definitely didn't hurt," Jack said, waiting for his boss to stop beating around the bush.

"And Wayne probably has his own contacts there, too—especially now that he's moved back."

Jack nodded patiently, knowing exactly where this conversation was headed.

"You know," Chastain continued, "Oxford is one of the towns I'm visiting next week and I need all the support I can get there. Would you give Wayne a call for me and see if there's anything he can do?"

"I'll call him right now," Jack said, heading out the door. He phoned his friend minutes later with the DA's request.

"Jeez, Jack, I'd love to help him out, especially since he taught me so much. But my agency has a policy against our openly supporting political candidates," Wayne said with some disappointment.

"Oh, I understand. No problem," Jack replied.

"But, you know, during my off time, I could personally introduce him to my father-in-law. He knows everybody who's anybody in politics," Wayne offered, truly wanting to help Chastain in any way he could. He knew there were complaints and rumors against Chastain's character but nothing ever proven or even suspected by those who knew him best, so he gave Chastain the benefit of the doubt.

"That'd be great. I'm sure John would really appreciate it," Jack said.

"Well, he's a good man, Jack, and we need all of those we can get in politics. Heaven knows there aren't many."

"Uh, Wayne?" Jack said, laughing. "Anyone ever tell you you're starting to sound just like your old man?"

Chapter Nineteen

The Election

The whole problem with the world is that fools
and fanatics are always so certain of themselves,
but wiser people so full of doubts.
—Bertrand Russell

With the election only a few weeks away, Chastain desperately needed his airplane. However, it would take time and money to repair—and the DA didn't have enough of either.

Already short of much-needed political donations, Chastain had started loaning personal funds to his own campaign war chest and was reluctantly selling off his father's prized cows. The markets were low and he knew he was taking a beating but needed the cash desperately.

"I should prosecute you for highway robbery," he told the buyers.

He was also pushing Amway sales to the distributors below him in what some said was a legal pyramid scheme, but the costs associated with campaigning and traveling were by then enormous. He knew the law and would not have participated if it had been illegal. His schedule was so full that he didn't even have time to deal with bringing the plane back. To make matters worse, he was still behind in the polls and the bank was breathing down his back.

"Betty Sue, what's today's date?" Chastain yelled through the open door of his office.

"You didn't see the pumpkin? It's Halloween, silly," the secretary said as she snapped her gum and unwrapped yet another miniature candy bar meant for trick-or-treaters.

"Oh, my God! You've got to be kidding me," Chastain said, standing up suddenly. "I still have to visit Southaven, Hernando, Senatobia, Batesville, Grenada, West Point, Starkville, Columbus, Tupelo and Corinth. Get my campaign manager over here now! We have to hit the road. There's not even a week left."

Betty Sue had stopped listening somewhere around "Grenada." But she snapped back to attention when she heard her boss barking about calling the campaign manager. She was used to that. He said it almost every time he was in his office—and each time was more urgent than the one before.

Within minutes, the campaign manager showed up looking spent. Betty Sue figured her boss had him on call twenty-four hours a day by then, like a heart specialist dealing with life and death; he was trying to revive his failing campaign. She sympathetically handed the man a small Snickers bar, hoping the sugar rush would give him the energy he'd need to deal with Chastain.

"John, we need to talk about money." It was the first thing the campaign manager said when he walked into the office. "Many of the pledges we got haven't materialized. Ever since that newspaper article questioning your campaign expenditures, a lot of 'loyal donors' have been hard to find. We're in debt up to our eyeballs and it's not getting any better. We don't even have the funds for your trips."

"Look, I'm going to make those trips. I have no choice. There isn't much time—it's my last shot. I have to get out and see the people—get them excited, get their votes."

"What you have to get is their cash," the campaign manager responded.

"Who says?" Chastain scoffed. "I'll put everything on my credit card."

"You realize you're going to have to pay that off, too."

"Yeah—but by then I'll have something more important than money. I'll have a seat in the US Senate," Chastain boasted proudly.

"I don't know," the campaign manager responded skeptically. "How much is that worth these days?"

―――

Entire days seemed to pass by as quickly as hours as the election drew nearer. Chastain's incessant campaigning did a lot to boost his image in those final moments, and Wayne's father-in-law's careful introductions and well-placed connections certainly helped the cause as well, to the point where a radio station in Tupelo reported that Chastain was neck and neck with his opponent. Of course, there was always at least a five-percent margin of error in such polls, and Chastain was hoping for last-minute donations to help cement his status.

Because this was a special election due to the resignation of the incumbent amid questionable legal issues and his association with corrupt lawyers from Jackson (who were then all serving time), the turnout at rallies was low. It was a sign that turnout would also be low at the polls—but it was a crapshoot as to which party would have the lower vote. As far as Chastain was concerned, he'd take fifty-fifty odds any time. It was what he faced in the courtroom each day. Guilty or innocent. Winner or loser.

―――

When the day of the election finally came, Chastain made it back to Stonewall County and was getting ready for his victory party at the local Holiday Inn. Early results looked good and by 8:49 p.m., when Chastain had changed into his impeccable suit and tie, the polls had been closed for almost three hours.

Because it wasn't an election that held a huge amount of public interest, only sporadic results were being broadcast on the local news stations. Still, the news—what little there was of it—couldn't have been better. By nine o'clock, Chastain was leading by nineteen percent.

"Come on, staff members. Let's go address the media," Chastain announced.

He wasn't bothered one bit by the fact that most of the results already in were from the state district where he was serving as DA. The challenge, of course, was to get votes in the federal congressional district outside those counties as well, but he was confident.

"Reporters are already chomping at the bit for an interview. I'm gonna try my best to sound humble, but it won't be easy." Chastain laughed. He took one last look in the mirror, straightened his tie and headed to the hotel banquet room downstairs.

Staffers and volunteers were all smiles as the crowd of reporters made its way toward Chastain. He accepted a microphone and news cameramen converged in front of the podium. The theme from *Rocky* was playing on a boom box nearby. After all his years of hard work and tireless service, it was Chastain's moment in the limelight, and he was ready to make the most of it.

"Ladies and gentlemen, I'd like you to know how much I appreciate all your support tonight and over these last few months. As you might have heard, things are looking good right now."

Chastain smiled at the round of applause he received then held up his hand to quiet it down.

"However, we don't want to open the champagne bottle just yet. So before we get to the good stuff, please continue to help yourself to the snacks and less-expensive refreshments we already have out for you." There was a smattering of laughter from the crowd. "No, seriously, y'all just enjoy yourselves. We'll continue to monitor the results and notify you when the final tally is in. Thank you again for your support."

Chastain left the podium with his arms raised in victory. When he returned back to his room, however, the mood inside was less than jubilant. It looked as if they were attending a wake.

"What's going on?" he asked some staffers who were huddled around the TV.

"Boss, the ten o'clock news is reporting an earlier error in the polls and it may take a while to straighten the mess out. Won't be done 'til midnight according to the media and the election-commission representative," the campaign manager glumly announced.

"You mean there wasn't a nineteen-percent lead?" Chastain asked nervously.

"Yes, sir, there was." The campaign manager kept his gaze fixed on the carpet. "Only thing is, it doesn't look like it was for you."

"What?" Chastain uttered. It was clear the news wasn't sinking in.

The campaign manager looked up and said softly, "It's your opponent who has that lead, not you."

"Goddamn local news!" Chastain said, striding over to the TV. For a moment it looked as though he would punch the screen in; instead, he pushed the "off" button.

No one said a word while the candidate just stood there, absorbing the news as if it had been a body blow. "You have got to be kidding me," he hissed. "Those results were mostly from my state judicial district. You mean my own people didn't vote for me? Hell, I thought my problem would be in the US congressional district, where there were so many people I didn't know."

"Sorry, sir. I don't know what to say," the campaign manager replied. He wasn't looking Chastain in the eye. Instead, he was studying the alarm clock perched on the end table as it ticked closer to the final midnight tally.

An hour before midnight, Chastain had taken up permanent position on a stool in the hotel's small back bar, hidden discreetly away from the main banquet hall. The campaign manager found him there, nursing a tall glass of whiskey. From the looks of things, it wasn't his first.

"The eleven o'clock news just reported that eighty-eight percent of the votes throughout the entire congressional district have been finalized. As of now, our opponent has forty-eight percent. We only have thirty-nine, but the rest haven't been counted." The campaign manager took a seat next to him, holding up a finger to indicate to the bartender that he'd have whatever Chastain was having.

"Guess we'll know soon enough whether I need to concede," Chastain said quietly.

"We still have our fingers crossed," the other man said.

"Well, uncross them. This has nothing to do with luck…" Chastain downed the rest of his drink before adding bitterly, "I would have to get almost all of the remaining uncounted votes. Figure the odds. It's the will of the people."

———

When the twelve o'clock news came on, a hush fell over the crowd still assembled in the hotel banquet hall. The large, flat-screen TVs on both ends of the room had been turned on for the final announcement and both candidates were at their respective victory parties, though Chastain's immaculately pressed suit now looked as if it had fallen off the back of the drycleaner's delivery truck. All the cheering and chanting had stopped, and the smiles had turned into cold expressions of anxiety.

"And this just in, ladies and gentlemen," the newscaster announced. "We finally have an official winner in the closely contested senatorial race…"

Chastain stopped listening; in fact, he seemed to have stopped breathing altogether as he nervously watched the percentages appear on screen. When the numbers showed him with forty-one percent of the vote compared to the opponent's fifty-eight, the booing from his supporters began. Chastain had only been credited with two percent of the uncounted votes.

Chastain took the stage once more—this time with apparent humility. He stood there for a few seconds without saying a word or showing any expression until, finally, he waved his hands, gesturing for the booing to come to a stop, as he had done earlier with the cheers. His concession speech was very short.

"Ladies and gentlemen, thank you for your support. The voters have spoken and it looks as if those in my own state judicial district have sent me the message that they want me to remain their district attorney and not go running off to Washington. I take it as their vote of confidence in me and not as a defeat. Thank you."

Though Chastain—professional prosecutor that he was—had managed to twist the outcome in his favor, he couldn't entirely mask the crushing disappointment in his voice.

Chapter Twenty

The Bank's Land

*The shaft of the arrow had been feathered
with one of the eagle's own plumes. We often give
our enemies the means of our own destruction.*
—Aesop

By late November, Chastain had gotten over the pricking of his pride that the election had caused. He had other, more-urgent things to worry about now—namely, his expenditures.

Along with the congressional race, he had lost all of his supporters' money as well as his personal savings. He had hocked his father's land, sold cows at rock-bottom prices and still had that wounded albatross of an airplane hanging over his head, costing him more and more money every day in storage, repairs, loan payments and insurance.

It had gotten so bad that Chastain took desperate measures, hoping to find almost any way out. He actually stooped to returning the call of an old friend turned real estate developer, Stanley Reynolds, who was known as the "motor mouth" of the county. Chastain should have known that telling him anything was like taking out a full-page ad in *USA Today*. But what choice did he have left?

"John, thanks for inviting me over," Stanley said as he walked into the office that afternoon. "I didn't want to discuss this over the phone, but I was wondering if you'd be interested in selling me that land your daddy left you. You know how I've always been asking about it."

"Yep, Stan, I sure do know," Chastain said, doing his best not to roll his eyes.

"I have a great plan for a new residential subdivision… We could even dig that old cow pond out into a nice lake," Stan said. He was so excited that he was tripping over his own words.

"Stanley, my daddy is probably just about rolling over in his grave right now. I can't sell you that land. Hell, I might even lose it."

"Lose it? What do you mean, buddy?" Stan pulled up a seat, looking both concerned and comfortably at home.

"I mean I put it up for collateral on that airplane and now I'm so deep in the hole, I may never get out. That damn thing's draining my bucket dry. I've got to sell it so I can get my daddy's land title back."

"Why don't you sell your land instead? I'll make you a good offer," Stan said.

"No, I'm not willing to do that yet." Chastain had lost almost everything but wasn't ready to part with family pride. His father had worked his whole life for that land. It wasn't his to throw away.

"I want to get rid of that damn plane, Stan. Don't you know anybody in your dealings who might be interested in it? I mean, hell, man, you had fun that one time flying to the Ole Miss game with me. Maybe the buyer could work out the same kind of charter deal for people with season tickets."

Stan sounded skeptical. "I'll ask around, John, but I don't know anybody offhand who might be interested. I mean, especially after that near crash and all. You keep me in mind about that land, though, you hear?"

Chastain's guest got up to go, confident he'd be hearing from him soon. In the doorway, he said, "Take care, John. I'll see you later. See you later, too, Betty Sue—*if* I'm lucky."

Stanley made his way across the square. Before getting back into his car, though, he decided to go into the coffee shop for a nice, steaming cup while he thought over his conversation with his old friend.

Man, ol' John really looked miserable, he realized. But what had really gotten to him was the distraught look on Betty Sue's face. She was clearly worried about her boss—and most likely her own job as well.

If John really does go under, he may have to quit being DA and move to a bigger city somewhere to go into private practice, Stan thought. *He may take Betty Sue with him—or the new DA may bring in his own people. Then I may actually never see her again.*

It was during this unsettling revelation that Stanley was joined by another friend of his, local ambulance chaser T. Carson Whittington III, who was carrying *The Wall Street Journal* and looking for a seat in the crowded shop.

Whittington was more interested in the stock market than the goings-on in the rural county of Stonewall. But he was willing to strike up a conversation with Stanley if it meant he could have a comfortable seat in the booth. He sat down and the two exchanged small talk, neither noticing that Patty Franklin was sitting nearby at the counter, eavesdropping.

"Carson, you go to New York pretty often, don't you?" Stan asked.

"Yeah, I go pretty regularly." He was glad to have the chance to talk about his experiences in the city rather than the usual small-town stuff. "My son goes to Rutgers University in New Jersey, just a hop, skip and a jump from Manhattan. My wife's originally from there, you know, though I met her at Ole Miss. She and I like to take in a Broadway play every now and then when we visit our son or her family. We even have a summer cottage on the Jersey shore, in Ocean County. I go up there to check on it twice a year and write the trips off my taxes, you know."

"Man, I didn't know you did all that," Stanley said.

Whittington was clearly pleased with the other man's interest. But for Stanley, it was his chance to try to help out an old friend—and the old friend's hot secretary. Even though he wanted Chastain's land—and figured he could still get a piece of it, especially out of gratitude—he said, "You know, Carson, you ought to go over there and buy our buddy's airplane."

"Airplane? What the hell are you talking about?" Whittington asked.

"I'm talking about John Chastain. You lawyers are all thick as thieves, aren't you?" Stanley laughed out loud. "So why don't you help old Johnny out of his troubles with Consumer Bank? You may even help him save his daddy's land, which I need at least a part of for some new development. Hell, who knows? I might even let you in on that."

At the counter, Patty was listening in intently. The coffee shop was her favorite place for intelligence gathering and she didn't have to go far since it was just next door.

"What on Earth am I going to do with an airplane, Stan?" Whittington scoffed. "Can't even fly one."

"Man, think how easily you could get back and forth to New York," Stan said. "No crowded airports, no delays… Heck, I've been on that plane with John, along with a bunch of politician friends of his—members of the board of supervisors and businessmen. We all flew to an Ole Miss away game. I'm telling you, you don't know what you're missing." Stanley chuckled to himself. "Shoot, I bet you could even work out a sweet deal with John to be your personal pilot. 'Name your own price,' like Captain Kirk says in those commercials. Heck, John would probably jump at the offer since he's in the old hurt locker, if you know what I mean."

"No, I don't know what you mean," Whittington said, fully aware that "Motor Mouth" Reynolds would fill him in.

"Well, he bought the damn thing thinking he was gonna be our new US Senator. Now he doesn't need it anymore, but it's costing him an arm and a leg to keep and he's got big loans to pay back. He told me he'd do anything to get rid of it, so you could probably buy it," Stanley explained.

"No," Whittington stated. "As I said, I ain't interested in an airplane, especially one that had a crash landing."

"Oh, don't you worry about that. Chastain's getting it all fixed. Plus he's sworn off drinking and flying, from what the guys told me." Stan grinned.

If Patty had been facing him instead of keeping her back turned stealthily, he would've seen her eyebrows shoot up in surprise.

"Sorry, still not interested," Whittington said. "But I'll ask around to try to help out a fellow member of the Bar."

Stanley didn't give up quite so easily. As he got up to pay for his coffee, he asked the proprietor standing behind the cash register, "How about you, Ray? You need an airplane, don't you? You could fly some of this topnotch coffee around the country and maybe put Starbucks out of business."

"No, not me," Ray said laughingly. "The wife was mad enough when I went out and bought her a new skill saw. I don't know what she'd do if she saw an airplane parked out back."

A few seconds after Stanley and Whittington left the shop, Patty hopped off of her corner stool (what the regulars referred to as "rumor control central") and headed back to the newspaper office. She couldn't wait to start putting out leads—so much so that she forgot to pay for her coffee. Ray didn't mind, though. He knew she'd be back at least two or three times before the day was done.

The first call Patty made was to her friend Kathleen at Consumer Bank. "Kat, it's Patty," she whispered excitedly. "Listen, is anybody there with you?"

"At the bank? Well, of course. We've got customers, tellers…all sorts of people." Kathleen fit the stereotype of a dumb blonde perfectly.

"No, I mean is anybody near enough to you right now to overhear our conversation?"

"Oh, no. I'm in my own little office, preparing loans for Mr. Buchanan," she chirped. "Why? What's up?"

"I need some information. I'm sure this will be a touchy subject, but you know I'd never burn you, right? I've got to find out about an airplane John Chastain bought through your bank. Would you have access to that on your computer?"

"Probably," Kathleen said, shrugging—though, of course, her friend couldn't see her over the phone. "What kind of information do you need?"

"Things that identify the plane, like a serial number and stuff, as well as any other collateral he put up for the loan, such as land. Actually, anything you could tell me about the transaction would help," Patty said.

"Okay," Kathleen agreed. "You know I can't give you copies, but I'll try to get the information for you." Before Patty could thank her, she added, "Now, you swear I'm not going to be reading about this in the paper on Thursday, right, Patty?"

Patty had never seen her friend read anything except celebrity-gossip magazines, but she assured her, "Of course not, Kathleen. I'm not even sure there's anything to this story. But if those sons of bitches on the board of supervisors that put me out of business are involved, who knows where it may lead?"

Chapter Twenty-One

The Felons

*Be courteous to all, but intimate with few, and let
those few be well tried before you give them your
confidence. True friendship is a plant of slow growth,
and must undergo and withstand the shocks of
adversity before it is entitled to the appellation.*
—George Washington

That afternoon, County Investigator Randy Wood was at his usual spot behind his desk in the sheriff's office. For all his efforts, he hadn't gotten any closer to the indictment against Gaddy's girlfriend or any further in the case of Buford Lancaster, the missing businessman. The ergonomic chair he had bought recently for lower back support already had well-worn grooves in its cushions that matched the exact shape of his rear end, making it uncomfortable for anyone else to sit in.

"Randy," the jailer called over the intercom, "you have a visitor."

Randy looked up, rubbing his overstrained eyes. He was expecting it to be one of the newspaper reporters who dropped in from time to time to cover the crime beat, but the visitor turned out to be someone he'd never seen before.

"Investigator Wood, I'm A.D. McMillan. How are you?" the tall man, sleazily dressed in what looked like a forty-year-old leisure suit, said by way of introduction.

"I'm fine, Mr. McMillan. What can I do for you?" Randy asked.

"Oh, just wanted to drop by and meet the county investigator," the man said casually. "You drive that blue, unmarked Ford out there, don't you?"

"Yes, I do. Why do you ask?" Randy's tone changed from curious to hesitant.

"Well, son, I don't know if you've heard of me," McMillan said, clearly expecting that Randy had, "but I'm a pretty prominent businessman in this county and I'm staunchly pro-law-enforcement. I actually bought that car for the sheriff's department, delivered it here myself and donated it to help in the battle against illegal narcotics. I believe that was shortly before you came to work here."

"Yes, it was," Randy said, "but I sure do appreciate it."

"I'm glad to hear that, son, because now I've got a little problem I wonder if you could help me with."

Ah, so that's his game, Randy thought. He was relieved to get down to business finally but refused to feel beholden. "What kind of problem is that, sir?"

"You remember Dennis Riley, that ol' boy you indicted not long ago for possessing a concealed weapon as a convicted felon?" McMillan asked with a smile.

"Yeah. What about him?"

"Well, he works in my electrical business. I was trying to give him a break after he first got out of prison, y'know?"

"What are you getting at, Mr. McMillan?" Randy asked, ready to lose his patience with this now obviously slimy, self-professed humanitarian.

"I was just wondering if there was any way you could help him out. You see, if he gets another conviction, he'll go back to prison and I'll lose one of my best electricians after putting in all that time and money to train him."

"Mr. McMillan, I appreciate your interest and concern, but Dennis Riley ain't never held a job in his entire life. He is a hey boy for a big fish, a half-ass dope dealer and a wannabe fur-and-diamond broker of hot stuff. As far as I'm concerned, he's better off in prison. It seems to suit him," Randy said angrily.

"Now, Mr. Wood, maybe you think I was too presumptuous to come in here asking favors without you knowing me and all, but I do know quite a bit about you. For instance, I know about that undercover operation you worked in the bar and I know how much the county needed help with narcotics when you came here. You're acquainted with Jack Taggart of the Tri-State Organized Crime Strike Force, aren't you?" McMillan asked.

"I am," Randy said, trying to let his temper cool down.

"Well, listen, son, talk to him later and he'll vouch for me," McMillan said, stepping within inches of where Randy was seated. "I'm about to tell you something nobody else knows, not even your sheriff, who's a darned good friend of mine. Mr. Wood, I'm a paid federal informant in addition to being a successful businessman. You see, my daddy died of drug abuse and I want to see all those pieces of garbage who sell that stuff cleaned up off our streets."

Randy was too surprised to speak, so he let McMillan continue his passionate speech.

"You can check me out for yourself, Mr. Wood. I help out law enforcement however I can: wearing wires, letting them wire up my car, all kinds of stuff. I'm a true friend of law enforcement—and I can help you, too. Got a motor home you could use for surveillance, which is something I know all about. Dennis Riley can even help me wire it up for you."

"Mr. McMillan," Randy said, standing up to stare the other man straight in the eye, "I don't drop charges on felons. I'm sorry I can't help you. But I will definitely talk to Mr. Taggart about your *offer* and if he feels your friend might be of some assistance to law enforcement, I'll consider asking the district attorney about an informant deal. For now, though, I'm going to have to ask you to excuse me."

"I'll leave, Mr. Wood," McMillan said with a sneaky smile. "But you don't mind if I go over your head on this, do you?"

"What do you mean?" Randy challenged.

"Like I said, your boss is an old friend of mine." With that, the businessman nodded his head, turned and left.

Within seconds, Wood was on the phone with Jack Taggart, getting some truthful information about this McMillan guy. He knew in his gut that something wasn't right about him.

"Yeah, McMillan's a snitch, but not a paid one," the Organized Crime Strike Force officer said. "He was turned over to us by the Bureau of Alcohol, Tobacco and Firearms, who investigated him three times for conspiracy to commit bombings. He was only convicted the last time on arson charges for setting fire to his own business and trying to commit insurance fraud, but he was a suspect in the fire bombings of some Memphis nightclubs a few years ago. To tell you the truth, I don't trust the guy. Think he might be a double agent. We're getting ready to cut him loose completely."

Randy barely had time to thank Taggart before getting on the intercom to speak to Sheriff "Doc" Sanders. He was sure that the sheriff wasn't the type to get in thick with someone like McMillan but, knowing Doc, it wasn't too much of a stretch to believe that he'd been duped by the bogus son of a bitch.

"Sheriff, I have something to tell you...quick," Randy said.

"Sure, Randy," Doc replied in his slow, affable drawl. "You know I'd always make time for my number-one county investigator. 'Course, you're the only full-time county investigator we got, but you know what I mean."

"Yes, Sheriff, thank you," Randy said, rolling his eyes in exasperation. He wanted to warn Doc not to accept McMillan's impending visit but was running out of time. "Listen, Sheriff, a man named A.D. McMillan is on his way up to see you. Says you and him are good friends—"

"McMillan?" Doc interrupted. "I know him. Wouldn't say we're exactly friends, though. Acquaintances, more like it. I met him during the election last year and he donated some money to my campaign.

Wonder what he could want? Thanks for letting me know, Randy. I'll see if he's here."

"No, no, no, Doc, wait!" It was too late. The sheriff was already ambling toward his office door, having left his intercom on. Randy could hear him asking his secretary, Nancy, if he had any visitors.

"Yes, sir. There's a man waiting to see you," she said.

Randy shook his head, knowing the sheriff would forget to turn off the intercom. Listening in, he could hear McMillan make his way into the office.

"Sheriff Sanders, long time no see. Unfortunately, though, this isn't a social call. Your investigator arrested a friend of mine for carrying a concealed weapon—a damn nickel-plated, five-shot thirty-eight he has for protection, not to hurt anyone with, just like the one I gave you when you won the election."

Randy's eyes widened and he felt a little sick to his stomach. He liked the sheriff very much but believed that Doc might have fallen for a scam artist and could soon have his reputation ruined.

For fear of hearing more than he wanted to, Randy quietly got up and left the office to be out of earshot of that infernal intercom.

Chapter Twenty-Two

Up for Sale

We desire nothing so much
as what we ought not to have.
—Publilius Syrus

Randy went over to the local pizza shop and ordered a whole pitcher of beer for himself. It felt good just to be out of the office but he couldn't stop thinking about what the sheriff might've gotten himself into—and, frankly, he wasn't quite sure who he could trust anymore.

The last time Randy had drinks there was months earlier with Wayne Lott, and that got him thinking about what the anticorruption assistant US attorney would do in this situation. The answer came to him about an hour later, after the pitcher was empty and he had put away four pints.

Randy got up a little wobbly and headed out to see John Chastain. The only problem was that someone else had already beaten him there.

———

Dennis Riley knew anybody who had anything for sale and often bought whatever he could—particularly if it had been stolen—at wholesale or yard sale prices. He used his electrical skills to refurbish the items then sell them for profit.

It just so happened that Riley had mentioned to his boss, "Word on the street is that a DA in Stonewall County is willing to do anything to sell his airplane." And it just so happened that McMillan was in the market to buy one. So, after leaving the sheriff's office, the businessman went straight in to see Chastain.

"Hello," McMillan said, eyeing Betty Sue like a starving man looking at a T-bone steak. "Is the DA available?"

"Sorry," the secretary said uncomfortably, adjusting her tank top so that less cleavage showed. "Mr. Chastain's busy getting ready for a trip."

"Well, would you be kind enough to relay a message for me? I've heard he has a plane for sale and I'd really like to speak to him about it before he leaves."

Unlike most men, there was just something about this stranger that Betty Sue didn't like, but she was pretty sure her boss would want to talk to anybody with an interest in buying his plane. "Wait here," she said before walking into the district attorney's office. McMillan watched her all the way.

"John, some guy's here about buying your plane."

Chastain nearly barreled her over in his haste to get to the door. "Hello, sir. I hear you have an interest in aviation." He smiled, motioning for McMillan to come into his office.

Betty Sue tried to squeeze out and shut the door behind her but McMillan's foot was in the way, ensuring that he'd have at least a partial view of her walking back to her desk.

"That's correct, Mr. Chastain," he answered distractedly before turning his full attention to the DA. "My name's A.D. McMillan. Now, I don't know you and you don't know me, but I'm a friend of Jack Taggart," he said confidently.

"Old Jack's a good man," Chastain said. "Any friend of his is a friend of mine. Quite frankly, though, if Charles Manson were interested in that airplane I'd probably sell it to him."

"Well, fortunately for both of us, I'm not at all like Manson. I'm a respectable businessman who sometimes gets called away on trips for work—much like yourself, as your charming secretary informed me," McMillan said, craning his neck toward the slightly opened door.

"That trip was scheduled for me to go get the plane but if you're serious about buying it, I'm more than happy to unpack my bags. What do you say you take a seat and let me sell you an airplane?" Chastain said, shaking his new friend's hand.

McMillan smiled and made himself comfortable. "You'll find I am quite serious, Mr. Chastain, but I do have a few questions first."

"Fire away," Chastain said. "But please, call me John."

"I'd like to know about the layout of the plane, John. Are the seats reconfigurable?"

Chastain assumed that the man's business involved some heavy transport, so he started in on the sales pitch. "Mr. McMillan, the seats can be taken out completely to haul cargo and the plane can accommodate up to six fully grown Ole Miss fans, so you know it can handle some serious weight," he laughed. "Hell, if it's too heavy, drain some fuel."

"That's fine," McMillan said, before launching into a lengthy discussion about payments and bank loans.

Betty Sue sat behind her desk, continuing to ignore the voices coming from her boss' office and hoping that Chastain would stay so occupied that he'd forget to ask her to do any work. She looked up only when she heard the cowbell announcing that Randy Wood had just walked in.

"Hey, Randy. What can I do for you?" she practically whispered.

Randy shot a look through the partially opened door to Chastain's office and saw a pair of fancy cowboy boots belonging to some man sitting in a chair with his legs crossed.

"Who's he got in there with him?" Randy slurred.

"Some guy interested in his airplane." Betty Sue shrugged. "Hopefully they'll be in there all afternoon, and then I'll be left in peace when John goes on his trip tomorrow."

"That's right. I forgot he was leaving again." The disappointment was evident in Randy's voice.

"Don't worry, sugar, I'll still be here. Maybe we can go for a liquid lunch together, which it seems you've just enjoyed," she flirted.

"We'll see," he said, suddenly feeling much more sober. With the DA constantly so preoccupied with his plane and other personal problems, Randy knew there was only one more place for him to turn.

He went back to his office, took out Wayne Lott's business card and dialed. "Wayne, it's Randy Wood."

"Randy, good to hear from you. Sorry I haven't been in touch but I haven't made much progress on the missing-man case," Wayne said.

"Oh, that? Don't worry about it," Randy replied. "Actually, I was calling to find out if there are any more jobs available down by you."

"As a matter of fact, there are," Wayne said, surprised. "We'd love to have someone like you here in Oxford, Randy, but won't the sheriff be after my butt if I take his county investigator?"

"Well, the two of you might just have to fight it out over me," Randy responded. "And may the better man win."

Chapter Twenty-Three

The US Attorney's Office

Anyone who goes through life
trusting people without making sure
they are worthy of trust is a fool.
—Elizabeth Aston

The next morning, Randy called in to work saying he'd be out of the office most of the day and went instead to the circuit clerk's office to get copies of indictments that had been dismissed for mysterious reasons. He knew that nothing would be done at the local level to fix the political climate in Stonewall County and thought that Wayne might just be the one who'd pursue it, given all the information.

Looking over the docket book in the clerk's office, Randy was shocked to see that one of the most-important recent indictments had been quashed.

That's the last straw, he thought to himself determinedly. More than determined, he became defiant but tried to hide it as he approached the circuit clerk.

"Ms. Fortenberry, I'm going to make some copies of a couple indictments," Randy told the clerk. "I'll put your books back when I'm through."

He didn't want a soul to see what he had uncovered. He pulled several other indictments that had nothing to do with what he was looking for so nobody could see who he was targeting. As far as he was concerned, corruption in that county could involve anyone from the county clerk all the way up to the sheriff himself.

Randy left the circuit clerk's office with an armload of evidence, which he packed in his car before driving to the US attorney's office in Oxford.

An hour and a half later, Randy arrived in town. He parked on Oxford's renowned square then walked to the lobby of the federal building with a large, overstuffed folder under his arm. He left his badge and gun locked safely in his vehicle, knowing he'd have to go through a metal detector. Besides, he wasn't so sure he'd need the badge much longer.

After being granted access to the elevator, Randy rode up to the US attorney's office, aware of the camera hidden in the vented light fixture above him. He smiled into it once before stepping off the elevator.

"I'm Randy Wood, here to see Wayne Lott," he told the receptionist, handing her his identification.

"Yes, sir. He's expecting you. Please have a seat while I page him," she said politely.

Randy sat quietly on the couch, fidgeting slightly while waiting. After a few minutes passed, the cipher lock opened and Wayne stepped out with a big smile on his face.

"Randy, it's good to see you again." Noticing the very-full folder his friend was holding, Wayne joked, "I see you brought your résumé."

"No," Randy said, shaking his head. "I may have jumped the gun a bit in asking for a job just now, but I might need one for real before this is over."

"That doesn't sound good," Wayne said, noticing his anxious expression. "Come into my office and tell me what it's all about."

As soon as they settled in, Randy said, "I have some bad news for you, Wayne. I know you think a lot of our little Podunk county and I know y'all are doing some investigating there, but I'm not sure you're looking into the criminal cases closely enough."

"I figured Chastain has those all under control," Wayne answered sincerely.

"No, I mean as part of your corruption investigation. Cases are falling off the docket and never getting heard, and now we've got guys coming in and asking point blank if we'll drop felony charges. I don't know who's responsible," Randy explained.

"Huh... I don't think our investigators heard about any such recent developments," Wayne said. "Our primary focus is on the supervisors' self-dealing."

"I know that's what Patty thinks but I don't trust anybody in our local or state agencies either at this point. The evidence I have here is only the tip of the iceberg," Randy said, waving the folder.

"If these are ethical issues you're talking about you may want to file a complaint with my old buddy Jimmie down at the Mississippi Ethics Commission," Wayne said. "But if they're criminal violations, you came to the right place."

"I know I did," Randy said, exhaling. "But that's just about the only thing I know. It's going to take some deeper investigating, but the violations are there."

"Is it all right if I get Tischner in on this?" Wayne asked. "He's the best investigator I know."

"I think that would be a great idea," Randy said. "We've traded phone calls back and forth about Buchanan for a while now but I've been looking forward to meeting him in person."

"Don't let looks deceive you." Wayne laughed. "He may not realize that his socks don't match but he really is a sharp investigator."

Wayne gave Tischner a quick call to fill him in and, minutes later, the man appeared in the flesh. "Howdy, neighbor," he said to Wayne.

Randy had to stop himself from looking down at the man's ankles to see whether or not Wayne had been exaggerating.

"Agent Tischner, meet Randy Wood of the Stonewall County Sheriff's Department," Wayne said.

"Nice to finally put a face to the voice, Randy," Tischner said, shaking his hand.

"Good to meet you, too," Randy responded.

"Now all we need is for Buford Lancaster to come walking through the door and our job here is done," Tischner joked.

"Not quite," Wayne interjected. "Randy here has some information that might help us on the corruption case we've been investigating in Stonewall County."

"I've got a lot of stuff in that file I'd like to show the two of you," Randy said.

"Why don't we move to a conference room so we can spread it all out on a table?" Tischner suggested. There was nothing he loved more than having evidence laid out like a battle plan.

As the three men walked downstairs, Randy started a brief synopsis of what was going on. "Gentlemen, as I've said, I believe some of our county officials are part of corrupt activities involving criminal charges that drop off or never appear on the docket. I think they're using their offices for personal gain and to obstruct justice."

When they arrived in the room, Randy immediately opened the large file and started removing papers and laying them out across the table. "These are indictments issued by the grand juries in Stonewall County over the last couple of years. In the seven here, the Tucker and Tatum Law Firm represented each of the defendants and filed a motion to quash the indictment rather than take it to court. And, in each case, the charge either never appeared or eventually dropped off the docket."

Wayne and Tischner, sitting next to each other, exchanged glances. Then Wayne asked Randy, "Is it possible that some of these indictments were pursued in Chastain's absence, maybe when Jack Burchfield was handling the grand jury? Could it be that Chastain wouldn't have allowed the file to be presented in the first case, had he been there, and it was all a misunderstanding or miscommunication?"

"Yes, that was the case on at least one occasion, but not all." Randy paused before bringing out the *pièce de résistance*: the file on Gaddy and the girl who gave him the information about the county investigator's undercover agent. "She was the personal secretary of a county supervisor," he explained. "I was still waiting for an indictment against her—until I found this."

He held up a piece of paper. "The grand jury issued a true bill, but apparently it later got quashed and I never heard a word about it. I don't know who concurred with the motion and, frankly, I'm tired of asking. I'd rather just turn it over to y'all and let the chips fall where they may."

"Randy, you've done a great job," Tischner said. "But Wayne told me there's one more thing."

"Yes, and it scares me the most. I arrested Dennis Riley, a convicted felon, for carrying a firearm on a grand jury indictment. Later, his boss, A.D. McMillan, came to try to get me to drop the charge. After I said 'no' I found out a whole lot more about him than I would've liked to know. I found out more about Sheriff Sanders, too."

"You don't think the sheriff's involved in any corrupt activities, do you?" Wayne asked.

"No, but I think he's fallen victim to something that could adversely affect his career, his decisions and possibly justice as a whole in our county," Randy said.

"What do you mean by that?" Tischner asked.

"I mean this guy who came to see me about dropping the charges on the convicted felon is a convicted felon himself. I mean he bought and paid for the county investigator's car and he knows all about my background in an undercover operation before I went to work for Stonewall County. I mean that even though he's a convicted felon, he gave the sheriff a pistol as a gift, just like the one I took off the other guy I arrested, and he also gave the sheriff campaign contributions. I think he did all those things to get the sheriff in his back pocket," Randy said disgustedly.

"Do you think he *does* have the sheriff in his pocket?" Tischner asked.

"Hell no. But this is one of your boys I'm talking about: a snitch for the feds assigned to the Tri-State Task Force for Organized Crime."

"Who is this guy again?" Tischner asked.

"A.D. McMillan. I'm not sure what the initials stand for, but he's a white male, mid-sixties, five-foot-ten, and weighs about a hundred and sixty-five pounds soaking wet. He owns an electric company but has been a suspect in numerous fire bombings."

"Hold on," Tischner said. "I'll be right back."

The special agent went to his office to run a check; he returned a few minutes later with a full file himself.

"This guy's a real winner—a double agent in drug cases. He's suspected of giving law enforcement only partial information about drug dealers—probably his competition—and dealing on the side with some heavyweights that have South American connections. They don't use him much as an informant anymore but there's a note that he's an electronics wizard who likes to play with tracking equipment and listening devices and is very skilled at that stuff," Tischner said.

"Did you say he bought the car you were supposed to use in your duties?" Wayne asked Randy.

"Yes. I am using it. In fact, it's parked on the square right now."

Tischner ran out of the room without a word and returned ten minutes later with a team of officers holding electronic bug tracking devices.

"Call it a hunch," Tischner explained. "Let's go take a look at that car."

Randy drove the vehicle back behind the federal office building, where the team of technicians began to comb every inch of it. In less than three minutes they found something.

"What's that?" Randy asked as one of the agents pulled a small, black box from underneath the car; it had been hidden near the gas tank.

"Tracking device," the tech said. "Looks like it's been there quite a while."

"You mean…" Randy couldn't quite finish his sentence.

"Your every move has been tracked via satellite through a GPS system," the tech said.

"Randy, that guy has known every time you were getting close to one of his deals He can pull you up on his computer any time he wants," Tischner explained.

"Damn it," Randy said, looking sick. "That's why some of my stings went wrong. How could I be so stupid?"

"Don't blame yourself," Tischner said. "These guys are pros. We're going to photograph the bug and check for prints on the interior of the battery cover. There's too much wear on the outside, but I wouldn't hold my breath that your buddy's fingerprints are on the inside, either."

"Then what do we do?"

"Then we put it back on your car and have you out of here in a jiffy," Tischner said. "Just don't drive your car on surveillance for now."

"What?" Randy exclaimed. "That's all? Isn't there anything we can do?"

"Only thing we can do is keep our eyes open and wait," Tischner said. "He'll trip up eventually."

"How do you know?" Randy asked.

"Guys like that always do."

Chapter Twenty-Four

The Florida Connection

*He has all the virtues I dislike
and none of the vices I admire.*
—Sir Winston Churchill

Weeks Later

Randy was sitting in his office, working on some of the cases that still hadn't been solved. It had been months since he'd first met Wayne Lott but nothing so far had come of the US attorney's office and FBI's joint investigation into the corruption of Stonewall County.

When the phone rang, Randy hoped to hear some new developments. Instead, it was a voice from the past.

"Randy, is that you?" the caller asked.

"Yes. Who am I speaking with?"

"This is Investigator Ron Stevens at the Miami-Dade Drug Task Force. Remember me? We went to DEA class together in Washington, DC, last year then went to that crab house over in Maryland, ate all those crabs and drank lots of beer."

"Oh, yeah, I remember. They'd never seen Southern boys eat that many crabs or drink that much beer, either." He laughed. "There was another guy from Miami with you, short with an afro. I think his name was Lane, wasn't it?"

"That's right. Sorry to say we lost him six months ago in a drug raid. Got hit just above the vest from a downward-trajectory bullet," Stevens said. "Poor guy had two little kids who really do miss him."

"Oh, sorry to hear that," Randy said. "Y'all really have a bad problem with major drug dealers down there."

"You got it, brother. Keeps us busy."

"So is there anything I can do for you up here?" Randy asked.

"Well, not so sure right now, but I'm working on something that might involve some people in your area. I told my boss about you and he wants me to fly up there tomorrow so we can talk," Stevens said.

"Sure, bubba, it'd be nice to see you, but I can't imagine what Stonewall County could have to do with Miami-Dade."

"Can't really say over the phone," Stevens replied. "But, due to the number of cases in Florida, we have trouble getting them all prosecuted. We're hoping that maybe we can get your US attorney's office interested and prosecute it there. Do you have any contacts?"

"Absolutely. I just met with them a while ago," Randy said.

"Well, what would they say to a big drug-smuggling case that involves some corrupt, well-known public officials? You know, headlines and that kind of stuff," Stevens asked.

"They'd say, 'Welcome to Mississippi,'" Randy replied.

⁓

The next day, Ron Stevens landed at the Memphis airport, then found his way in a rental car to the small sheriff's office in Stonewall County.

"Thank heaven for GPS," he said to Randy as soon as they met and shook hands.

"I used to think that myself until a few months ago," Randy said, laughing, though he didn't elaborate. "Listen, Ron, before we take the ride to the US attorney's office in Oxford, let's go visit a newspaper editor nearby. She won't print anything you don't want printed and I'm sure she can provide you with some much-needed information about our local politicians. What do you say?"

"I'll say 'yes' to anything that'll let me stretch my legs for awhile," the six-foot-one officer said, glad to be out of the economy Dodge hatchback for which his department had sprung.

"Great. Let's take a short walk," Randy said.

They stopped for a quick coffee to catch up on some small talk, then Randy called Patty to tell them they were coming before they ducked into the newspaper office next door.

"Patty, I'd like you to meet Ron Stevens, an investigator from south Florida," Randy said, handing her a cup of take-out coffee.

"Glad to meet you, Ron."

"Likewise."

"Listen, Patty," Randy said, "Ron needs some information from you about your favorite people…"

"So you figured you'd bribe me with caffeine?" she joked, taking a gulp from the Styrofoam cup. "Smart man."

Randy smiled. "Seriously, though, we need you to hold the presses on anything we say until we give the word."

"Of course," Patty assured them. "Don't know why a Florida investigator would be interested, but I would welcome an investigator from the moon at this point. What do you need?"

"Just general info about public officials, their associates and whatever you know about their business dealings," Ron answered. "But first I'd like to know about the bone you have to pick with these guys."

"Oh, it's nothing—besides the fact that they all conspired to get me out of business. I sent in a bid to print county notices and the county attorney made me provide a full list of my subscribers, which I usually keep under tight control. The attorney assured me it was confidential but not long after that, all my readers received anonymous letters smearing me and strongly suggesting that they don't buy my paper or take out any ads. Then, to top it all off, their buddies at the bank gave all their customers free subscriptions to my competitor newspaper. The bank president's brother, a local lawyer, provided them with a new space for a newspaper satellite office here in town and the bank president gave them sixty thousand dollars to renovate it. I've filed a lawsuit alleging violations of the Sherman Antitrust Act but so far, nothing has been done."

"Those are some pretty strong connections between county government and the bank," Ron said. "What else are they working on together?"

"Deals of all kinds, from fixing criminal charges to bogus land deals and even bogus loans."

"What do you mean 'bogus loans'?" Ron asked.

"Loans that were really for something like a hundred thousand dollars but showed up on paper at the bank as being for ten thousand. Somehow, all those good ol' boys who were in on it split up the remaining ninety thousand," Patty said.

"How did you get all this information?" Ron asked. "Do you have a connection at the bank?"

"Yes, I have a source. I also have some documentation about these bogus loans but I'm sitting on that right now. Ron, are you really going after these guys? They have so many connections and have done too many favors for people in high places—plus they've got some things to hold over their heads," Patty said.

"What I'm really after is drug smuggling," Ron admitted. "I'm sure some of that money they split up went into the operation."

"Really?" Patty asked, wide-eyed. "I hadn't even considered that. But anything I can do to help, just ask."

"Thanks," Ron said. "Tell you what… In return, I'll save their mug shots for you to run on the front page of your paper one day."

"I hope like hell it's still around," Patty said with a smile.

Chapter Twenty-Five

Coming Full Circle

History is the version of past events
that people have decided to agree upon.
—Napoleon Bonaparte

Randy and Ron stopped for lunch at the McDonald's drive-thru window outside of Oxford on their way to the US attorney's office.

"I can't believe that of all the great places to eat in Mississippi, you want to stop for a Big Mac," Randy said, shaking his head.

"My wife doesn't let me have them at home," Ron admitted. "Besides, I was rarin' to go—that is, until you told me you were driving a compact rental car, too. What's with that? Good thing you are using a hand-held radio. If that equipment were in this thing too, neither of us would be able to move." He squirmed in the front seat, trying to get comfortable without much leg room.

"Well, you're not gonna believe this, but my official car was bugged. Then the transmission went out. The dealership gave me the rental. Lucky for me the transmission specialist at the dealership got injured the day my car went into the shop. He won't be back for a couple of weeks. In the meantime, the feds are watching the dealership to see if anybody interested in my movement shows up to get the device off the car and move it to this one."

"What?" Ron said. "Who would do that to a county-owned vehicle?"

"Some thug named A.D. McMillan, an informant for the Organized Crime Strike Force in Memphis."

Ron spit soda all over the windshield.

"Are you alright?" Randy asked, patting his friend on the back.

"Fine, fine. It just went down the wrong way."

"Well, it came out the wrong way, too," Randy said, grabbing a few napkins to clean up. "Now I'm glad we didn't take my car."

"How much further before we get to the US attorney's office?" Ron asked anxiously.

"We're almost there."

"Good, Randy. 'Cause I've got a lot to fill you in on."

<hr />

Upon their arrival in Oxford, Randy parked on the square. It was a beautiful, sunny day without a cloud in the sky—perfect for a short walk. Ron, however, was practically sprinting with his briefcase.

When the two visitors cleared the security checkpoint, they made their way up to the US attorney's office, where they met Wayne and Tischner, who were already waiting for them.

"Come in, gentlemen. How was your trip here?" Wayne asked.

"Not bad at all, other than the fact that my new partner here washed the inside of my windshield with some Diet Coke," Randy said.

"You'll understand soon," Ron assured him. "Agent Tischner, AUSA Lott, I'm Ron Stevens from the Metro-Miami/Dade Aircraft Drug Smuggling Task Force."

"Man, that's a real mouthful," Wayne said.

"Yeah, well, he sure is good at spitting things out, so I guess that handle's no problem," Randy said.

Ron shot him a look and continued. "We're having trouble getting a case prosecuted in our area because of our workload and some lack of evidence."

"What makes you think we can help up here?" Wayne asked.

"I think you'll understand when I present this to you. We think the first overt act of the conspiracy began in Mississippi," Ron said, holding up his briefcase.

Tischner and Wayne led their guests to the conference room, where Ron took out folders filled with papers and photos.

"My unit tracks private airplanes suspected of drug smuggling throughout southern Florida. In the first four months of this year, in my county alone, we seized seventeen planes and made a hundred and forty-four arrests, mostly American businessmen and smugglers from Central and South America as well as from Caribbean islands. The planes typically have no records onboard. They may be worth tens of thousands of dollars but most are sold at auctions for less than ten thousand. Recently, we'd received confidential intel from an informant that a planeload of cocaine was coming in at a small field."

Ron showed them a picture of investigators dressed in camouflage, lying facedown in some tall grass.

"We were waiting for the plane to land and had Humvees hidden with spotlights, snipers, the whole nine yards. We'd been quietly watching a couple of Hispanics rig running lights from their old truck batteries down to the other end of the field."

Ron showed them another picture of two Hispanic men unloading bricks upon bricks of cocaine from the aircraft. "They had a shitload onboard," he said, "and our captain—Captain Veazey— old the sniper to take out the guy on guard if he turned his weapon in our direction when we turned on the lights to rush them."

The next photo caused Wayne to wince. It showed a man with a bandolier of bullets whose head had been blown off. He was lying on the ground in a puddle of blood, illuminated by lights from an army of Humvees.

"We rushed the plane but the pilot tried to escape," Stevens said. He showed them a photo of the plane after it had spun around at the edge of the field, having been stopped by a specially configured explosive-round shotgun. The landing gear had collapsed and the right wing was drooping toward the ground.

"The coke was stacked on top of a huge, collapsed bladder tank, and we noticed that the N number had been altered. One of the guys who surrendered said the plane wasn't stolen. It belonged to some big businessman who paid them to haul the drugs—millions of dollars' worth."

"Did you trace the ownership records through the Federal Aviation Administration?" Randy asked.

"Yep, and it came back registered to two parties. One was A.D. McMillan," Stevens said.

Randy jumped up from the table in excitement. "Hot damn, I can't believe it! We got him! We got him! You were right, Wally. We just had to wait." He gave Tischner an unwelcome hug.

"Who's the other one?" Wayne asked.

Stevens handed him another photo, turned facedown. When Wayne looked at it, Randy and Tischner could see his expression transform into a combination of confusion, horror and disgust.

"No," Wayne uttered, slowly shaking his head. "It can't be."

"Who?" Randy asked softly.

Wayne looked at him a moment before turning the picture around. It showed a smiling, still-hopeful senatorial candidate: John Chastain.

Chapter Twenty-Six

The Guilty

Evil deeds do not prosper;
the slow man catches up with the swift.
—Homer

W hen the shock wore off, Randy finally spoke. "Everybody in town knew Chastain had been making comments that he'd do anything to sell that airplane."

"Guess he finally found a buyer," Wayne said with disappointment.

"Apparently, he sold half his interest in the plane to McMillan. Our check on the aircraft showed it was first registered to Chastain and the Consumer Bank, then to Chastain and McMillan, with the bank holding a lien on it in both their names," Ron said.

"Do you happen to know the date the registration was changed?" Randy asked curiously.

"Sure, take a look." Ron handed him the documents as Randy thumbed through his little pocket notebook.

"Holy crap! That was the day I visited Chastain's office and saw the cowboy boots."

"What?" Wayne asked.

"McMillan was in his office! He must've gone to see him as soon as he left the sheriff. That was the day he came to me about

153

dropping the charges against Riley. Don't you see?" Randy asked excitedly. "Doc must've turned him down, too."

"So naturally his next stop was the DA," Tischner said.

"Wait a second," Randy said, grabbing his car keys. Clearly, something had dawned on him. "I'll be right back."

Minutes later, the county investigator returned out of breath. He was carrying a file retrieved from the backseat of the car. "Here's the indictment I had gotten on Riley that I refused to dismiss. And here's a motion to quash filed by the lawyers next door—it was submitted on the same day Chastain sold half his interest in the plane to McMillan."

"Who are these lawyers?" Ron asked.

"One of them's the county attorney for the board of supervisors," Randy said. "Remember what Patty told you? Those are the guys we're after. But it gets worse." He held up another piece of paper. "Here's the order entered into the record to dismiss the indictment…and there was no hearing, even though it's required by law. Chastain just let it slide through the system without any challenge. It was simply dismissed for half a share of an airplane."

"But it cost him so much more," Wayne said sadly. "His integrity and an entire career fighting against drug dealers." He picked up the picture of the damaged plane. "And look how it all came crashing down."

"Well, Randy, it looks like you've solved the mystery of the 'lost' indictments and cases falling off the docket," Tischner said.

"As much as I hate to admit it, John Chastain's our prime suspect, working in conjunction with the private practice next door," Wayne said. "I never dreamed the guy I admired most as a prosecutor would potentially be a defendant for me to prosecute."

"We still have to look at the other cases that fell off the docket to see what connections these bankers, newspaper owners, the board of supervisors and private attorneys had with the county attorney and DA," Tischner added. "Randy, why don't you try to maintain a low profile? That way we can continue to rely on you for information."

"No problem," Randy agreed. "Doesn't matter to me who slams these guys—as long as they get slammed."

"So where's the plane now?" Wayne asked, shaking off his initial surprise. He was ready to bring in the bad guys, regardless of who they were.

"In a warehouse just off the general aviation tarmac in the Miami airport. It has a seizure notice in the window and we're planning on pursuing the seizure," Ron said.

"Seizures under federal statutes require notice to the owners and lien holders so they can claim an interest in the plane and seek a hearing to dispute the action," Wayne said. "Have McMillan, Chastain and the bank president been served notices of the hearing?"

"Yes, they have," Ron replied. "They were all served via registered mail, restricted delivery. Each of them verified and accepted receipt."

"I can't wait to find out what their response was," Wayne said.

"You really want to know?" Ron took another file out of his briefcase; this one contained the aircraft seizure documentation as well as a lengthy police report of the incident, arrest records complete with fingerprints and photographs of the defendants, and the coroner's report on the deceased defendant shot by narcotics agents at the scene. All those arrested in the field that night had long criminal histories and intelligence information about their drug-smuggling activities. They were all Colombians.

"Here's a copy of the seizure notice taped to the plane window," Ron said, handing it to Wayne. "And here are the individual notices that were sent to the two registered owners and the lien holder. These are return-mail receipts signed by Chastain, McMillan and Buchanan, indicating they were served."

"How about their responses?" Wayne asked.

"No responses were ever received defending their interests in the airplane," Ron replied.

"What does that mean? Are they just waiving their appearance and forfeiting the plane?" Randy asked.

"Could be. They were given thirty days to respond but didn't.

However, the auction for the plane is scheduled for next week, along with seven other aircraft. Anybody with the money can go buy it but since it has wheel damage, bullet holes and no records, it won't be very attractive to anyone other than drug smugglers. Of course, the owners could send a representative to buy it back for pennies on the dollar and never show their faces but still get it back," Ron reasoned.

"You mean you actually have drug smugglers showing up at police auctions?" Randy asked.

"Oh, yeah. Parts dealers and drug smugglers are the only parties interested in this type of plane."

"Guys, there has to be something else to tie Chastain to McMillan other than their being registered partners in ownership of the plane," Wayne said. "Randy, since you're always going through old court cases in your position anyway, will you see which other documents you can get from the clerk's office—and I don't want copies, I want originals. Can you do it?"

"Sure. I'll tell the county clerk I'm making copies and give her receipts for the originals. Then I'll give her the copies to put back in the file—don't want an evidentiary chain of custody issue to come up."

"Good. And what will you do with the originals until I see you?"

"Keep 'em in my car," Randy said. Scared to leave any files in the sheriff's department, fearing those he might not be able to trust, the county investigator had already turned his rental into a mobile file system.

"Okay," Wayne said. "If you're sure they'll be safe. Pay particular attention to any motions to quash indictments that had been issued by the grand jury."

Randy nodded his understanding before he and Ron hit the road once more.

"What are you gonna do now, Wayne?" Tischner asked when they were alone. He was worried about how his friend and neighbor would react to his mentor's betrayal—but Wayne's response quelled any concern.

"I'm going to call my old friend Jack Burchfield." Wayne began to think that the assistant DA couldn't have been oblivious to everything that was going on around him. "And if I have to, I'll take him down with the rest of them."

Chapter Twenty-Seven

Law and Loyalty

Nearly all men can stand adversity,
but if you want to test a man's
character, give him power.
—Abraham Lincoln

Wayne made the call from the privacy of his office. The conversation wouldn't be easy, but he was spurred on by his belief that no man was above the law.

"Jack, how are you, buddy?" Wayne began in a friendly tone.

"Fine, bubba. What's up in Oxford?"

"Well, I need to talk to you about something. I'd prefer to do it in person, but we can start over the phone."

"What's this about, Wayne?" Jack laughed. "You sound all official. Are you going to interrogate me?"

"You know the old saying, 'Where there's smoke, there's fire,' right, Jack? So let's just say I'm investigating a fire."

"What do you mean, Wayne?" Jack asked in a serious voice.

"You've been working for Chastain for a while now. What do you know about cases dropping off the docket or suddenly disappearing?"

"Wayne, you know very well that this is a political position. The district attorney has a great deal of discretion in what he prosecutes. I'm not going to tell you that he never refused to prosecute a case that might have had merit but in which the defendant had major political connections. I don't like it any more than you do but that's just the way it is," Jack reasoned.

"I'm not talking about discretionary authority, Jack. I'm talking about cases disappearing after indictments have been issued by the grand jury and the defendants' names and evidence are known," Wayne persisted.

"Wayne, come on. I could get fired for—"

"Worse yet, you can get indicted yourself for conspiring to obstruct justice or as an accessory to the crime after the fact," Wayne interrupted.

"Are you threatening me?" Jack asked. "Look, Wayne, we may be friends but I don't like your tone."

"So you're not willing to help me out?"

Jack exhaled. "I am, but not because you threatened me. It's just that the charge of obstructing justice really strikes a nerve with me."

"I'm listening," Wayne said, softening his tone. "Jack, we've been friends for a long time. I need you to be straight with me."

"I will…don't worry." Jack paused for a few seconds, then continued. "Here's the deal, Wayne. Randy Wood brought a case about conspiracy to obstruct justice in front of the grand jury when I was in charge. Chastain was out of town campaigning. Anyway, turned out a secretary who worked for a county supervisor gave up an undercover agent's identity and Randy wanted me to give him the indictment to serve on her personally. I intended to do that the following Monday since it was late on Friday when I finally got the grand jury foreman's signature."

"You *intended* to? Does that mean you didn't?"

"Yes, Wayne, I did. Hear me out. Chastain came back over the weekend and confronted me about how the grand jury went. At first he thought it was great that somebody was indicted for conspiracy to obstruct justice—you know, a headline case and all. Then I told him the defendant's name."

"What happened after that?" Wayne asked.

"Chastain was furious when he saw the indictment. Said he was close to this girl's family. His wife had been her babysitter and her dad and Chastain hunted together—even bought a Jeep together to use for deer hunting." Jack took a deep breath. "He refused to allow me to give the indictment to Randy and didn't want him to process her in the jail."

"But the sheriff's department has a policy that anyone arrested for a felony charge must be fingerprinted, photographed and interviewed," Wayne interjected.

"I know that, but Chastain wouldn't allow it. He said he'd call her dad personally and get him to bring her to his office to spare them the embarrassment. He had me call the sheriff to tell him to call Randy off the case."

"And did he bring her in to serve the indictment like he said?"

"Yep. You can see on the back that it was served by Chastain's investigator. But the day Chastain was leaving to go get his plane, there was a motion by the lawyers next door to quash the indictment," Jack said.

"Okay, Jack," Wayne said, rubbing his forehead. "I want you to start looking for these documents in the DA office files as well as the circuit clerk's office. I'll send an FBI team to help. I want you to pull anything that doesn't look right, whether you had any involvement or not."

"Alright, Wayne," Jack said, sounding resigned. "But I want you to know I've never done anything wrong—not intentionally. You've gotta believe me."

"I hope not, Jack. But what I believe doesn't matter—it's all about what the evidence shows. You of all people oughta know that by now."

Chapter Twenty-Eight

The Files

Necessity has no law.
—William Langland

Later that day, Jack went through Chastain's files, determined to uncover anything that showed an obstruction of justice. Wayne's words had lit a fire inside him and he was no longer worried about who would get burned.

When he found an item of interest he called Wayne right away, unaware that the DA's investigator, Pierce Milton, was listening in outside the door. He had noticed Jack rifling through some papers and was starting to get suspicious himself.

"Wayne, it's Jack. I've been going over the documents like you said and I think I might've found something in the motions to quash. Is there any way you can come here to talk about it?"

"Nice work, Jack, but I'm still in Oxford and it'd take me some time to get there. Special Agent in Charge Tischner is on his way to Stonewall County right now with a team. You can talk to him about anything you've found."

"Okay, but I don't want them to come to my office," Jack said in a low voice. "Tell him to meet me south of town behind the old cotton gin. He won't be able to see me until he goes behind the building. Let him know I'll be sitting in a blue Ford Mustang, newer model."

"I'll pass it along," Wayne said. "Give him about an hour to get there."

"Alright," Jack said, checking his watch. "So I'll expect to see him around two o'clock." With that, he hung up and headed toward the door.

As soon as Milton heard him coming, he ducked into a side office and waited for Jack to go into the copy room. Then he snuck into Jack's office, picked up the phone and hit redial. The secretary answered, "US attorney's office, Oxford."

Milton hung up, rushed out of the office and met Jack head-on as he was walking away from the copy machine. Startled, Jack dropped several papers he was carrying—one of which was the indictment that had been issued on the daughter of Chastain's friend for obstructing justice in the narcotics-agent case.

"Sorry. Didn't mean to make you jump," Milton said, stooping to help Jack recover the documents while getting a closer look at them.

"Th-that's okay," Jack said nervously, grabbing the papers as quickly as possible and stuffing them into his briefcase.

"I was looking for you to see if you want to go get a late lunch," Milton said, putting on a friendly smile.

"Oh, I can't," Jack said, starting to calm down. "I already made plans to meet a friend."

"Alright. Maybe tomorrow then." Milton watched him walk down the hall and close his office door. Then he went into his own office and made a call.

"Boss, Burchfield's acting strange. I saw him with the indictment you told me about and I think he's planning to turn it over to the US attorney in about an hour."

"Damn," Chastain swore on the other side of the line. He tried to compose himself then said, "Okay, this is what I need you to do. Get your hands on another car, not yours, as quickly as possible. Preferably with dark windows so he doesn't see you following him."

"Then what?" Milton asked.

Chastain took a deep breath. "Then do whatever you have to do to keep him from delivering those papers."

———

Minutes later, Milton drove down to Leroy's Garage and Car Sales behind the square.

"Hey, Leroy," he said, getting out of his car to greet the oil-covered owner.

"Hey, Milton. How's the car I sold you?"

"Great. I brought it by for you to do a tune-up, but I'm kind of in a hurry. Any way you can get me a loaner off your lot, like last time?"

"Sure, man. Anything you want," Leroy said. "You know I try to keep my customers happy. Especially the good ones that pay upfront, like you."

Milton took a quick look around at the vehicles parked outside. "How 'bout that big, black Dodge over there with the tinted windows?"

"The one that looks like an old police car? Like I said, man, anything you want. I gotta tell you, though, that one's already been sold to a cat called Pinkie. He made one down payment and we drew up the bill of sale, but he ain't comin' back for it until next Saturday, when he's got the rest of the money. You'll have to bring it back before then."

"No problem," Milton said, smiling. He knew Pinkie—he'd helped send him to the big house a few years back. He also knew how he'd gotten that name: from snorting a half a gram of coke from the nail of his little finger. That was the last person he'd have to worry about. With everything Milton had on him, Pinkie was in no position to give him a hard time about borrowing his car—or anything else, for that matter.

"Alright. Give me five minutes and I'll have a dealer tag on it," Leroy offered, turning to walk inside.

"No, that's okay, Leroy. You know I'm working at the DA's office. Nobody's gonna bother me if I get stopped without a tag."

"Suit yourself," Leroy shrugged. "The key's already in it."

Moments later, Milton drove the car down a side street around the corner from the DA's office, where he waited for Jack to start driving. It wasn't long before the blue Mustang made its way out onto the two-lane highway, with the big, black Dodge close in pursuit.

At first, Jack didn't notice anything. He was too focused on getting the papers into the right hands. Then he looked into his rearview mirror and saw the Dodge getting closer. His first thought was that he was getting pulled over by an undercover policeman.

"Great," he said under his breath, checking his speedometer. He was doing over seventy.

When no police lights came on and the Dodge started tailgating within inches of his back bumper, Jack figured it was some kid showing off his used car and his brand-new driver's license. He slowed down to change lanes then looked over toward the other vehicle, yelling obscenities. Unfortunately, he couldn't see the kid's face because of the dark windows and because the visors were down, nor could his shouts be heard.

"Goddamn stupid kids," Jack muttered to himself, accelerating to get back in front.

The Dodge slowed down for a little while then sped up toward Jack's bumper, to the point where it was almost pushing him. Jack kept an anxious watch on it in the rearview mirror but when he turned to look at the road, he saw a concrete bridge coming up quickly over a small creek.

At eighty miles per hour and climbing, the Dodge whipped up beside Jack again to terrorize him. The car suddenly jerked to the side, striking the Mustang with its fender in an attempt to force it to hit the bridge railing. In a split second, Jack pulled his steering wheel to the right and hit the brakes, missing the bridge railing but slamming into the banks of the shallow creek, less than half a mile from the cotton gin where he was supposed to meet the agents.

Another driver, who had been about a quarter of a mile behind the two vehicles, saw smoke and steam rising from under the bridge and pulled over immediately to call 911 on his cell.

"Send an ambulance right away," the driver said.

"Sir, what is the emergency?"

"Somebody ran off the road into the creek a half mile north of the old cotton gin south of Stonewall."

"Are there any injuries?" the dispatcher asked.

"Yes. There's a man slumped over the wheel. Smoke's pouring out of the hood, so you'd better get a fire truck here, too," the driver said in alarm.

"Okay, sir. Please don't go near the vehicle. Just stand by while we dispatch emergency vehicles."

Within moments, police cars, ambulances, fire trucks and a tow truck were called to the scene of the accident from both directions. The sirens in the distance caught the attention of Tischner and his agents, who were already waiting behind the gin.

Tischner checked his watch to see that Jack was already fifteen minutes late. Figuring the assistant DA was caught in traffic, he wrinkled his brow and picked up the receiver on his car radio. "What's the nature of the emergency near Highway Fifteen?"

"Guy just ran off the road into a creek," the voice came back. "Driver of a blue Mustang."

"Jack!" Tischner said, starting up his car.

With the other agents following, he sped north until he saw the first emergency vehicle pulling over to the side of the road. When they got there, a ball of flames suddenly burst from below the bridge.

Chapter Twenty-Nine

The Rescue

*The policy of being too cautious
is the greatest risk of all.*
—Jawaharlal Nehru

The agents quickly pulled to the side of the road and ran over to the bridge.

"Jack's trapped," Tischner yelled, moving toward the burning car. "We've got to get to him."

"Don't!" a policeman called out, stepping in front of him. "He may already be dead and we don't need another casualty. Wait for the fire truck."

Tischner pulled back his jacket to show his FBI badge, pushed past the officer and jumped with another agent into the muddy, shallow creek. Picking up a large stone, he slammed it into the driver's-side window as flames washed across the windshield from under the hood. The fire was so close that it singed Tischner's hair as he grabbed at Jack's seemingly lifeless body, slumped back against the seat. The other agent reached in and disconnected the seatbelt, then the two of them lifted the body through the window.

When the ambulance arrived, the car was engulfed in flames almost up to the back tires. But through the thick, black smoke, EMTs could make out the two agents dragging Jack's body away from the creek.

"He's alive," Tischner yelled out as ambulance workers ran down with a stretcher.

"Let's get him a safe distance away from the fire," an EMT said. As they loaded the body onto the stretcher and carried it up to the road, Jack's eyes opened.

"What happened?" he moaned. Blood streamed down the center of his face.

"You had a bad accident," Tischner said, standing over him.

Jack's eyes focused first on Tischner's FBI badge, then he moved his head slightly to the side and saw the smoke streaming up from the creek. "Oh, shit! My briefcase is in the trunk. Get it, get it!" he screamed.

Tischner understood. By that point, fire was covering the entire body of the car except for the trunk and taillights, and flames had just burst out the back windshield.

"Get back! Everybody get to the other side of the road," Tischner yelled, removing his weapon from his holster and running toward the car.

"Tisch, what are you doing?" one of the other agents yelled out as emergency workers swarmed around Jack to carry him into the back of the ambulance.

"Shooting the lock off," Tischner said, squinting toward the trunk

"But what about the gas tank?"

Boom! Tischner's handgun went off and the lock disappeared, replaced by a hole five times as big as the bullet. The trunk popped open and flames immediately began to enter the space through the back windshield.

Tischner ran to the trunk, reached in and grabbed the briefcase. Sooty and sweaty, he slipped in the mud as he made his way up the creek bank, where the other agents offered him a hand.

Just then, the ambulance started up, ready to pull away.

"Take my keys and follow us," Tischner said, handing them to an agent before stepping onto the back of the ambulance.

"Sir, you can't ride with us," one of the attendants told him.

"FBI! Get out of my way," Tischner flashed his badge as he stepped inside. "This is a federal investigation now."

The ambulance sped away toward the hospital with FBI agents and police following close behind. Tischner watched silently as EMTs assessed Jack's condition by checking his pupils and blood pressure.

"Sir, do you know where you are?" an attendant asked.

"In an ambulance," Jack replied groggily.

"And do you know what your name is?"

"Look, man, I know where I am and who I am and how old I am," Jack snapped, much to Tischner's amusement. "What I want to know is *how* I am."

The attendant stepped to the front of the ambulance and radioed in. "H one, this is alpha four en route to the ER. We have a white male, approximately thirty to thirty-five years old—car accident victim with laceration on upper forehead, normal pulse and normal blood pressure. Victim is now conscious and coherent but was unconscious on scene. May have suffered a concussion from impact with the air bag or steering wheel. Laceration will require several stitches. Forehead is swollen, eyes appear to be bruised and possible fractured nose. ETA to ER approximately four mikes."

"Sounds like I'll live," Jack said to Tischner when the assessment was over.

Upon arrival at the hospital, Jack was wheeled into an emergency room, where he was quickly examined by a doctor and found to be in good health other than the laceration, which was quickly sutured by an intern.

"Where are my glasses? I can't see a damn thing," Jack mumbled.

"Are you having trouble with your vision?" the intern asked.

"Of course I am. I don't have my glasses."

Tischner, standing nearby, smirked. "Hey, Jack, I remember seeing them in your lap as I pulled you out of the car. If it makes you feel any better, they were broken."

"Well, that explains the laceration between his eyebrows," the intern said. "The air bag must have pressed the broken glasses against his head."

"Good work, Quincy," Tischner said. The intern, too young to understand, gave him a puzzled look.

Just then, the attending physician came back into the room and told Jack everything was normal. "We can keep you overnight for observation if you'd like or we can release you to your friend here and I'll give you some pain medication for your head."

"I don't want to stay here. I feel fine. Thanks for patching me up, but I'll be in good hands," Jack said, glancing at Tischner.

When the doctor and intern left, Tischner asked, "Do you want me to take you home now, Jack?"

"Do you really think I should go there? I mean, someone was trying to kill me," Jack said, hopping off the exam table.

"What?" Tischner was shocked. "You mean that wasn't an accident?"

"Hell no. That son of a bitch tried to run me into the bridge railing."

"Did you get his license-plate number?" Tischner asked.

"I never saw the back of the car. Man, I'm starting to think we should put tags on the front in Mississippi."

"What did the car look like?"

"It looked like a police car—a big, black Dodge with windows so dark I couldn't see the driver," Jack said.

"A police car?" Tischner repeated. "Did you happen to notice if the antenna was long or short, or if it was mounted on the trunk, the bumper or on top?"

"I don't remember seeing an antenna, but that doesn't mean there wasn't one. I was trying to save my life more than get a sketch of the car," Jack said sarcastically.

"Got it," Tischner said, putting a stop to his investigative instincts. "Tell you what. We'll find you a hotel for the night in another town. Hope you don't mind if one of my agents sleeps in the same room, but I'd feel better posting him there. We'll get two beds—don't worry. You won't have to snuggle."

"That's fine." Jack smiled in appreciation then pointed to the slightly charred briefcase Tischner was holding. "And when we get there, I'll show you what you risked your life for."

Chapter Thirty

Files Reviewed

Be smart, be intelligent and be informed.
—Tony Alesandra

After settling in at the hotel, Tischner called his two remaining agents into the room while Jack took a hot shower to clean off. Realizing that they had a murder attempt on their hands, Tischner had slipped into special-agent-in-charge mode, chain smoking and barking out orders to his agents while the victim wasn't around to see him lose his calm demeanor.

"I want you to locate any black, unmarked Dodges at police and sheriff departments as well as any state law-enforcement agencies in the area. Check out the state tax commission, alcohol beverage control, the highway patrol and any others that use that type of vehicle," Tischner said while the other men took notes.

"I also want you in every body shop around, looking for a vehicle that meets the description with any damage at all to the right side. Have our helicopter unit comb a twenty-five-mile radius of the accident, looking for any such abandoned vehicle, then get to the tax collector's license-plate division and get a listing of all full-size Dodges that have been issued car tags within the last three years."

Deep in thought, Tischner lit another cigarette before finishing the first one. "Run an ad in the paper looking for anybody in the area who might have seen a vehicle fitting our description and offer a reward. Also, get paint scrapings from Jack's car if you can find a spot where it wasn't burned. If we find a suspect vehicle we can see if it has any paint from his Mustang by comparing the samples. We sure as hell won't find any of the Dodge's paint on Jack's car since the front end burned like the toast my wife made me for breakfast, but the other way 'round is worth a try."

Just then, Jack stepped out of the bathroom, looking refreshed in a plush, terrycloth robe. "Were you guys just discussing room service? I thought I heard someone mention toast."

"You can order something in a little while," Tischner assured him. "Right after you tell us what you know."

"Gentlemen," Jack began as if he were in a courtroom instead of a Courtyard by Marriott. "I'm not sure what happened today, but I do know one thing: Somebody tried to kill me. Whether it was just some stupid redneck, a crooked cop or a piss-poor driver, I don't know. But I'm beginning to believe you're of the opinion that it could be tied to what I was about to deliver to you. Am I right?"

"Anything is possible, Jack. Did anyone know you were meeting with us?" Tischner asked.

"Nobody should have known," Jack said, taking a seat on the bed.

Tischner walked to the trashcan to empty his ashtray. "Well, was there anybody else near you when you retrieved those documents?"

"No, I was by myself."

"Could anybody have overheard your conversation or listened in to the phone call when you said you had something important?"

"I only told Wayne and he told you."

Tischner walked back to the table by his agents. "Where were you when you called Wayne?"

"At my desk with the door closed. Our secretary, Betty Sue, was still at lunch, Chastain hadn't been in all day and his investigator, Milton, was in his office."

"Is he trustworthy?" Tischner asked, raising an eyebrow.

"Well, he is an investigator—but he's also close to Chastain, who I *thought* I could trust until I looked over some of his files," Jack said. "But I don't think Milton's got anything to do with it. For one thing, he doesn't drive a Dodge. He bought a used, white BMW convertible from a local car lot a couple of months ago."

Tischner glanced at his agent and gave him a nod to make sure he had written that down. Then he looked at Jack and casually said, "Well, we're gonna get all cell phone numbers and records of every staff member in your office anyway, just in case someone overheard something or saw you going through the files."

"Ah, yes," Jack said, getting up to grab his briefcase. "Speaking of the files, I want to show you what I found that seems suspicious."

"You sure you feel like it tonight?" Tischner asked.

"I played for Ole Miss. Six stitches in my forehead is nothing," Jack replied.

Tischner smiled and said, "Okay, let's see what you've got."

Jack handed him a piece of paper. "It's a letter to the crime lab. I printed this on the secretary's copier this morning."

Tischner read it and then looked up, puzzled.

"The letter itself means nothing," Jack explained. "But look at the dark smudges on the back of the paper caused by the printer. The wheel that feeds the paper through was once cleaned with a solvent that softened the rubber. Ever since then, it has made these marks."

"What are you getting at?" Tischner asked, growing curious.

"Now look at these motions to quash supposedly filed by the law office next door, where the county supervisors' attorney works along with a couple of other lawyers." Jack handed Tischner more documents.

"They all have the same mark," Tischner said, turning them over.

"Exactly. That means these motions likely were typed by our secretary and printed on our printer. What almost always happens when other attorneys file motions to quash, postpone or dismiss is that we either get them in the mail or they're hand delivered by the defense. We should never file a defense attorney's motion to ourselves."

The agents looked at each uncertainly.

"Don't you see?" Jack continued. "Chastain must be getting pressure from other politicians or businessmen to dismiss cases, so he pretends they're represented by the lawyers next door. He has our secretary print the motions, takes them over there for his lawyer buddies to sign, then either doesn't contest them or recommends the action to the judge."

"Have you seen him with any politicians or businessmen you may suspect?" Tischner asked.

Jack looked thoughtful. "All I can say is that the entrance to his office is like a revolving door for members of the board of supervisors, bankers, real estate agents, builders and those types… So it'd be hard to narrow it down."

"We have indictments pending on some of the supervisors for receiving interest-free loans," Tischner said, stroking his chin in thought. "Now you say Chastain was also meeting with bankers…"

"Are there any loans from the Consumer Bank?" Jack asked.

Tischner nodded.

"Well, the chancery clerk serves for the board of supervisors and he's also, by state statute, the county treasurer. That means he decides where county funds are deposited, and the board of supervisors supposedly confirms his decision. That decision is worth millions."

"Let me guess," Tischner said. "He decided to deposit them in the Consumer Bank."

"You got it," Jack said. "And the vice president of the bank just so happens to be the chancery clerk's son."

"That makes perfect sense," Tischner said with some disgust. "It's like one big circle of thieves. The bank hires a flunky and makes him VP. He gets his dad, who's the chancery clerk, to convince the supervisors to deposit millions of dollars in his son's bank and they, in return, get interest-free loans. Then, if any of these so-called friends or supporters of the supervisors, who somehow helped with the loans, have friends or family members who end up in jail, they go see the supervisor, who then goes to the DA to take care of the charges. The DA uses his lawyer buddies next door to sign motions that he drafts himself and the charges simply go away. Everybody either gets money or a get-out-of-jail-free card."

"That seems to pretty much sum it up," Jack said, barely able to believe it himself. "Man, Patty had it right all along. She said the supervisors, bankers and businessmen were involved in underhanded dealings."

"Yeah, we've been investigating some of her allegations," Tischner said. "Jack, let me ask you something. Where did Chastain finance his airplane?"

"Take a wild guess. You get three tries...and the first two don't count."

"The Consumer Bank," one of the agents said.

"Give that man a trophy," Jack said.

"Sounds like we need to investigate the whole damn county instead of just the supervisors," Tischner said, standing up to leave. "But first we need to find the asshole who almost killed you."

Chapter Thirty-One

Looking for Leads

The more original a discovery,
the more obvious it seems afterwards.
—*Arthur Koestler*

When Tischner left the hotel room, he pulled out his cell phone to make one more call.

"The wife, huh?" Agent Kent Jackson asked knowingly.

"Don't remind me," Tischner responded. "While Jack and Agent Malone order up filet mignon from room service I get to drive home to a dried-up old bird." Catching the stunned look Jackson gave him, Tischner added, for clarification, "I'm talking about the turkey she made for dinner...not my wife."

"Oh," Jackson said with a smile.

"Anyway, I'm not calling Ann. I'm calling someone I've worked with who might be able to help us on this. You'll find out tomorrow when you meet with him."

———

The next morning, Agent Jackson joined Randy Wood at a truck-stop café off the highway, not far from town. Randy's blue Ford, back from the dealership, with a low-band antenna on back and SO-2 license plates, was one of the few cars in the parking lot, surrounded by a small army of eighteen-wheelers.

"Figured this was a good place to meet," Randy explained after their introductions. "No one here 'cept long-distance truckers—and they don't have eyes for anything but the waitresses and the home-made pies, so no chance anyone'll notice us."

"Good thinking," Jackson said. "Special Agent Tischner said you were on the ball."

"Ah, he's being kind," Randy said, taking a sip of steaming, black coffee. "But it's a good thing he caught me when he did. I just turned in my resignation yesterday."

"That's too bad," Jackson said, diving into the plate of fried pork chops, mashed potatoes and hot rolls he'd ordered. "We hate to lose a good man in law enforcement. What's next for you?"

"I'm hoping to start with a bondsman as soon as I get my license. Have to look out for my family and pay the bills, you know. Local law enforcement just doesn't pay enough—and any notions of social justice have gone by the wayside recently, too. I think criminal justice is just an oxymoron."

Jackson nodded. "I understand."

"But Wayne and Tisch are two of the good ones, so I'd like to do whatever I still can to help them," Randy said.

"Glad to hear that," Jackson responded. "Tisch says you're familiar with the Dodges many departments bought a couple of years ago when Chrysler won the state bid for police vehicles."

"Sure am. We had those when I was with my last agency. They were fast, tough cars. Wish I still had mine." Randy motioned for the waitress to refill his coffee.

"Well, we know there are a few still around that haven't been replaced by the new Fords like yours. Do you know of any agency nearby that uses them?" Jackson asked.

Randy thought for a few seconds before shaking his head. "No, Kent, I don't. There were a few around here up until three or four months ago but most of the local agencies sold them through auction."

"How many auction houses are in this area?" the agent asked, pushing his empty plate away.

"There's only one, about fifteen miles from here. Jack the Ripper's place," Randy said.

"What does that mean?"

"Guy named Jackie Johnson owns it. Gets a lot of cars that don't move off the lots and they usually arrive with prices still taped to the windshields. He prides himself on ripping off the old price tags and selling them for much less. Says if you want a good deal without being cut to the bone by some cutthroat, come see Jack the Ripper," Randy explained with a laugh.

"That's original," Jackson replied. "So, wanna go see old Jack the Ripper with me?"

As they pulled into the auction parking lot, Jackie was out front ripping price tags off a new batch of cars he had just received.

"Hey, Randy, long time, no see," Jackie said when the two men got out of Randy's car.

"Yeah, it's been a while, Jackie. Got time to talk to us for a minute?"

"Sure. Always got time to talk to you. But who's the other guy?" Jackie asked, eyeing Agent Jackson.

"This is Special Agent Kent Jackson with the FBI," Randy said. Jackson held one hand out to shake Jackie's and displayed his credentials with the other.

"Whoa, I must be big-time now—you bringing the FBI here. Looking for stolen cars, are you?" Jackie asked.

"No. Looking for an unmarked black Dodge police car that was most likely part of the state-bid program a couple of years ago. It may have been auctioned off in the last few months. Remember anything like that?" Agent Jackson asked.

"Yeah. We've had quite a few of those come in spurts over the last year. Haven't had any in a while, though. Most of the ones we had were marked. They had damage from where the light bars were and you could see where the department stickers had been on the doors. Let me check my inventory and sales records to be sure, though."

The three men walked into Jackie's office, where he called the info up on his computer.

"Three months ago, we sold two old black-and-white marked units to a cab company. Hell, they're probably egg-yolk yellow by now," he said with a laugh. "Here's one I don't remember." Jackie squinted at the screen. "It must have been a pretty clean car because I don't recall it as a police vehicle and it brought almost twice as much money as the others. It was black and unmarked."

"Who bought it?" Randy asked.

"Shoot, you know the guy who runs the little car lot and garage next to your office—Leroy Robinson? He bought it about three weeks ago. It might still be on his lot," Jackie said.

"Jackie, you're a gentleman and a scholar," Randy said with a smile.

"Can I get a copy of the sales record?" Jackson asked.

"Yes, sir. Anything I got is yours. Don't need no run-ins with the FBI, that's for sure," Jackie replied. "I may be known as Jack the Ripper, man, but I ain't got nothin' to hide."

***

Randy and Agent Jackson left the auction lot shortly afterward. "I know exactly where that garage is," Randy said. "What do you say we drive by?"

"I say Tischner sure set me up with the right guy."

After driving a few miles they passed Leroy's Garage and Car Sales and saw only about eight cars on the lot. There was no black Dodge among them.

"Sorry," Randy said disappointedly as he turned by the square and passed the district attorney's office. "But it was worth a…"

"Everything okay, Randy?" Jackson asked, wondering why Wood had suddenly stopped mid-sentence.

"Yeah," he said tentatively. "Kent, we're gonna pass that car lot one more time."

"Sure, man. What are you thinking?"

When they got in front, Randy pointed out the window. "See that white BMW convertible off to the side?"

"Pretty sharp looking for an older model," the agent replied.

"Yeah, well, it usually sits out in front of the DA's office we just passed. Belongs to the DA's investigator, Milton. He hasn't been on the radio at all today—yesterday afternoon, either—and he *never* misses work." Randy gave Jackson a meaningful look. "Could be nothing…"

"But could be something," Jackson said, finishing the thought.

Chapter Thirty-Two

One Man's Trash

The only thing that makes life possible is permanent,
intolerable uncertainty; not knowing what comes next.
—Ursula K. LeGuin

After dropping Jack Burchfield back at home that morning, FBI Agent Sandy Malone followed Tischner's orders and went in search of local body shops.

So far that day he'd visited three. He'd gotten spray paint on his car from parking in front of the first shop; accidentally touched wet paint on a car that had been freshly touched up at the second one, pissing the owner off to no end; and slipped in oil, almost busting his ass, at the last one, only to be attacked by a junkyard dog while trying to get up.

Other than that, things have gone well, he thought to himself. *Except I'm no damn closer to finding that car.*

He checked his notes and saw that he still had two left on the list: Stonewall Body Shop and a place called Fast Eddie's.

I think I'll hit Fast Eddie's first, he thought. *If I were looking for a quick job, that's the name that would attract me.*

Resigned to seeing the job through, Malone drove down several country roads and behind a residential area until he found Fast

Eddie's shop. It was an old, detached garage in a rundown area of the county.

As soon as he saw a potential customer pull in, a thin, wiry, black man with a receding hairline and a little gray, in his mid-sixties, walked over. "Fast Eddie Jameson here. What can I do for you, sir?"

"Agent Sandy Malone, FBI. Need to ask you about some work you may have done recently." His voice was stern, reflecting the type of day he was having.

"Yes, sir," Eddie replied helpfully. "Don't want no trouble with the FBI, but this ain't no chop shop, mister."

"No, I didn't think it was," Malone replied.

"You see, we ain't like most body shops around here that spend a lot of time beating and banging on them old fenders and doors, trying to straighten them out, or filling them dents with Bondo and fiberglass. Takes too long to dry and sand, prime and paint. No, we just go down to the junkyard and get another fender or door, paint it the same color you've got with fast-drying lacquer paint and bolt it on. We can usually have you out of here the same day," the owner said proudly. "That's why they call me Fast Eddie."

"How about a big, black Dodge that looks like a police car?" Malone asked. "Worked on any of them lately?"

"Sho' did, mister. Just got it out of here a little while ago, matter of fact. Had to paint that thang twice, though, 'cause the old fender was white and it was showing through the black," Eddie explained.

Malone raised an eyebrow in interest. "Got a repair bill with the owner's name?"

"Mister, I'm gonna be honest with you. That black fellow who brought it looked like a pimp—gold teeth in the front, scars on his face, wore a lot of gold chains and had plenty of money. Told me he'd pay cash and a big tip if I hurried up. I don't know who he was but his money was good, and I didn't make out no bill." Eddie shrugged, smiling. "Now, I don't want no trouble with taxes, y'know. I just got him outta here and threw that old, bent-up fender behind the shop."

"You mean you have still it?" Malone asked with excitement.

"Sho' do. I'll get it for you, if you come on 'round here," Eddie said, leading the way.

During the short walk, the agent took down the shop owner's description of the man who'd brought in the car. He was busy writing in his notepad when he heard Eddie say, "Here it is."

Agent Malone's day suddenly got much better when he looked up and saw the fender. It was from a large, black Dodge and had light-blue paint on it that matched the shade of Jack Burchfield's Mustang.

"Mr. Jameson, I'm going to need you to do me one more favor," Malone said. "Can you dip that paint-stripping brush over there in white paint and sign your initials and the date on the inside of this fender, please?"

Fast Eddie was more than happy to do so, like an artist signing his name to a masterpiece.

"Thank you very much, Mr. Jameson," Malone said before placing the fender into the trunk of his FBI car. "You've been a lot of help."

"You sho' are welcome, sir. But I don't know what you'd want with a beat-up old fender like that," Eddie said, smiling.

"Well, you know what they say," Malone replied. "One man's trash is another man's treasure."

Chapter Thirty-Three

Sunny Beaches

He that is of the opinion money will do everything
may well be suspected of doing everything for money.
—Benjamin Franklin

After helping Jackson out with as much information as he could
on the DA's investigator, Randy left the agent on his own to continue a background check on Milton and to meet with his partner,
Malone, about the fender he'd found. Besides, the county investigator had some last-minute packing to do.

He was planning an overnight drive to Florida to meet his friend
Ron, who had offered to show him around the Miami facilities. The
drug-task-force agent was also going to show him Chastain's shot-
up plane before it got sold in the auction or reclaimed. It was a rare
opportunity, and Randy realized it was best to get down there before
his friend heard that he'd left the sheriff's office. He wouldn't offer
that kind of all-access tour to a civilian, after all.

Randy wasn't exactly looking forward to the sixteen-hour drive
down the highway but there was one thing he couldn't wait to do: get
exclusive pictures of Chastain's drug-running plane to send to Patty
for the front page of her newspaper. It was a scoop that CNN, *60
Minutes, Nightline* and the *Memphis Commercial Appeal* would all kill

to have, but he wanted to give her the opportunity to trump the big boys one last time before she was forced to close up shop.

He haphazardly stuffed some clothes into an overnight bag—after making sure they passed the smell test—then checked around for his digital camera.

"Honey," he called to his wife after rooting around in a couple of drawers, "have you seen my camera?"

"You took it in to work a few weeks ago," she called up from the bottom of the stairs.

"Damn, that's right," Randy cursed to himself. "I'll swing by the office to get it when I start out on my trip."

"All right," his wife answered. "Do you need anything else…like clean shirts?"

"Nah, the ones I have are clean," he lied. "Besides, they'll just get wrinkled on the way down. But there is one thing you can do. Try to keep the kids off me for a few hours. I'm going to take a nap before I head out."

"Okay, sweetie, I'll stand guard."

———

Hours later, Randy was awakened by the unwelcomed buzzing of his alarm clock. It was eight in the evening and he was feeling a bit disoriented from waking up after the sun had gone down. He turned the alarm off, rubbed his face and stretched, then went downstairs in search of leftovers from dinner.

After a quick meal, he tucked his kids into bed, kissed his wife and headed out on the road. At nine o'clock there weren't many people at the sheriff's office to disturb him when he ducked in to get his camera.

But something definitely did disturb him when he left and drove past Leroy's Car Sales and Garage. Milton's BMW was no longer there, but the black Dodge they were looking for was.

Since the business was closed and there were very few cars on the road, Randy decided to pull into the lot discreetly and turn off his headlights. He got out, put his keys in his pocket and walked over to the car's right front fender. It smelled like fresh paint.

Ducking down, Randy reached into his pocket and removed his keys, using one to make a small scratch on the fender near the bottom so it wouldn't be easily seen as he held an open envelope underneath to catch the scrapings. Underneath the new black paint, a slash of white appeared.

Looking over his shoulder to make sure he hadn't been spotted, Randy went back to his car, removed his camera and took a few photographs of the Dodge, making sure to get a close-up of the scratch he had made. Then he returned to his front seat and called Special Agent Jackson on his cell phone.

"Kent, I've got good news. That black Dodge you were looking for is back on the lot here in town—and its fender got a nice, new paint job. Looks real good in the pictures I took," Randy said.

"You found the missing piece of the puzzle, friend," Jackson replied.

"Tell you what. I'm on my way to Florida but I'm not far from home. I'll stop by real quick, download the photos and e-mail them to you."

"Please do. And send me a few from the sunny beaches of Florida, too," Jackson laughed.

———

Randy made it to Miami in record time. *State troopers must've all had the day off,* he thought to himself happily as he pulled into his hotel's parking lot.

He was exhausted but too excited to take a nap. He wanted to see Chastain's plane as soon as possible and it was already almost 3:00 p.m. So he splashed some water on his face to reenergize, made himself an awful cup of hotel-room coffee and gave Ron a call to come pick him up.

Ron couldn't help but laugh when he saw his friend standing in the lobby a half hour later. "Welcome to sunny Miami," he said, giving Randy a firm handshake and a strange look. "Hell, we're going to check out drug dealers' planes, not ride the coasters at Disney World. How come you're dressed like a tourist?"

"Uh…my wife packed for me," Randy stammered, hoping to hide the truth. He was wearing a wrinkled Hawaiian shirt and plastic sunglasses and his camera was strapped around his neck, and all those long hours working in the sheriff's office had left him with a pale, almost grayish complexion.

"Man, you'd better put on some SPF forty so you don't sizzle like bacon," Ron said as they walked out toward his car. "Only make sure you rub it all the way in and don't have any of that white stuff left on your nose. Then I'd have to pretend like I don't know you."

"Funny," Randy said, taking a tube of sunscreen from his pocket. He applied it as Ron narrated some stories and they drove to the Miami-Dade facilities.

When they arrived, Ron took him on a very quick tour of the offices before they closed. Randy had lost all track of time and suspected that the brief visit was due in part to Ron's embarrassment to be seen with him.

No matter, he thought, wanting to move on to the airplanes anyway.

Back outside, they got into the car and Ron drove him to the nearby airport, where they kept most of the planes they had recently seized.

"We sell most of these to drug smugglers," he said bluntly.

"You mentioned that when you were up at Stonewall," Randy said, shaking his head. "That just amazes me."

"Think that's amazing?" Ron asked. "See that big old King Air over there?" He pointed toward a blue-and-white plane. "We've seized that plane and resold it to drug smugglers three times. We went to a judge to try to get approval to install a tracking device so we could follow the next load it picked up. We've got a similar plane we could use to follow it but the damn judge said that was against the law. Believe that? Unlawful search and seizure."

"That's the problem with the laws," Randy said. "They're designed to protect the criminals, not law-abiding citizens. You know how you just said that criminal justice is an oxymoron? It should be called 'victim justice.'"

"Know what my boss said?" Ron asked with a smile. "That he didn't give a rat's ass what that old-fart judge said. He doesn't know who did it but somebody put the tracking device in there anyway. My whole team's on rotating standby out at the field just waiting to get in that other plane and track 'em down."

"Good for you guys," Randy said, nodding his approval.

"The boss said we might not be able to use it in court but we'll seize the dope and not tell anybody how we knew it was there. Since the drugs are contraband, we won't be able to give them back to the bad guys even if we can't show probable cause for the search."

"That's great. But what'll happen to the smugglers?"

"That's the real kicker. We won't be able to prosecute them but when those assholes go back to their boss and tell him they lost the plane and his dope, not to mention returning without any money, they'll be shark bait the same day," Ron said with a laugh. "Then they're the Coast Guard's problem, not ours."

"Man, I love the tactics you guys use," Randy said.

"We don't have a choice." Ron fixed his friend with a serious look. "Let's go check out Chastain's plane before it goes up for auction tomorrow."

"You don't mind if I take a few pictures of it, do you?" Randy asked. "Call it a personal keepsake."

"Take all you want," Ron said, motioning out the car window. "There she is."

Ron parked the car and they got out to examine the damage. Randy let out a low whistle. "Man, that exploding shotgun round did a number on the landing gear," he said. "Check out those bullet holes. I gotta get a close-up of them, along with the seizure notice in the window." Snapping away with his camera, he said, "What a souvenir!"

Afterwards, Randy was antsy to get back to the hotel. He told Ron he was feeling tired from the long drive and was going to take a nap before they met up again for dinner.

When Ron dropped him off, Randy really was beginning to feel the effects of his overnight drive. He went straight to his room, opened his laptop, plugged in the photo card and attached the file to an e-mail addressed to Patty. He wrote a quick message explaining the images and what she should do with them. In the subject line, he typed: "Because of What Those Bastards Did to You…" Then he hit "send."

Within minutes, Patty sent a return e-mail. There were only three words in the subject line: "OH MY GOD!!!" Her message told Randy that he was the best for sending her the exclusive pictures and that they'd make it onto the front page of Thursday's paper for sure—which would probably be her best-selling issue of all time. But her final question left him a little perplexed: "The guy in the background checking out the plane looks familiar—who is he?"

"What the hell is she talking about?" Randy said to himself, yawning. He glanced at the photo and noticed a few blurry images of random people looking at the plane—no one rang a bell.

He considered shooting her a quick e-mail back but the brightness of the computer screen was beginning to bother his bleary eyes and he decided to get some much-needed sleep before Ron came to get him for dinner—and what would most certainly amount to more than a few drinks.

He shut his laptop, intending to write to Patty the next day, then fell asleep the second his head hit the pillow.

Chapter Thirty-Four

Disposition of the Plane

*The greatest events occur without intention playing
any part in them; chance makes good mistakes and
undoes the most carefully planned undertaking. The
world's greatest events are not produced, they happen.*
—Georg C. Lichtenberg

On the day of the auction, Randy awoke at 8:00 a.m. with a sore head from too many drinks, which matched his sore muscles from too long a drive. He scowled into the mirror, brushed his teeth, then threw on another brightly colored shirt—wishing he had brought just one white button-down. He had no time to check his e-mail, let alone take a shower or comb his hair, since he was supposed to meet Ron at the auction site at eight-fifteen.

By the time Randy had finished the short drive to the hangar—with a little help from his GPS—his friend was already waiting there, looking remarkably tanned and well rested.

"How the hell do you do it?" Randy said, shaking Ron's hand.

"You Mississippi guys need to learn how to keep up with us in Miami," the agent replied, restarting the old rivalry.

Randy took a look around the auction hangar. There were six planes being offered, with Chastain's fourth on the list.

"What do you think that first plane will go for?" Randy asked, checking out a six-passenger aircraft.

"Well, it has plenty of room in the back for drugs but it's only got a single engine," Ron said after doing a brief assessment. "Just like the rest of these planes, it has no papers—and that's the biggest expense. My guess is ten thousand bucks, max."

"That's all, huh?" Randy replied. He glanced around, half expecting to see Chastain or one of his crew turning up with a bid on his old plane. At those prices, it was a pretty affordable way to get back into the drug-smuggling game, if that was indeed the DA's new business.

At that point, it hadn't yet been determined whether or not Chastain had prior knowledge of the plane's being used for drug smuggling. Randy knew the worst-case scenario was that he was just as involved as McMillan and knew about the contraband cargo. The best-case scenario was that he'd made some very poor errors in judgment—first by partnering with a known felon like McMillan, then by arranging for the charges against McMillan's associate, Dennis Riley, to be dismissed. In either case he had let down his voters, possibly obstructed justice and could have been charged with drug smuggling, against which it would cost thousands of dollars to defend himself.

Florida authorities had served notice on Chastain, A.D. McMillan and Bill Buchanan at the Consumer Bank to let them know the airplane would be seized and sold at a public auction. Almost $300,000 was still owed on the aircraft, but none of them had shown up for the in-state seizure hearing, refusing to acknowledge ownership.

Now that it had gone to auction, they had a better chance of getting the plane back affordably—and anonymously.

Within moments, the auctioneer started addressing the small crowd that was bidding on the first plane. "We're starting it off at eight thousand. Eight thousand, gimme nine, gimme nine... Do I hear nine? No? We have eight going once, going twice, sold to the bearded gentleman in the striped shirt."

The whole thing took less than a minute. "You were pretty close on the price, Ron, but I thought your guess was a low ball," Randy said. "I didn't think it would come in under ten."

"I'm telling you, these things go cheap. It's good for the drug trade, not so good for my task force. Well, maybe…" Ron paused. "After all, it *is* job security."

Both men paid little attention to the next two sales; instead, they drank coffee and ate doughnuts from the corner table. However, their interest piqued as Chastain's plane came up for sale.

The plane had dual engines and plenty of room in the back; it was by far the largest and could carry the heaviest load. As a group of spectators crowded around to inspect the plane, Randy could hear them commenting on what a good aircraft it was, how forgiving it was and how little field was needed to take off and land. There were obviously several people who were seriously interested in buying.

"If any of those guys are drug smugglers they may pay big bucks for this old workhorse, even without papers," Ron whispered to Randy as they watched the small crowd. "They can overcome their investment with one load on this plane, so having to get papers won't mean much to these guys."

"I see what you mean," Randy replied.

"Randy, let me borrow your camera," Ron said, snatching it from around his neck. "I'm going to take some pictures of the plane."

Inspired, Ron walked over and snapped a few shots with the lens focused in the direction of the crowd, zooming in on particular faces. It was obvious that a few of the potential bidders felt uncomfortable, but nobody tried to hide their face or walk away.

"Gentlemen, this is without a doubt the finest airplane you'll see today," the auctioneer announced. "The retail value of this plane—with all its avionics—is around three hundred fifty thousand dollars. That's with the damages repaired, of course, but the mechanic said it would only cost around twenty-five thousand. So whatever you bid, I'm sure you'll get a good deal."

The crowd was getting worked up. "Let's get the show on the road!" one guy yelled out.

"Okay," the auctioneer agreed. "We're going to start this bid at ten thousand. Do I hear twenty?"

Several hands went up and the auctioneer pointed to the first one that was raised. "Twenty. Do I hear twenty-five? Twenty-five it is. Let's see fifty... Fifty to the gentleman in the white suit. Seventy-five, seventy-five... Okay, you, sir. Do we have a hundred?"

Not a hand was raised.

"Okay, gents, we have seventy-five, going once, going twice..."

Suddenly, the man in the white suit, who had recently been outbid, yelled out, "One hundred!"

"One hundred," the auctioneer repeated. "Do we have a higher bid? No? Two hundred going once, going twice... Sold to the gentleman in white."

Both Ron and Randy took a good look at him. He had bleached-blonde hair and a goatee that didn't hide his scar. "Well, Ron, what do you make of that?"

"Bottom line—either this guy knows who has the papers and can get them, or he's a smuggler. Doesn't look like anybody I've dealt with before or that we have intel on. Could be from out of state but we almost always get local buyers at these auctions. I'll check the papers he filed to qualify as a bidder, along with any bank letters he may have."

Randy squinted at the man in the white suit to get a better look. He might have been there the day before, checking out the merchandise.

"I have a hunch he knows McMillan and will put his hands on the papers before the week is gone," Ron continued. "He'll invest twenty-five grand on repairs and will have one hundred twenty-five thousand invested in a plane that should cost three hundred fifty thousand. That's *if* he's legitimate. Otherwise, we'll probably seize it again in a few months."

Ron and Randy made their way through the small crowd still gathered around Chastain's plane until they got up next to the winning buyer. He had finished giving the auctioneer his name and information and was now swamped by people wanting to shake his hand and congratulate him—most of whom were clearly envious despite their pasted-on smiles.

Randy pretended to be just another guy interested in airplanes, which made it easy for him to move in close. With his gaudy shirt and somewhat-disheveled appearance, no one there really noticed him, let alone took him for a law-enforcement official. But there was something of which he took notice.

He motioned to Ron that it was time to leave. When they stepped far enough away from the group he said, "I got something. While the guy was busy shaking hands I could see a plane ticket sticking out of his pocket. I couldn't catch the name but he's flying to Memphis tomorrow morning at seven. That'll put him close to Chastain and McMillan."

Ron looked impressed. "Good work. Listen, you go back to the hotel and get some rest. You seriously look like shit, man. I'll stick around here and get the guy's name from the auctioneer after everybody leaves. Then I'll call my boss to get approval to tail him, which shouldn't be a problem."

"You'll get no argument from me," Randy said. "I'm gonna drive back home later tonight, which means I'll see you in Memphis."

"Yeah," Ron said with a smile, "but I'll probably beat you there."

After Randy left, Ron copied down the man in white's information from the auctioneer's log book. He ran the information through his office's criminal-justice center and soon found out that the man's Social Security number was bogus. The name he'd used was Austin J. McBrayer II. It turned out that there was nobody in the state of Florida with that name—at least no one with a driver's license.

Ron gave Randy a quick call.

"Sorry to wake you up, bubba, but I got some info on the buyer of Chastain's plane," Ron said.

"Oh, crap," Randy said groggily. "I was going to get in touch with Patty. She said the guy in the picture that I emailed her looked familiar. But I fell asleep before I found out what she was talking about."

"Well, you might want to find out because all the info he gave was bogus. Apparently, the auctioneer just let him fill out all the information without verifying it. He probably has ID with the phony name anyway."

"Alright. I'm hitting the road anyway. I'll call her on my way to Memphis and get back to you with any info."

"Okay, bubba," Ron said. "And if we do wind up having to follow this guy around Memphis, you may want to rethink the Hawaiian shirts. They're not all that inconspicuous, y'know."

Chapter Thirty-Five

Local News Story

Modern man must descend the spiral of his own absurdity to the lowest point; only then can he look beyond it. It is obviously impossible to get around it, jump over it, or simply avoid it.
—Vaclav Havel

That very same day, Patty's newspaper, *The Stonewall Times*, hit the street. The front-page photo took up the entire top half of the cover and showed so much detail that the bullet holes in Chastain's plane were obvious even to the untrained eye. So was the seizure notice in the window, on which the names A.D. McMillan and John Chastain could be seen clearly by anyone who bothered to look closely enough.

Sadly, though, that wasn't many people. The subscription list for *The Stonewall Times* had dwindled to 118 residents and the advertising list was down to twelve. The paper was already in the red and going down the tubes fast.

But there was at least one reader at the Consumer Bank.

"Mr. Buchanan, did you see the headlines of *The Stonewall Times* this morning?" the bank president's secretary asked, walking into his office.

"Now, Ellie, you know damn well I don't read that woman's trashy paper. And why would you, when you know our bank gives away free issues of the *Tribunal*?" Buchanan chastised her.

"Well, when I went by the coffee shop I saw one on the stand and the headline caught my eye—as did the picture of our collateral," Mrs. Swindol said.

"What are you talking about? Let me see that trash," Buchanan scoffed, reaching for her paper.

He unfolded it and read the headline: "DA Plane Seized in Colombian Drug Operation!"

"Oh, Lord, that damn woman will print anything," Buchanan said, looking up from the paper. "Get Chastain on the line for me now!"

As soon as the secretary made the call, Buchanan blurted into the phone: "John, have you seen the Stonewall paper?"

"Yes, Billy, I've seen it. Calm down. I've already talked to a defense lawyer and a publicist who thinks we should lay low and not say a word. Just laugh it off," Chastain said soothingly.

"*Laugh* it off? You think this is something to laugh about?" Buchanan asked angrily.

"Nobody's going to read that paper, Billy. Hell, she doesn't have any subscribers left to speak of."

"I wouldn't worry about her subscription rate if I were you, John. What I'd be worried about is the Memphis papers picking this story up. Then it'll reach everyone and their brother—maybe even go out over the AP wire. People will start asking questions about ownership and liens and that damn felon friend of yours," Buchanan said, cupping his face in his hand.

"Billy, I'm going to tell you something that I have never told anyone else, okay? But this doesn't leave our conversation, understand?"

"Of course, John," Buchanan said with some hope.

"Several months ago, the editor of the biggest Memphis newspaper got into some pretty serious trouble down here. I was contacted by a friend of mine on the Memphis Organized Crime Task Force, who asked me to help this guy out. So I did, and it saved his ass. He said if there was ever anything he could do for me, I could just say the word," John said smoothly.

"You mean he can keep it out of the papers?" Buchanan gasped.

"Let's put it this way, Billy. I got wind of this article coming out from one of the printers, so I already called the Memphis editor and said the word. According to my publicist, none of the smaller papers there will be interested in the story either since the big one passed on it. They'll think it has no merit and it'll all blow over in a couple of weeks." Chastain laughed. "I'll tell you, it sure helps to help other people sometimes."

"You know, John, that's what got you into trouble in the first place."

Chapter Thirty-Six

Expanded Investigation

There is no odor so bad as that
which arises from goodness tainted.
—Henry David Thoreau

After her front-page scoop had been printed, Patty was at her wit's end. This was the story that should have blown the lid off the county corruption plot and restored credibility to her failing paper. She had expected her phones to be ringing off the hook with calls from new subscribers and larger news agencies and was sure there'd have been FBI agents lining up outside her door. Instead, nothing happened. Not one damn thing.

She kept pacing the floors of her empty office, trying to think of what had gone wrong. When it hit her, she decided to call Wayne Lott at the US attorney's office in Oxford.

"Wayne, this is Patty Franklin from the Stonewall paper. Did you hear about my story where you are?"

"What story is that?" Wayne asked.

"I can't believe it," she said frantically. "I had a picture of Chastain's airplane plastered across the front page, right along with the seizure notice. I'm not sure what he's up to but he must have done something to keep major media outlets away from this story. I don't know if he's planning to sue me for slander, promising an exclusive to any paper that doesn't print it or doing something worse, but he's quashing this piece the same way he does indictments. He thinks he can get away with anything—and up to this point, he's been right."

"Patty, try to take it easy. I'm driving up with Agent Tischner in a little while for some investigations into your favorite bank, so we'll look into this issue while we're there."

"Thanks, Wayne," she said, exhaling with relief.

"No chance you'd tell me who sent you that photo?" Wayne asked, not expecting an answer.

"Sorry. You know I never give away my sources."

"That's okay," he replied. "I think I have a pretty good idea who it is."

After hanging up with Wayne, Patty was beside herself. She kept staring at the front-page picture, trying to figure out what had gone wrong. The longer she looked, the more her attention was attracted to the man in white.

To keep herself occupied, she decided to recheck the original photo Randy had e-mailed her. She sat at her computer, blowing the image up to four times its original size. Studying it as intently as a germ beneath a microscope, Patty suddenly gasped.

She went to another file immediately to compare the images—and there she had her answer.

Wayne waited until he and Tischner were on their way up to Stonewall County to follow his hunch about the source of Patty's photo.

"Randy," he said, putting his cell phone on speaker as Tischner drove. "It's been a while, buddy. Tisch and I are riding together and decided to give you a call. What have you been up to?"

"Hey, Wayne, Tisch. I'm in Memphis now. Just got back from Florida. You know, trying to use up my vacation days before I start the new job," Randy casually replied.

"That's great. Well, with all that traveling, I'm sure you're taking a lot of pictures," Wayne said.

"You mean like the one on the front page of Patty's paper?" Randy asked with a laugh.

"That's exactly what I mean."

"Yeah, I just got off the phone with her. She had something to tell me and also mentioned that you didn't sound too happy about the photo."

"What gives with that?" Wayne asked.

"That was my last-ditch effort to take one last jab at Chastain on my way out. Since it doesn't seem like anything's going to happen to him, I figured the least I could do was spread the word to the voters—hit him where it really hurts. Losing the next election could be the only way he gets his just reward," Randy said.

"Randy, don't take that attitude," Wayne said. "You know we're working on it. Chastain's just a part of the corruption cases we're looking into up there."

"I know, guys, it's just that I'm so fed up with politics. I don't think they have any place in law enforcement. Now, you know I have the utmost respect for both of you, and I don't mean no offense, but it takes your agencies forever to do anything. Chastain will be dead of old age before y'all get to him. Tisch, you'll be retired and, Wayne, there's no telling where you'll be. Hell, Chastain will probably even have contacts at the US attorney's office by then and will never be prosecuted. I'm sick of the whole system," Randy said in an impassioned voice that showed his disgust.

"Keep your chin up, bubba," Tischner said. "We'll work through this. I know how much you love law enforcement and I agree that politics shouldn't enter into the equation, but they do. That's going to make it very hard to show that Chastain knew about this drug-smuggling deal but Wayne and I are going to burn the midnight oil until we can prove it."

"They lost a good man when you quit, Randy. Tisch and I are going to stay with this thing to make sure all your efforts to fight corruption weren't in vain," Wayne added.

"Thanks, guys. I appreciate it. I really do," Randy said, sounding choked up. "And since you're both doing so much for me, I want you to know that I've got something for you, too…"

"What?" Wayne asked.

"Buford Lancaster," Randy said. "Our missing man."

Chapter Thirty-Seven

The Final Straw

Disappointment is a sort of bankruptcy—
the bankruptcy of a soul that expends
too much in hope and expectation.
—Eric Hoffer

Wayne and Tischner were by stunned by Randy's news and couldn't wait to get to Patty's office to ask her how she'd made the identification. But they were so busy with the bank investigation and the conspiracy against the newspaper that they wouldn't have time to focus on Lancaster just then.

"We've been looking for him for months on end. Waiting a few more hours won't kill us," Tischner reasoned. "Besides, Randy's on his trail. He'll follow him wherever it leads."

"True," Wayne agreed.

"Our plates are so full that I hardly know where to start," Tischner said with a shrug.

"Don't worry. I do."

They drove into Stonewall and purposely avoided the square, parking instead on a side street. Wayne led the way directly to Patty's office. He could hardly believe it was the same place he'd been before. It was as empty as a ghost town. Gone were the clutter and the yellowed articles tacked to the walls. In their place were a quick coat of whitewash paint and just two or three lonely looking cardboard boxes filled with papers.

"Patty, how are you?" Wayne asked sympathetically.

"Not worth a damn," she said sadly. "They have beaten me down to almost nothing."

"What goes around comes around, darling," Tischner said, stepping forward to offer her a handkerchief.

"You must be Agent Tischner, who Wayne has told me so much about," Patty said, trying to muster a smile while dabbing at her tears. "Thanks. I've run out of Kleenex and was about to start using copies of past issues to dry my eyes. I've already put them in the bathroom in place of toilet paper." She was so emotional that it was hard for them to tell whether she was laughing or crying.

"Look, Patty, if you still have some fight left in you there's something you can do for us now," Wayne said. "I know you have a source at the bank. Did you get any documents that would prove a particular bank officer's involvement in making interest-free loans to members of the county board of supervisors?"

"Hell yes," Patty, said, clearly cheering up. "And that's not all I have." She rummaged through the few boxes on the floor, took out a file and handed it to Wayne.

"We really appreciate your providing this information," Tischner said.

"No problem. I just wish I had some assurance that it would do any good." She walked to the window and looked over at Chastain's office. "These people have ruined me just for exercising my First Amendment rights."

"Well, don't worry," Wayne said, skimming quickly through the papers in the file. "What you just handed me is as hot as a smoking gun—and Tisch and I intend to use it."

"Listen, Patty," Tischner said, trying to cheer her up. "These guys might have you against the ropes but you've done something that even an FBI special agent couldn't do. You found Buford Lancaster. How did you know it was him?"

Patty smiled proudly. "In the photo, he looked like he'd lost a lot of weight, grown a goatee, bleached his hair and put on a nicer suit than I'd ever seen him in before, but I knew that was him. He had a scar on his face from a propeller, from when he was trying to hand start an old, vintage airplane he had. I have his missing-person picture and put them side by side. It was a match. I knew that bastard looked familiar the second Randy e-mailed me the photo from the auction in Florida."

"Well, when you're done with the newspaper business, you may want to think about an investigative career," Tischner said.

"No, thanks. I've already found all the criminals I ever want to find in one lifetime." When she said it, she was staring across the street, at the DA's office and the Consumer Bank on the corner.

Armed with copies of the interest-free loan papers made to the supervisors by the chancery clerk's son, Tischner went to interview the big boss at the bank.

"Mr. Buchanan, we've heard rumors that you or some other officers in your bank have made interest-free loans to the members of the board of supervisors. Is that true?"

"Of course not," Buchanan said, squirming in his chair. "We'd never do that. We're in the business of making money, not making loans for free."

"Is it possible you're just not aware of it?" Tischner asked, watching the other man's face turn red. "I'd like to talk to all of the VPs and your CEO."

"Fine," Buchanan said, though he was clearly irritated by having his authority questioned. "They're all in the conference room right now...where I was *supposed* to be five minutes ago."

Buchanan led his guest to the conference room, where he gave him a brief, less-than-cordial introduction. "Gentlemen, this is Wallace Tischner, special agent in charge of the FBI's Oxford office. He so kindly dropped in today to question each of us about a particular matter so if you don't mind putting off our pressing business for a while, I'll turn the floor over to him."

For the next half hour, Tischner took copious notes while he questioned the bankers and secretly recorded their answers with a small device hidden inside his jacket. A microphone on a long wire attached to a recorder ran down the sleeve and fit under his stretch watchband. It recorded each and every VP—as well as the president and the CEO—denying any knowledge of the loans.

Once the evidence was collected, Tischner warned them again: "I just want each of you to know that lying to a federal officer about an incident under investigation amounts to obstruction of justice, which will be prosecuted."

No one said anything further, but it appeared to Tischner that at least two of the men looked nervous, as if they were almost about to speak up. They exchanged glances and then hung their heads mutely.

Tischner knew he had all of them by the balls. Their names either appeared directly on incriminating documents or bank policy required their approval. Some of the loans needed the green light from the entire board because of the amounts involved. These guys had been had already—they just didn't have the brains to realize it.

"Well, gentlemen," Tischner said, looking around one last time, "I appreciate your cooperation and I want to give each of you my business card with my cell phone number on the back. If any of you recollect something you forgot to mention here today, it would be in your best interest to call me so we won't need to press criminal charges." He walked around the table with a tight smile, handing each person a card.

When he left, the CEO gathered all of the business cards together and threw them in the wastepaper basket. "Y'all won't be needing these. I will not stand for these strong-arm techniques. I'm calling my lawyer."

Tischner went back to brief Wayne on what had transpired, and what he heard really pissed the assistant US attorney off.

"Look, Tisch, this whole thing burns my ass. Not only do these bankers conspire with the board of supervisors to make illegal loans but then they go and deny it even when they must realize that they've been caught. They really do think they're above the law."

"What do you want to do about it?" Tischner asked, half expecting what Wayne's answer would be.

"What I *want* to do is close the doors of that bank forever. But what we will do, since we've got enough evidence, is recall the federal grand jury and present these cases."

Chapter Thirty-Eight

Federal Grand Jury

Obviously crime pays, or there'd be no crime.
—G. Gordon Liddy

"Ladies and gentlemen of the grand jury, I'm Donald Spillers, United States Attorney for the Northern District of the State of Mississippi. I understand you were compelled to be here today but I would like to thank you for exercising your right to vote and willingness to serve the courts of this district."

Days after Wayne and Tischner presented their evidence to US Attorney Spillers he stood in front of the assembled group of men and women in the grand-jury conference room, eager to let justice take its course.

"What we have to present to you, however many days it takes, is a complicated web of bribery, corruption and conspiracy that started out as a simple case targeting county supervisors using their positions for personal gain. It has since escalated to include other county officials as well as bankers, lawyers and newspaper editors. My assistant, Wayne Lott, who is very accustomed to working corruption cases, will provide you with all the information, and investigators, FBI agents and other witnesses will be on hand to help you determine whether or not to issue a true bill."

After further instructions about the grand-jury process—a less-formal precursor to a courtroom trial—he graciously turned the floor over to Wayne.

"Thank you, Mr. Spillers. Ladies and gentlemen, I would like to echo the thanks Mr. Spillers gave you for being here today. Without you, this process would not be possible. It is a very important part of our judicial system and you are very important people for making it happen," Wayne began.

After a brief introduction he fielded the first question from the group. "Excuse me, Mr. Lott, I'm Cliff Cooper, the foreman of the grand jury. I just want to know, will there be individual charges on each defendant or conspiracy charges on all of them?"

"That's a very good question, Mr. Cooper, and the answer is yes and yes," Wayne said.

After some laughter from the group, Cooper asked, "What does that mean?"

"It means we have individual charges on county supervisors that range anywhere from selling personally owned bulldozer engines to the county for individual gain to taking kickbacks on ballpoint pens bought from undercover FBI agents. Other violations include accepting bribes, such as expensive kitchen appliances, football tickets and trips to the Caribbean, from real salespeople—and sometimes from undercover federal agents posing as salespeople. We even have instances of lying to federal agents in attempts to obstruct justice. Those are all individual charges," Wayne explained.

"How about the conspiracies?" Cooper asked.

"They get a little more complicated. Just to give you a brief run-down, let's take the chancery clerk first. He decides where to put the county's money—millions of dollars per year, enough to keep a bank afloat—and the county supervisors concur. In this case, the chancery clerk's son is a senior officer at the bank where they chose to deposit the money—and, to show its appreciation, the bank decided to give them all interest-free loans. Now, you and I couldn't get those kinds of loans, could we?"

A few groans came from the group.

"Y'all with me so far?" Wayne asked.

"I certainly am," the foreman said. "Sounds like a den of thieves scratching each other's backs. The bank probably even raises *our* interest to cover their losses on those loans."

"I wouldn't be surprised, Mr. Cooper, but it gets even more complicated. You see, the conspiracy also involves a hard-working, small-town newspaper editor…"

Wayne went on to discuss Patty's persecution by the county supervisors, the bank president and other businesses and advertisers. The members were very interested in the story, although they were only getting an overview without the benefit of witnesses providing details yet.

When Wayne was finished describing the conspiracy case it was time to move on to the individual charges—starting with who he felt was the worst offender: John Chastain.

"Ladies and gentlemen, the next person we'll discuss is the district attorney of Stonewall County. Seems he had a habit of dismissing charges on people or having his lawyer buddies next door to his office file phony motions to quash indictments. He even dropped a concealed-weapon charge on a convicted felon as a favor to a man who came to him with a little proposition about his plane. That's what we call an obstruction of justice and using his office for personal gain."

Wayne could see the shocked expressions on the grand jurors' faces but he knew they hadn't heard the worst of it yet.

"Turns out that later, the plane was used to transport drugs. When it was seized, it was registered to both the DA and the fellow who got him to drop the gun charges on his buddy."

Everybody in the room was speechless when Wayne completed the story. Within a minute, however, when everything he said had sunk in, there was a loud roar of discussion in the room from people who couldn't believe what they had just heard.

"I'm ready to indict them now," Cooper said. "We don't need all the details or additional witnesses."

"Thanks for your vote of confidence," Wayne said, shaking his head. "I just wish it were that easy."

———

The grand jury listened to witness testimony for three days; when it was over, they had no hesitation in issuing true bills on all of the defendants for each of the charges. The FBI was given the arrest documents and quickly formed a team to carry them out.

The county supervisors were aware by then that their days were numbered. They all got lawyers, expecting to be arrested at any time because they knew the federal grand jury was in session and the feds seemed to have exhausted all their leads. Their arrests were simply formalities and everything went well.

The lying bankers were a different story.

Chapter Thirty-Nine

The Arrests

*There are more fools in the world
than there are people.*
—Heinrich Heine

When the FBI agents walked up to the bank with their raid jackets on, a bank officer saw them coming and quickly ran to the door and locked it in an attempt to keep them out. Although the agents had the authority to kick in the new glass doors of the building, they were so stunned and amused by the idiot's actions that they just stood there for a moment, looking at each other and laughing.

Tischner put up with the situation for all of thirty seconds. "Give me one of those papers," he said gruffly to an agent next to him as the stupid banker stood there, looking at them through the glass.

Tischner flipped the document over and wrote a message on it in large, capital letters, then placed it firmly against the glass: "OPEN THIS DOOR NOW OR I WILL BLOW IT OPEN WITH A SHOTGUN!"

Luckily for the bank, a young, female teller with a brain walked up beside the idiot and turned the key to unlock the door. Tischner walked in first, pushing the guy against the wall.

With his thumb pressing on the man's throat, he hissed, "You know what, asshole? We don't even have a warrant for you but I may just charge you with felony stupidity and take you to jail. Don't you know that interfering with FBI agents falls under obstructing justice?"

Tischner reluctantly released him and walked over to the CEO of the bank. "You, you and you are all under arrest for lying to a federal officer during the conduct of an official investigation," he said, pointing to the familiar faces. "You have the right to an attorney—"

"I was going to call you, Mr. Tischner, I swear," Buchanan said, shaking.

"That's Special Agent Tischner to you, scumbag. What you were *going* to do and what you *did* are two very different things."

"No, listen…please. Can we talk a minute in my office?" Buchanan begged.

Tischner practically railroaded him into the office and closed the door behind them. "You want to talk to me so bad now. Why didn't you talk before, Buchanan?"

"I don't know," the president said, looking scared. "But I think I have some information you need to know about the DA's airplane."

"Oh, yeah? What might that be?" Tischner asked skeptically.

"You saw the name A.D. McMillan on the paperwork, right?" Buchanan waited for the agent to nod. "Well, there was no way our bank would do business with that thug. It's his son who signed the loan. They have the same name and don't use 'junior' or 'senior.' I don't think the son would be involved in drug smuggling but I have no doubt his dad would be."

"Is that right?" Tischner asked.

"Yes, sir. We had an old loan gone bad that the father had signed and I compared their signatures. You can see the difference. I made the loan to the son and I'm willing to testify…*if* it will help me," Buchanan stated.

"Help *you*, huh? Guess you don't care about helping *us* at all," Tischner scoffed. "Well, I'll talk to the US attorney to see how much *help* you can actually provide. No promises, though."

Tischner walked out of the office and gave the US marshals the signal to make the arrests. All of the bankers who had lied would be taken to Oxford for an immediate appearance before the US magistrate to set bond and make arraignments. Tischner himself, however, decided to take another agent with him to the electrical-parts factory that A.D. McMillan, Jr. owned.

As they walked from the parking lot to the building, still wearing their blue raid jackets with "FBI" printed on the backs in bold letters and FBI emblems on the left front breasts, people started to get antsy—one person in particular.

"If they're looking for me, tell them I left a little while ago," A.D. McMillan, Jr. told his employees. "You won't be lying 'cause I'm leaving now."

McMillan ran out the back door, got in his sports car and drove around the back of the large warehouses, exiting on the opposite side of the office.

Meanwhile, Tischner and the agent were inside, questioning the workers. Scared they'd get in trouble, they immediately identified McMillan to the agents, pointing out his car through the large window.

Tischner and the younger agent were both back outside within seconds, jumping into their car and pursuing the fleeing suspect. They drove across a field and caught up with him rather quickly. However, McMillan began to speed up. They were driving in excess of a hundred miles per hour on a two-lane highway.

The FBI car was bouncing all over the road. Just ahead was a narrow bridge—and a truck was coming. Tischner slowed down but began to cuss and pound on the dashboard. He remembered Jack Burchfield's car bursting into flames and didn't want the same thing happening to them.

As both cars entered town—with McMillan a distance ahead—one of the local policemen recognized the FBI car in pursuit with the dash light on. He called ahead for another officer to put out spikes to flatten the tires on McMillan's car, but they were too late. He soon pulled out of sight and was nowhere to be found.

"We're going to get a bench warrant on that bastard," Tischner said to the other agent. "He'll be going home soon—and we'll get him there."

～～

In less than an hour the FBI office in Oxford called Tischner's cell. It wasn't the news about the warrant he'd been waiting for.

"Special Agent Tischner, this is Elizabeth in the Oxford office. We have a phone call for you from an attorney from Memphis by the name of Ralph Golden. He said he represents A.D. McMillan, Jr. and would like to talk with you about making him available for an interview or for surrender if you have a warrant for him."

At this point, Tischner would rather have arrested the jerk but he played along. "Go ahead and patch him through, Elizabeth. I'll talk to him."

"Agent Tischner, this is Ralph Golden. I represent A.D. McMillan, Jr. and understand you might be looking for him."

"You could say that," Tischner answered snidely.

"Is there anything I need to know? I mean, is he in any trouble?" Golden asked.

"Well, he could be. I just wanted to interview him today but then he decided to evade the police—a pretty stupid move," Tischner said.

"Yes, sir. I agree with you on that, but the FBI is not in the business of charging people for traffic violations now, are they?"

"No, not unless we have to. We'll do what it takes to complete our investigation—and if that means chasing somebody down, we'll do that, too."

"Oh, I have no doubt about that," the attorney agreed. "But, you know, if somebody had told me his daddy had done something to get the feds chasing him, I wouldn't doubt that, either. You'd have to know this young man. He ain't like his father at all. He's an honest, straightforward businessman who thankfully takes after his mama."

"Yeah? Then why did he run?" Tischner asked.

"Hell, he was scared to death. He came straight to my office, shaking like a leaf. He said y'all came skidding up in the parking lot and jumped out with those raid jackets on, walking fast toward the door with guns in hand. When he saw you out the window, he panicked. He's never been in trouble before but he knew his daddy had been—plenty of times. He's willing to help you out any way he can," Golden said. "Is he a suspect in a crime?"

"No, he's just a person of interest who might have some information on an ongoing investigation. We'd like to talk to him, but you'd better come along. If at some point we feel he has become a suspect we'll stop and advise him of his rights, and you two can determine what you want to do. Most of the information we need is documentary evidence and we have access to it through subpoenas anyway," Tischner said.

"Tell us when and where to meet you."

"In an hour at the truck stop on the east side of the highway just north of town," Tischner replied.

"That's fine," Golden said. "But could you do us a favor and dispense with wearing the raid jackets and holster your weapons? That really makes Junior nervous. He might have a heart attack and I don't know CPR."

"Okay," Tischner said. "But if he tries to run again, he's gonna have a hell of a lot worse than a heart attack to worry about."

Chapter Forty

Retribution

If an injury has to be done to a man it should be so
severe that his vengeance need not be feared.
—Niccolo Machiavelli

When Tischner met with McMillan, Jr. and his attorney as scheduled, he found the young man to be rather likeable but scared out of his wits. A.D. looked a lot like his dad but with bigger ears, a longer neck and a skinnier frame, like a puppy that hadn't quite grown into its limbs.

"My mother told me not to get involved with my dad in any kind of business deal," Junior admitted, shaking his head. "She was divorcing him and didn't want him corrupting me. But somehow I let him talk me into signing the loan with Chastain."

"Did you sign any FAA papers?" Tischner asked, holding a hot cup of coffee. "As far as we know, you're not listed as part owner of the plane."

Junior glanced at his lawyer, then said, "All I know is that I'm listed as fifty-percent responsible for the loan, which my dad would pay off. Chastain owes the other fifty percent."

Tischner believed the young man's story. Addressing Golden, he said, "We'll get in touch with you if we need to talk again after briefing the US attorney." Then he turned to Junior. "As for you, don't ever run from any law-enforcement officer again—and mind what your mama told you."

"Yes, sir," Junior agreed. "That's some excellent advice. I apologize for what I did."

Tischner nodded his acceptance. "We do have a warrant for your dad, though, and would like your assistance in locating him."

"He called me this morning before y'all got to my workplace. He heard you had been at the bank and was running his mouth about what he was going to do. He's just a big blowhard, though. He didn't mean anything by it," Junior said shyly.

"What exactly was he running his mouth about?" Tischner asked.

"Well, I think he was still drunk from the night before. He was calling y'all a bunch of Keystone Kops, saying he had worked with good investigators as a snitch and that y'all couldn't bust a pimple on a good cop's ass. He said he wasn't going back to jail and he'll do whatever it takes to keep that from happening."

"So, where do you think he is?" Tischner asked, trying to ignore the insults.

"Sir, I don't know, but I'm sure I can get in touch with him," Junior said sincerely. "I'll make sure he's sober and bring him in for you, if you'll let me. I'm afraid that if he's drunk and you approach him, you may have no choice but to kill him—that's how ornery he gets. Now, I don't like some of the things he does, but I sure don't want to see him shot down like an animal."

"Tell you what. I'll give you forty-eight hours to find him and get him to our office. After that, he'll be pursued by federal-marshal SWAT teams and there's no telling through which window in whose house—or factory—those gorillas will come swinging with their concussion grenades." Tischner looked the young man straight in the eye. "Trust me, son. You do not want to deal with them."

That evening, A.D. McMillan, Jr. received a phone call from his father. He was used to these almost-nightly drunken phone calls, though he was never sure at which bar in what town his dad was drinking. When he told McMillan, Sr. what had happened with the agents, the old man was furious.

"Those sons of bitches ain't gonna use my own flesh and blood to try to capture me! And I sure as hell ain't letting them go after you, boy. Now, listen, don't you tell them one damn thing. They ain't taking me down. I've done all the time in prison I'm gonna do."

"Dad, listen, you need to turn yourself in," Junior said calmly. "I told the FBI agent I'd bring you. If I don't, he's going to make trouble for me... I could lose the business. And he'll make worse trouble for you, I guarantee it."

"Son, no low-life bastard is gonna make no trouble for neither of us."

Junior ignored his father's ranting. "Even said an assistant US attorney, Wayne Lott, would work with you."

"Wayne Lott?" McMillan repeated in a slurred voice. "I've heard all about that snot-nosed politician hunter. He's using you to get to me and he's using me to get to the district attorney. If he wants trouble, I'll give him trouble. Ain't nobody gonna use my boy against me!"

"Dad... Dad, please," his son said before the phone went dead.

Within seconds Junior was dialing Tischner's number. "Agent Tischner, I'm sorry. I just talked to my dad, who's really pissed off. Couldn't talk no sense into him."

"What did he say exactly?" Tischner asked.

"Exactly?" Junior asked, reluctant to repeat it. "Well, he told me that you and that 'snot-nosed' assistant US attorney are trying to use his kid to get to him and that if you're looking for trouble, he'll give it to you."

"Well, son, you've done all you can do," Tischner said. "Don't worry about it anymore. We'll do everything we can to bring your dad in safely—I promise you that. But I also promise we'll be bringing him in."

The next evening, Wayne met with Tischner and the deputy US marshals who'd be helping with McMillan's arrest. They had received word of their task the night before and had gone to a bail-bonding business that had bonded their suspect out of jail previously.

Today, they brought with them McMillan's application for the bond, which listed every known associate, relative and hangout. Apparently, he'd wanted out of jail so badly that he hadn't been shy about giving that information to the agency for them to check out.

However, he'd never suspected it would wind up in the hands of law enforcement, who would then harass every friend, neighbor, family member and business associate he had, with teams of heavily armed goons showing up to look for him. Nobody wanted those guys around—and if they had any idea where he was, they would tell just to keep the goons away. The tactics they used weren't playful by any means and could sometimes last for hours.

In fact, the team leader was fond of saying, "We don't play—ever. We quit school just because of recess."

Just before they were ready to head out on business, Wayne's secretary stopped him in the hall. "Mr. Lott, I hate to interrupt," she said, "but your wife is on the phone—and she's hysterical."

They had not told anybody yet but Julie was pregnant, and all Wayne could do was hope she wasn't having a miscarriage. "What's wrong, honey?" he asked, snatching up the phone in his office as quickly as a man trying to swat a fly.

Julie was crying so loudly and desperately that she couldn't even speak.

"Julie, calm down, sweetheart... Tell me what's wrong. Do you need an ambulance? Just answer 'yes' or 'no.'"

"No, no, not me," she sobbed. "Wayne, they've got her."

"Got who, honey? What are you talking about?"

"Dawn… They've got our baby!" she cried.

"Who has her?" Wayne asked, gritting his teeth. "What happened?"

"I don't know, I don't know," Julie said, breaking down uncontrollably.

"Honey, have you called the police?" he asked, trying to keep the panic out of his voice.

"Mr. Lott?" a male voice said over the phone.

"Who is this?"

"Sir, I'm a police officer. Your wife is at the Kroger Grocery Store on Main Street. She reported that someone took your child out of the buggy while she had her back turned to put in some bags and straighten out the straps on the car seat."

"Do you have any idea who did it?" Wayne asked.

"She didn't get a good look at the guy as he was running away, or at the driver as she ran alongside the moving van, clawing its side with her fingers. She's going to need some minor medical attention for lacerations, bleeding fingers and broken nails, but she's refusing to go to the hospital until you get here."

"I'll be there in five minutes," Wayne said, hanging up.

He ran into the hallway and filled Tischner in on what was happening. "I gotta get there right now," Wayne said, punching the elevator button to make it arrive faster.

"Give me the keys, pal," Tischner said. "I'll drive to make sure you get there alive. You won't be any good to Julie or Dawn otherwise."

"Thanks," Wayne said, handing over the car keys. "And you guys don't go anywhere," he shouted to the US marshals. "We may need you."

Upon their arrival they found Julie sitting in the back of an ambulance, unconsciously rubbing her baby bump; a plain-clothes police investigator was asking her questions while medics were rendering first aid as best they could to her bleeding hands.

Wayne stepped inside the ambulance and Julie stood up to hug him. Then she pulled back and said, "They got her, Wayne. They've got our baby. They took her away. My back was turned for two seconds. There wasn't anything I could do." Her mouth was trembling and her eyes were swollen but she didn't seem to have any tears left.

"Don't worry, honey, we'll get her back," he said, glancing at Tischner for support. "Did you get any kind of description of the van?"

"It was dark with no back windows or license plate. I think I saw it near our house before I left and again behind me when I pulled into the store lot."

"We've put out a BOLO alert for all departments to be on the lookout and we're initiating an Amber Alert," the detective chimed in. "You could get a ransom note in a matter of days or hours, but so far we don't have much to go on."

"There was one more thing," Julie added urgently. "Before the van took off, the man who took Dawn yelled out, 'Tell your snot-nosed husband our boss says hi.'"

"What?" Wayne asked, truly confused.

"Were those his exact words?" Tischner asked. When Julie nodded, he added solemnly, "Then there isn't going to be a ransom note."

"What do you mean, Tisch?" Wayne asked. He could feel his heart drop into his stomach.

"I may know who has your daughter," Tischner said. "Let's get the marshal SWAT team on a new assignment—now!"

Chapter Forty-One

The Hunt Is On

Violence is the last refuge of the incompetent."
—Isaac Asimov

When detectives retrieved the video from the store's security department they saw that the van was exactly as Julie had described it. There was no license plate, but a distinguishing characteristic was visible on the driver's-side door: A trace of lettering showed that it had been used previously as a delivery or service vehicle. Tischner thought it looked similar to ones he had seen at McMillan, Jr.'s workplace.

The driver was only partially visible. He had long hair covering his ears and sticking out from the back of his white baseball cap. Neither Wayne nor Tischner recognized him.

"I'm telling you, it's an eye for an eye, a tooth for a tooth," Tischner explained. He was driving Wayne back to the office after Julie was taken to the hospital, where her parents would meet her. "What Julie heard were the same words McMillan's son passed along from his father. He was so pissed about the feds trying to use his son to get at him that he's using your daughter to get back at us."

"I'll kill him," Wayne snarled, staring at the road ahead. "I swear to God, if he touches one hair on her head, I'll kill that son of a bitch."

"I don't blame you for feeling like that, son," Tischner said, stealing a worried glance at Wayne. "But we've got to find him first. More importantly, we've got to find Dawn."

———

With the US marshals gathered around, Tischner made an announcement: "Gents, the FBI Hostage Rescue Team has been notified. They're on their way from Quantico now and will be here in the morning. Meanwhile, we need to make up a map showing all possible locations McMillan could be. We're bringing in the Organized Crime Strike Force agents who worked him as a snitch. They know him best."

"I have a feeling he's going to get in touch with us to tell us what he wants," Wayne stated, balling his hand into a fist. "I guarantee you it won't be money."

"What's he after, then?" one of the SWAT team members asked.

Wayne gave him a steely look. "His own brand of justice. Blood-stained justice."

———

Just before daylight—and after numerous pots of coffee—helicopters were heard hovering outside. The Hostage Rescue Team had arrived.

The lead assault helicopter landed on top of the building. Another one was being used as a command post and the other, larger chopper carried medical personnel, negotiators and equipment. These guys came loaded to hunt bear and ready to evacuate the injured if need be.

As the two other choppers landed at the local airport, HRT members filed into the conference room, dressed in body armor, combat boots and dark clothing. Small submachine guns were strapped across their chests, grenades hung from each of their vests, and handguns were slung low on their legs, in the old cowboy style. They knew what they were doing, and no one got in their way.

"We need full intel on suspect: photos, rap sheets, maps, addresses and anything else you have. We'll take it from there," the HRT leader said with a great deal of authority.

"The suspect's son has a factory in Stonewall. There's a chance he may have stolen a van from there," Wayne said.

"I'm afraid we can't fly out there now," the HRT leader said. "Severe thunderstorms are moving in. Our choppers have been grounded."

"Damn it," Wayne said, pounding the table in exasperation. "The longer my little girl is missing, the less chance she has to survive."

In the suddenly silent room, the only sound that could be heard was the ringing of Tischner's cell phone. He stepped out into the hallway to take the call.

"Tisch? This is Randy Wood. Listen, I followed Buford Lancaster back to Stonewall, where I believe he's setting up a meeting with Chastain. But over the police radio here I heard something about Wayne's daughter being kidnapped. Is that true?"

"I'm afraid it is, Randy," Tischner replied.

"Damn. I was hoping I got that wrong," Randy said. "The bulletin described a service van that sounded a lot like the ones sitting at McMillan Electrical Supply."

"It's very possible that McMillan, Sr. is behind all this."

"Well, I figured as long as I'm down here I might as well go check on it. So I'm outside the building now and nobody's at work yet. But there's a van like the one you're looking for alongside others in the fenced-in area in back. Difference is, this one has obliterated lettering on the doors," Randy said.

Tischner felt a stab of hope. "Randy, can you keep a watch on it and let us know if there's any movement or activity?"

"Sure can. I'll call you if there is," Randy said before hanging up.

Tischner practically sprinted back into the room. "Gentlemen, it looks like we may have the van spotted."

"Who the hell was that?" the HRT leader asked.

"The best cop in the county that ain't a cop no more," Tischner said, giving Wayne a knowing look.

"What?" the team leader asked.

"Don't worry about it. Just know I trust that guy more than I trust you," Tischner said, pasting up a Google Earth image of the McMillan Electrical Supply buildings and property, then pointing out the location where the van was located.

———

There was nothing they could do but wait for news. At eight-thirty the phone rang again. Tischner was expecting to see Randy's number. Instead, it was an anxious A.D. McMillan, Jr.

"Agent Tischner, I just got to work a little while ago and I think my dad has been on the property. He kept a pickup truck in back of the warehouse and it's gone. One of our old vans that we put out of service is parked there instead. He'd given that van to a couple of guys who did odd jobs for us. They had all been in prison together."

"Son, don't go near that van. It matches the description of a vehicle used by two men who kidnapped Wayne Lott's daughter yesterday. We've got a man watching it," Tischner said.

"Oh, my God," Junior gasped. "The two guys Dad gave that van to haven't shown up for work yet."

"Well, we aren't worried about their attendance. We just want to know if they've got that little girl."

"Agent Tischner, I don't think you understand," Junior said in a dreadful tone. "One of those men is a rapist and the other a child molester."

Tischner took down the names then dropped the phone. "I need one agent to stay here and get the info on these guys: mug shots, rap sheets—should be a mile long. E-mail the mug shots to each agent's cell phone." He turned to the HRT leader. "Guys, we've got to move now—weather be damned."

Despite the rough winds and almost-blinding rain, the choppers arrived in Stonewall County within thirty minutes.

The SWAT team members didn't think twice about having just risked their lives. The second they landed on solid ground they didn't hesitate for a moment; they swept into the electrical supply buildings, which were all systematically but swiftly searched. There was no sign of the little girl, McMillan or the two men anywhere.

The search moved to the back of the building, where the van was parked. It seemed to match the security photo exactly.

HRT members rushed to the van, but Wayne was the one to reach it first. He pulled open the door—and what he found inside was ghastly.

Chapter Forty-Two

Negotiations

If you have made mistakes, even serious ones,
there is always another chance for you. What we call
failure is not the falling down but the staying down.
—Mary Pickford

Although there was no one in the van, little Dawn's pink security blanket had been left behind on the floor in back. What was particularly troubling about that piece of evidence was the blood stain, the size of a quarter, soaked through.

Wayne's first instinct was to pick up the blanket and hold it close to him, as he would have liked to do with his daughter at that moment, but Tischner's hand on his shoulder held him back.

"We'll send it to the state crime lab for an immediate blood analysis," Tischner said. "And any fingerprints could help with an arrest."

"If I don't kill them first," Wayne said.

Although there wasn't sufficient time for DNA testing, evidence technicians could at least determine the blood type and if it was animal or human. Randy, who had been watching the van, volunteered to ride with the agent to take the evidence to the lab as quickly as possible, since he knew the lab techs.

Even with this case as top priority, however, the results wouldn't be immediate. Wayne would have to wait and he did so in Junior's office, with Tischner by his side and the HRT outside, ready to get into the chopper at a moment's notice.

After a grueling hour, Randy and the FBI agent reappeared in the doorway of the main office, his head hanging down.

"What's happening? Did you get it?" Wayne asked, jumping up from his seat.

"Afraid so," the agent said. "The serologist found that it's from a person with a rare blood type that less than five percent of the population has: AB negative."

"That's Dawn's type," Wayne said, as if in shock.

"I know." The agent walked over and handed him the results. "I'm sorry."

"Look, Wayne," Tischner said, trying to see the positives, "we have the van, we know the suspect and there was just a small amount of blood. We're going to get her back."

Just then, the private phone rang in McMillan Jr.'s office. Agent Tischner rushed Junior over and instructed him to pick it up as he, Wayne and Randy huddled around.

"Son, is something going on at work? I passed by a little while ago and noticed quite a ruckus," A.D. McMillan, Sr. said with a laugh.

"Dad, you know damn well what's happening. You had no right to take that little girl."

On cue, Tischner rushed out of the room to tell an agent to get a trace and triangulation on the phone.

"The feds have no right harassing my boy, either," McMillan, Sr. said.

"I'm not a boy. I'm a grown man who can take care of himself."

"Oh, yeah? You don't do anything yourself. In fact, I bet right now you're not by yourself. You've probably got the feds all around you." McMillan's sneering disdain was unmistakable.

"Dad, will you return that little girl, please?" his son pleaded. "You can bring her back to me."

"Nah, son, we're having fun," the father said, letting out another laugh. "Besides, I'm not walking into any trap. If your fed friends are so interested in me, why don't you put the phone on the speaker so they can talk to me now?"

Junior held his finger above the "speaker" button and shot a look at Wayne, who nodded in agreement. Just as he turned it on, Tischner came back into the room with the HRT negotiator.

"What do you want, McMillan?" Wayne growled into the speaker.

"I want you, my friend. Since you like to play games so much, we're going to play one right now. It'll be real exciting," McMillan taunted. "Life-and-death-type exciting, I mean. You could win your daughter's safe release—but it might cost you your life. And she could end up in about a thousand little pieces." He laughed mockingly. "What do you say? Wanna play?"

"You son of a bitch! I want to know my daughter's okay," Wayne insisted, refusing to get sucked into his twisted plans.

"You listen to me, you little snot-nosed bastard. You ain't in charge here—I am! You'll do as I say if you want her to live." McMillan paused, trying to gather his cool. "I figure that daughter of yours is just about shy of her second birthday, right? Well, don't worry about her. She's is in good hands with a friend of mine who gets along real well with little girls that age."

Wayne's face went red with rage. But before he could say anything, the HRT negotiator stepped in front of the phone.

"Mr. McMillan, this is Special Agent Dwayne Wyzenski. I'm a hostage negotiator. Is it alright if I call you A.D.?"

"I know how you guys operate," McMillan scoffed. "I ain't no amateur. You think you can give a little and get a little, huh? Well, I don't want no damn sandwiches brought to me in a cooler with no bug attached to it. I don't want no car, no airplane, no money or no getaway assistance. In fact, I don't want to move much at all, 'cause I don't want to be seen and have no sniper blow my head up like a pumpkin. Most of all, I don't want to talk to you." As he spoke,

McMillan was building up steam. "There's only going to be one give and one get—that little snot-nosed Lott can give his life for hers, no negotiating."

"A.D., we know you're no amateur. You're aware of how these things work. With your cooperation, I can see to it that you get minimum time to serve," Wyzenski said.

"Tell you what, smart boy, I'm going to fax something over to my son's desk that'll make you understand why I ain't interested in no stupid deals."

"Okay, A.D.," Wyzenski said, glancing over at Tischner. "Why don't I hang on while you do that?"

"Nah, why don't I give y'all a chance to read it in private? I'm about to leave from where I am so that trace of yours won't do you no good. But don't worry. I'll call you when I get near my new place."

As soon as he hung up, the agent trying to trace the call came into the room. "Agent Tischner, the phone's a pay-as-you-go cellular, so we we're having trouble tracing it. We're triangulating it through different cell towers in case he's on the move when he calls back."

"Okay," Tischner said, dismissing the agent.

Just then, the office fax machine came to life. Junior ran over to get the letter from his father and read it aloud:

Dear Mr. A.D. McMillan, Sr.:

Your CT-guided biopsy test results indicate a massive, rapidly growing tumor on the left side of your brain. The cancer also has spread from your lungs to your lymph nodes and is being deposited in all the major organs of your body. As your doctor has discussed with you it is imperative that you arrive at The Anderson Clinic immediately for radiation treatment. Failure to do so could result in your death within three months.

The doctor who had written the letter went on to explain about new, experimental treatments that might assure a good quality of life for up to a year, which could allow him to get his affairs in order, do the things he always wanted to and spend his last days with family.

The phone rang and Junior stopped reading, looking up with tears in his eyes.

"So, did you get the letter?" McMillan, Sr. asked when Wyzenski picked up. He was pulling his car up in front of a brick building.

"Dad," Junior said, racing over to the speaker, "this letter is over two months old! The doctor only gave you three months. Why won't you go get treatment?"

"Don't want to be no guinea pig," McMillan stated matter-of-factly. "But now you see I ain't got nothin' to live for, which makes it hard for you feds listening in. Can't offer me no deals down the road. I'm like a man committing suicide, 'cept I might take Lott and his daughter with me."

Wayne couldn't stand any more. "Listen, McMillan, I'm not sure why you hate me so much, but please don't take it out on my daughter. I beg of you... I'll do whatever you want."

"Well, aren't you cooperative?" McMillan said snidely. "Some of my friends in the legislature were cooperative, too, and you sent them to prison with your undercover sting in Jackson. Now you come to mess with my boy and serve warrants on my friends up here, too? Well, I'll tell you what—you ain't never gonna get to serve me!"

McMillan's maniacal laughter turned into a fit of coughing. When it was over, his tone turned serious for the moment. "I'll call you in the morning to tell you what to do next. In the meantime, get rid of those damn helicopters I seen and get away from my son. Believe me, I have friends everywhere and I'll know when you're gone. Y'all have a good night, now. I know all of us *here* will."

With that, McMillan threw his prepaid cell phone, still on, into the back of a garbage truck that was going down the street in the opposite direction.

Chapter Forty-Three

Mind Games

You can discover what your enemy fears most
by observing the means he uses to frighten you.
—Eric Hoffer

The command center at the federal building in Oxford was crowded the next morning with FBI agents, US marshals, hostage negotiators, members of the HRT and even a chaplain. Every couch was covered with wrinkled blankets and pillows showing signs of restless tossing and turning; most couldn't sleep at all, thinking about how a madman about to die controlled the destiny of an innocent child.

Tempers were fuming and everyone was exhausted—but ready. The negotiators would assume the first role when the call they had been waiting for came in. Assuming that talks would prove no more fruitful with this animal than they had before, the HRT was prepared to take over.

One conference room was now filled with A.D. McMillan, Sr.'s associates. It included anybody the negotiators could reach who might have had any influence whatsoever on McMillan. Personalities varied greatly. His soon-to-be ex-wife, his son, an old cellmate from federal prison, District Attorney John Chastain, McMillan's doctor and a neighbor, even Wayne's wife, Julie, were all there.

The other main conference room held the HRT members. They had brought their own folding cots, no bigger than lightweight lounge chairs, painted in camouflage. None were occupied now, though. Every member was crowded around the briefing board, where plans were being written out that looked like a football coach's pregame strategies. This was commonplace for these guys. However, the frustration certainly was mounting.

Though they had zeroed in on a likely location they still didn't know the specific building McMillan was occupying, nor its construction or layout. A few possibilities had been drawn but whatever area Dawn might have been kept in, that side of the board was blank. When they learned more, their breaching plans would be finalized.

"Just as soon as he tells us where that little girl is," the HRT leader said, "we'll be all over him. The helos are already warmed up and waiting."

———

At ten-fifteen, after a few tense hours of waiting, Wayne's office phone finally rang.

McMillan didn't even wait for a greeting. "I'm sure y'all have all the experts you think you need gathered together to defeat me by now," he said with a laugh. "But the thing is, I don't like to talk on cell phones around explosives—you never know what's gonna set them off—so I'll give you a landline number to call me back on. I've made it easy on you, Lott. You won't have to travel far."

Wayne took down the information without a word before McMillan hung up. The number was soon determined to be the pre-booking processing center for the local prison, an old federal facility that now belonged to the county and was undergoing renovations. McMillan had friends on the construction crew and had made sure they wouldn't be showing up for work that day.

Wayne dialed the number. "McMillan, where's my daughter?" he demanded into the speaker phone at the center of the main conference-room table.

"Oh, she's right here with me. I'm sure you figured out where I am by now."

"In the prison," Wayne replied. "Where you're gonna be for the rest of your life."

"Like I said," McMillan laughed, "I made it easy for you guys. Your SWAT team has only one building to deal with, just inside the fenced-in welcoming center, as it was called when I was first herded into here like an animal for in-processing eighteen years ago."

The HRT leader familiarized himself with that building: solid concrete, sturdy, with no windows and a couple of holding cells in the back monitored by cameras. He began sketching it on the board.

"Give us some proof she's alive," Tischner said into the speaker phone.

"No problem," McMillan said. "I just love this little game." He gave them a Web site and added, "Just ping it—one three nine dot one six five dot three three two—and you'll tap into the cameras monitoring the holding cell where Dawn is. Which, by the way, is the same one I occupied many years ago. Nice touch, huh, boys?"

He gave them a few minutes to find the image. When Wayne finally saw his daughter sitting in the cell, cradling a small dog in her lap, he broke into tears. It was the first time he was sure she was still alive. He wanted nothing more than to smash his fist into the monitor and reach in to free her.

"Isn't that sweet?" McMillan's voice came back over the speaker phone. "I even gave her a little puppy to play with. That's more than I got when I was inside."

"How do we know that's not a video?" Tischner asked.

"Simple," McMillan answered. "I'll walk back there and talk to you live on camera. I have something else to show you in her cell, anyway."

Suddenly, they could see McMillan appear on the monitor,

unlocking Dawn's cell with a key. When Wayne saw him walk inside and smile into the camera, he took a step toward the screen as if meaning to destroy it.

Tischner got in front of him and whispered, "Why don't you go tell Julie your daughter's still alive? You don't need to listen to this guy's mind games."

Wayne clasped Tischner's arm with gratitude then ran down the hall to the other conference room to share the good news with his wife.

"Hey," McMillan continued into the camera, "any explosive ordinance detachment experts with you? Those EOD guys will love this." He walked behind Dawn and lifted a blanket, exposing the area under the prison-style bunk bed; there was a hard-shelled suitcase underneath connected to the chain of a leg iron. The other end of the chain was attached to a metal bracelet around Dawn's right ankle.

McMillan pressed a button to activate an explosive charge and a digital counter began busily counting back in bright-red numerals. When he dropped the blanket, one hour, fifty-nine minutes and seven seconds were left—less than two hours to save that precious life.

"McMillan, my name's Ruben, the chief negotiator. Let's talk about what you want."

"What I want is for Lott to leave my family and friends alone—but it's a little too late for that."

"You worried about your friends in Stonewall getting prosecuted?" Ruben asked. "How 'bout we let you talk to John Chastain? He'll tell you everything's alright."

"You got Johnny boy there with ya, huh?" McMillan said, sounding pleased. "Know what, Mr. Ruben? I'm in a better mood today with all this excitement going on. I might just be willing to negotiate. Why don't you come on out here, along with my little snot-nosed friend and his old-fart FBI buddy, and I'll walk out to the processing yard to talk. Bring a couple more agents and some more of my friends along for the final party, if you want. Even those itchy-fingered SWAT boys and your EOD hot shots."

"We're on our way, McMillan," the EOD leader said. "But, listen, we know you're an explosives expert, so you wanna tell us about the bomb in the cell with Dawn first?"

Humoring him seemed to work. "I thought you'd never ask," McMillan said proudly. "It's my best creation yet. Anybody can make a bomb, after all, but it's the detonator that makes it interesting. You're limited only by your imagination. I've spent years working on this—learned how to do it from a real good ex-con. He used to be an EOD guy, too, but I bet he was better than you."

"No doubt," the EOD leader agreed, hoping to keep him talking.

"Here's the deal. You guys like to freeze bombs sometimes, right?" McMillan asked. "Well, I wouldn't try that on this one. If the temperature changes ten degrees either way, a thermostatic detonator blows the package."

The HRT leader took notes as McMillan went on, chatting away like a guest on a talk show.

"You like to move them to a safe location to explode them, too," he continued. "I wouldn't try that, either, 'cause this one has a motion switch. Think you're good enough to move it slowly without jarring it? Wouldn't try that! It has a pressure switch on the bottom. Lift it, no matter how carefully, and it goes off."

The EOD leader exchanged a worried glance with the head of the hostage-rescue team.

"Want to cut that leg iron chain and free the little girl? That would be a no-no 'cause it's a conductor. You'll break a circuit, causing a big boom. Wanna X-ray it to make sure there's really a bomb in there? That would be a dumb move, too, 'cause the outer package is wrapped in a special film. If it's exposed to X-rays, a rearrangement occurs in the silver particles, causing them to join together and form a closed circuit. You'll never even see the image before it blows. Stop the clock by any method and guess what, boys? It blows. Any questions?"

Onscreen, McMillan stood with his arms folded and a self-satisfied grin on his face, staring defiantly into the camera.

Tischner and the team leaders looked at each other, realizing they had underestimated the maniac's intelligence—at least when it came to blowing things sky-high. They quickly gathered everyone who was going together and headed out the door.

"Mr. McMillan, this is Ruben again. May I call you 'Mac'?" the negotiator asked.

"Sure, Rube, all my buddies do," McMillan said, clearly enjoying himself.

"The group you asked for is assembling and will be on their way soon in a mobile command-post motor home. They'll have radios, satellite phones and a video feed so they can hear everything you say. I'm going to stay here on the line with you."

"Good. I'm glad they won't miss out on our conversation," McMillan said, reveling in his captive audience and all the attention he was getting.

"Please have the gate open when they get there, since every second counts," Ruben said. "We can work this thing out, Mac. How much time do we have left?"

"Well, according to my trusty old Timex, looks like an hour and twenty-two minutes," McMillan laughed. "Did you hear that boys?" he screamed into the camera. "Better get your asses moving!"

Chapter Forty-Four

Impossible Odds

Nobody ever did, or ever will,
escape the consequences of his choices.
—Alfred A. Montapert

Everyone named by the HRT leader was in the van heading to the hostage area, including John Chastain. Electronic gear in the vehicle had been activated, sending a video signal back to the command post in the federal building so they would see everything as it occurred.

Only Ruben and a few command-center agents were left behind. McMillan's associates remained in the conference room.

Julie, however, had insisted on coming into the main room and watching the live feed along with the chief negotiator and several agents. Her eyelids were swollen and red, her eyes bloodshot and her hands shaking as she bit her already-torn fingernails to the quick.

"Are you sure you want to watch this?" Ruben asked her.

She nodded. "If these are my daughter's final minutes on Earth, I'm damn sure gonna spend them with her in any way I can."

After being briefed on the dire situation, Wayne was sitting in the mobile CP, across from Chastain. He'd been unable to look him in the eye at first but couldn't hold back his comments any longer.

"I thought you were a noble man, you piece of shit. You ain't nothin' but a dope-dealing, criminal-conspiring, soap selling, cow tending, worthless politician—and you make me sick," Wayne screamed. "As far as I'm concerned, you're the one who got my daughter into this—and if anything happens to her, I'm taking it out on you!"

Chastain was visibly shaken by Wayne's intensity and how far he had fallen in the estimation of someone who had once looked up to him. But before the DA could respond, the HRT leader interrupted.

"You can't do this right now," he said. "We're running out of time."

"You mean my *daughter's* running out of time. This son of a bitch's time is already over," Wayne said, pointing at Chastain.

———

As the CP got closer to the prison, McMillan was ready to talk once again. "Okay, Rube, old buddy, when they get here, I want Snot Nose and Old Fart out of the motor home and on foot in the yard, where I can see them. I'd like to spend a little time getting to know them better."

"What's your plan, Mac?" the negotiator asked.

"Well, Rube, the outer door of the facility is solid steel and uses a big, brass key, like a jail cell does, which I'll bring out with me when I meet the dynamic duo. Follow me on your camera."

Ruben, Julie and everyone at the command center, along with those in the van who were watching the monitor, could see him stepping out of Dawn's cell. He rifled through some keys on a hook, selected one in particular and took it off. However, instead of using it to lock the cell, he left it wide open.

"I told you I'd make it easy for you." McMillan said. He smiled grotesquely, holding the key up to the camera. "This is for the front door. Dawn's cell will be left unlocked and I'll hand this key to the two feds outside. All they have to do to rescue her is get through that big, old, steel door and find a way to free the girl."

While McMillan fell into a spasm of laughter, Julie and Ruben exchanged confused looks.

"I have to say, though, that I did hope to keep things interesting with a surprise," he continued once he'd calmed down. "You see, when I walk out to meet my two new friends and close the door behind me, it will activate another device attached to the entrance that'll kill the first person who turns the key or tries to breach the door."

As he playfully dangled the key in front of him, Julie realized what a deranged mind her husband and Agent Tischner were up against.

"Oh, my God," she gasped.

"Don't try to blow the door off, either, boys," McMillan continued, addressing everyone in the van, "'cause even the slightest movement will trip a much-larger charge. You could kill that little girl and her new pet, too, before you even have a chance of freeing her."

Now knowing that there were two trick bombs in place, Ruben began to run out of hope. "McMillan, please… Tischner and Lott will be there like you want, along with everyone else you asked for. Just tell me, what's the next step after that to make sure this will all work out?"

"The next step?" McMillan echoed. "The next step, Rube, old buddy, is to quit asking questions. We only have forty-three minutes left now and it shouldn't be long before my guests arrive. I'll be walking out soon and closing the door behind me. And once I do, even I can't get back in."

Chapter Forty-Five

Justice Served

*The difference between a moral man and a man
of honor is that the latter regrets a discreditable act,
even when it has worked and he has not been caught.*
—H.L. Mencken

After hearing the extent of McMillan's plan, everyone in the mobile CP fell silent. The situation they were heading into seemed more impossible than ever.

"If we can immobilize him and get that key we can rig some sort of long pole to attach to it and open the door from behind our portable ballistic panels," the EOD leader said over the radio.

The mobile command-post had just pulled up to the prison yard and the electrically operated gate slid open.

"I'm sure the charge on the door is rigged to blow outward to harm the intruder instead of the child," he hurriedly continued. "Then we can rush in as planned, rig a jump wire on the leg irons, cut the chain in the middle and free her."

"The long pole's a good idea," the HRT leader replied. "Start on it just in case, but we gotta move with plan A for now."

The van drove just inside the prison yard with the front of the vehicle facing the small, fortified-looking building where McMillan was hiding out. The gates shut ominously behind them.

"Ah, you made it," McMillan said over the monitor. "And not a moment too soon." He held the key up to the camera again as a final warning. "I can hardly wait to see Snot Nose and Old Fart outside. It's going to be such a *blast* watching you try to rescue little Dawn."

With a final wave goodbye, McMillan suddenly disappeared. All that was left in the corner of the screen was an image of a little girl happily playing with her puppy.

Tischner looked at Wayne. "I know you don't like giving guns to criminals like Chastain under any circumstances, but this is the only plan we've got. We have to do our part."

"Better work," Wayne snarled.

"Remember, you two keep a fifty-yard distance from McMillan. We don't know if he's armed, but snipers have him in their scopes either way," the HRT leader warned.

Just then, a few dozen yards in front of the van, they could see the door of the building open and McMillan walked out, waving the key.

"We're down to twelve minutes," he called out gleefully, locking the door behind him. "What are you guys going to do?"

"Let's go," Wayne said, setting his jaw, and he and Tisch stepped out of the van

"Well, well, my two favorite assholes," McMillan shouted. "And they say a man only has one." He laughed before becoming suddenly serious. "Guess it's just us three now."

"Not quite," Chastain said, jumping from the door of the mobile CP with a revolver in his hand. He quickly positioned himself between McMillan and the two feds.

"Isn't this a pleasant surprise?" McMillan said as he began to walk closer. "My old business partner, District Attorney John Chastain. They told me you came to the final game but I wasn't sure whose team you'd be on."

Chastain pointed the gun at him. "I don't care what your plan is, McMillan, I just want the pleasure of killing you myself. What happens after that won't matter because the next bullet in this gun is for me."

"I know you, Johnny. You're not the self-sacrificing kind."

"What have I got to lose?" Chastain asked. "You lied to me. Said you were going to ferry that plane to a shop in Florida for repairs. You ferried it alright, down to Columbia with your dope-dealing buddies. You smeared my name, not to mention your own son's name, you worthless bastard."

"My son's name *is* my name," McMillan jeered. "Who are you to talk to me about being a worthless bastard? You haven't made it far enough in your career to *judge* people, Johnny. You're just a redneck, beer-drinking, Ole Miss brat with expensive toys that could have made you millions. You know as well as I do that you were always up for sale—I just bought you at the right price."

Chastain hesitated a moment before lowering his gun. "You're right," he said. "Who am I kidding?"

"Now, get out of my way," McMillan said. "We're down to eight minutes and I wanna watch this. I'm sure the old FBI fart will be the one who tries to open that door. Then his little snot-nosed sidekick can step over whatever's left of him to have a crack at freeing his daughter and see what happens. Who knows? We might all get to witness a happy little reunion—but I'm betting we're gonna see this building go up in smoke."

"You want them dead so bad, McMillan? Then I guess I owe you that much for bailing me out." Chastain turned and fired two shots from the revolver. Both Tischner and Wayne fell to the ground.

"Now they're dead," Chastain said, throwing his gun away. "Your vengeance is served. That leaves just me and you again as partners."

"You son of a bitch, I wanted to kill those bastards myself," McMillan screamed. "You took my glory!" He ran toward Chastain like a madman, landing a punch on his midsection that surprisingly doubled him over. "You took my glory!"

Chastain suddenly stood up straight, holding a small, two-shot derringer he'd gotten out of his car when he'd left the federal building. He grabbed McMillan in a headlock and fired one round into McMillan's temple point blank, rendering him lifeless, then dropped him to the ground.

The last shot was still available for Chastain himself, but he didn't use it. Instead, in a last-ditch effort to redeem himself, he grabbed the key from McMillan's clenched hand and ran toward the door with less than six minutes to spare.

The EOD vehicle that had been following the main van busted through the prison gate just in time for the explosion to blow parts of Chastain's body all over its windshield.

Even before the smoke could clear, the EOD experts rushed inside with only four minutes remaining.

"Holy shit," the HRT leader said, standing outside. "Guess that damn Chastain had a set of balls after all."

Chapter Forty-Six

The Aftermath

Nothing in his life became him like the leaving it.
—William Shakespeare

Back in the command post at the federal building, agents were trying to get Julie out of the room. Only minutes earlier she had watched her neighbor and her husband get shot down. Now, an explosion occurred in the building her little girl was in. She had seen the worst but in her mind, her child still remained.

———

The EOD officers quickly attached a jump wire around the chain that held Dawn to the device and clipped the chain in the middle with bolt cutters to free her. Within moments, an EOD team member came running from the building, dressed in garb that made him look like a cross between a hockey player and a haz-mat specialist. In each arm he held a life: in his right one a small puppy and in his left, a frightened but otherwise healthy child. Her only imperfection? A lip that was split open from when her kidnapper first had grabbed her—and that was already healing over.

The EOD agent ran without stopping, with other team members

close behind. They made it to the opposite side of the mobile command post and dropped to the ground as another loud explosion was heard.

As the smoke cleared, Wayne and Tischner crawled away from the site where they had played dead, shot by blanks in the gun given to Chastain as part of the plan.

Wayne sat up and squinted through the mist. When he saw the small figure of a child, he ran to her, screaming, crying, laughing and thanking God.

Meanwhile, Tischner turned to the HRT leader and asked, "Did you know Chastain had that other gun hidden?"

"I had no idea. Guess he kept it to shoot himself just in case the EOD van didn't bust through the front door in time to save the little girl."

"It *was* getting close," Tischner said. "Who knows if we'd have made it without Chastain doing what he did?"

"We had a plan B—the long pole," the HRT leader said defensively.

"And what was plan C—the North Pole? You were hoping Santa and his sleigh would fly through the chimney just in time and save the day?"

Tischner walked away, shaking his head in disgust. "Wayne!" he called. "Hold that little girl up to this camera so your wife can see her. Let her see you, too, by the way. She didn't know that part of our plan was to have Chastain shoot us with blanks, remember?"

Wayne scooped Dawn into his arms and held her up to the camera in the command-center van. His face was pressed against hers, plastered with a huge smile.

As Julie watched from the main conference room in the federal building, silent tears of joy streamed down her face and her fingers lightly traced the images of her daughter and husband on the screen.

"Okay, get out of the way, you camera hog," Tischner told Wayne, stepping into the frame. "I want Julie to see me, too, so she can call Ann and tell her not to go out spending my retirement money just yet."

"Be a movie star all you want, Tisch," Wayne said, stepping aside. "I'm going home. No, I mean, *we're* going home, my little girl and I."

Chapter Forty-Seven

Finality

The world is a dangerous place to live; not because of the people who are evil, but because of the people who don't do anything about it.
—Albert Einstein

A few weeks later, with Wayne on indefinite leave, Tischner went to Stonewall County to tie up some loose ends.

He met with Randy at the coffee shop next to Patty's boarded-up newspaper office and filled him in on the whole hostage showdown.

"Man, I still can't believe Chastain did that," Randy said, shaking his head. "He's a hard one to figure out. You knew I was getting into the bonding business here but the law requires you to get a recommendation from the DA in the district you intend to work in. The last time I saw Chastain he was refusing to give me a recommendation since he figured out I'd taken that picture of his airplane for Patty's newspaper. He was even telling the police chiefs in the county not to hire me because he wouldn't prosecute any of my cases. I was gonna move down to Jackson, but I think I might just stay here. Maybe go back to the sheriff's office now that Chastain's pushing up daisies and I don't have to depend on him to prosecute my cases or recommend me for a bonding license."

"What a screwed-up state law," Tischner said. "Still, it'd be good to have you back in law enforcement. You know, that was the real

Chastain—petty and political. One last act doesn't make a hero out of him."

"I know," Randy agreed. "He began with a noble career but fell victim to a phenomenon that so many politicians do. He didn't have absolute power, but he had a taste of it—enough to corrupt him and make him willing to do anything for more."

"Yeah," Tischner said. "And his failure to gain the power he wanted so badly, plus his loss of income as a result, made him vulnerable to temptation. He used what power he had left to solve his personal problems, which only creates more problems."

"You mean like selling his soul to the devil by making deals with people like A.D. McMillan?" Randy scoffed. "He betrayed the people who elected him and the profession he swore to uphold. He became a disgrace."

"That's exactly what Wayne said," Tischner replied, wondering if his close friend would ever come back to work in the US attorney's office—or any law-related position again for that matter.

The bad guys were dead—Chastain and McMillan—but there would always be others to take their places. Wayne's child, however, lived and for that he thanked God, but couldn't bring himself to thank Chastain or think of him as having honor or nobility. Instead, Wayne chose to think of him as a coward. He had lost his credibility, his reputation, everything he'd owned and the confidence of everyone who ever had believed in him. If he hadn't died he would've faced losing his freedom and ending up in prison with the people he had put there.

Wayne thought of him as a man whose fear had overcome his guts and he couldn't take it, so he took the quickest—and, in some ways, easiest—way out instead. His life and reputation had been blown to bits already by then; it was only his body that followed.

When guilt tried to creep into Wayne's conscience from knowing that the DA had saved his child's life, he remembered that she wouldn't have been in that situation had it not been for Chastain in the first place. He'd reflect for a moment then say to himself, "He got what he deserved."

"What about Buford Lancaster?" Tischner asked, trying to shake off his thoughts about Wayne for the moment. "What ever happened to him?"

"Seems that when the rest of us were busy with the county corruption cases, Chastain kept trying to find him. He needed an outside connection since all of his here were under investigation. Who better than a suspected drug dealer who had already disappeared? Some of Chastain's friends who had underground ties themselves must've helped locate him."

"It's amazing what a desperate man can do," Tischner interjected.

"True," Randy agreed. "Turns out Chastain would've been an asset to us in law enforcement if he'd stayed straight. But when he finally tracked this guy down in the Cayman Islands, all he wanted was to strike a deal. Lancaster had pretty much run out of cash at that point, which was why he'd had to use his credit card. So Chastain promised him whatever money he had left to go to Florida, where he wouldn't be recognized, to reclaim his plane."

"It's not like Chastain could afford to repair it. What did he even want that wreck back for?" Tischner asked.

"I think he hoped it'd simply be a case of 'out of public sight, out of mind.' He just wanted it where no one could see it and be reminded of his failures," Randy explained. "So when Lancaster came here and got the cash, he bought himself a small plane and immediately disappeared again."

"Guess he *really* wanted to get away from his wife," Tischner said with a laugh.

"Yep," Randy agreed. "Who knows where he went? But at least we don't have to deal with the likes of him in Stonewall County."

Two weeks later, Buford Lancaster's plane was found crashed into the side of Mt. Alvernia on Cat Island in the Bahamas. His lifeless body was recovered inside, along with hundreds of dollars in cash. A few thousand more swirled in the swift breezes along the mountainside. It was all that was left of Chastain's legacy.

Epilogue

Disposition of the Co-Conspirators in Stonewall County, MS:

- Chancery clerk
  Died of cancer before going to trial
- Clerk's son
  Entered a plea to serve two years in federal prison
- Bank CEO
  Died of heart attack after being arrested
- Bank CEO's brother
  Went to trial and was acquitted
- Bank vice presidents
  All received three years in federal prison for lying to FBI agents
- Bank manager (Buchanan)
  Went to trial, was convicted and got five years to serve
- County attorney
  Surrendered his law license, entered an plea and got three years probation
- *Tribunal* editor
  Turned snitch on all the others, entered a plea and got five years probation
- DA investigator
  (Milton) Became a fugitive from justice and an interstate flight to avoid prosecution warrant was issued for him
- Co-kidnappers
  The convicted child molester got twenty years and the convicted rapist got fifteen for kidnapping and child endangerment

Of the Five County Supervisors:

Two entered guilty pleas to serve two years—one in the federal prison system, six months in a halfway house with freedom to come and go, and the last six months in their homes under supervised probation with ankle bracelets. They also agreed to testify against the other three.

The other three went to trial, were convicted and received five years to be served in the federal penitentiary.

Note: The two who only served one year in prison came back home when their positions were up for reelection. Oddly, they were qualified to run.

The US attorney argued against it, since state law prohibited them from running for reelection to any office in the state due to their felony convictions. However, the Mississippi State attorney general ruled that the law only prohibited them from running for reelection if they were convicted of *state* crimes. Since they were convicted of federal crimes the state statute did not apply.

One was reelected by a landslide and the other lost the election by only seven votes.

About the Author

Rick Ward was born in Tunica, Mississippi, on August 1, 1953. He has an associate's degree in law enforcement from Mississippi Gulf Coast Community College, a BS in criminal justice from the University of the State of New York and a master's in education from the University of Hawaii. He is a graduate of the Mississippi State Police Academy, the US Army Military Police School and the FBI National Academy.

Rick enlisted in the US Navy in 1971 and served four years on active duty during the Vietnam era. He remained in the US Navy reserves for twenty-five years and went back on active duty two more times while completing fourteen years in civilian law enforcement. He retired from the US Navy as a lieutenant commander.

Rick began his law-enforcement career in 1975 as a uniformed police officer in Moss Point, Mississippi. Three years later he became an undercover state narcotics agent, then the chief investigator for Desoto County, Mississippi. He later worked for the state attorney general, investigating white-collar crime and political corruption.

Rick's actual experiences have inspired him to embellish real-life events and write fictitious scenarios to be enjoyed by readers interested in legal thrillers, crime and politics, told from the perspective of a seasoned, well-rounded, retired senior law-enforcement officer.

This is Rick's second book, preceded by *The Lawmaker*.

Author's Comments

Although some of the events in this book are based on actual events that occurred during my career, this is a story of fiction. There is no twenty-third judicial district in Mississippi, no county called Stonewall and no town called Puknik. None of the characters are real; any similarity to actual people is a coincidence.

CASINO MEETS *THE FIRM*
IN THIS BRILLIANT SIZZLER

Wayne Lott is a young attorney out to make a name for himself. When a state legislature seat becomes vacant, Wayne jumps at the chance to run for office and enter what he thinks will be the glamorous life of politics. But he's in for a deadly surprise.

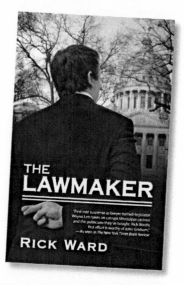

Naïve and idealistic, Wayne is a lamb being led to the slaughter. In no time, he becomes enmeshed in the violent, high-stakes underworld of a sinister casino lobbyist. Caught with a hired temptress and threatened with blackmail, Wayne is forced to choose between cooperating with federal authorities and succumbing to the dark side of Mississippi's gambling gangland.

Breinigsville, PA USA
24 March 2010
234814BV00001B/1/P